Their fingers met.

Mace felt cool, beautiful green energy flowing up his arm and, surprisingly, right into his heart. He hadn't expected this kind of feeling from Ana. After all, she was evil personified.

"Do you see that sun birthmark? Here, on my neck?" she asked.

No question, she had the *Tupay* or Dark Forces symbol. "Yes, I see it."

"It's a symbol of ultimate evil."

"What kind of evil?"

"I don't know. I don't want to believe I'm evil. I don't lie, cheat, steal or do things intentionally to hurt others."

Out of the corner of his eye Mace studied Ana's profile. He decided Ana had to be one of the best sorceresses he'd ever met, or she really was in pain. Impossible, Mace decided. He made a mental note to believe Ana not only knew who she was, but that she was consciously manipulating him until a time and place where she could kill him before he killed her.

LINDSAY McKENNA

is part Eastern Cherokee and has walked the path of her ancestors through her father's training. Her "other" name is Ai Gvhdi Waya, Walks With Wolves. At age nine, Lindsay's father began to teach her the "medicine" ways, or skills brought down through their family lineage. For nine years Lindsay remained in training. There was never a name given to what was handed down through her Wolf Clan family lines, but nowadays it is generally called shamanism. Having grown up in a Native American environment, Lindsay is close to Mother Earth and all her relations. She has taught interested people about the Natural World around the globe and on how to reconnect spiritually with the Earth. She is now infusing her books with her many years of experiences and metaphysical knowledge in hopes that readers will discover a newfound awe for the magic that is around us in our everyday reality. Paranormal was known as metaphysics in Lindsay's family. She considers herself a metaphysician and her intent is to bring compassion and "heart" through her storytelling, for she believes the greatest healer of all is love.

DARK TRUTH

LINDSAY McKENNA

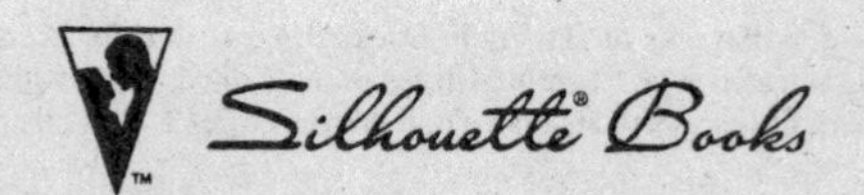

nocturne™

ISBN-13: 978-0-373-61767-8
ISBN-10: 0-373-61767-4

DARK TRUTH

This edition published by arrangement with Harlequin Books S.A.

www.silhouettenocturne.com

Printed in U.S.A.

Dear Reader,

I'm very excited about *Dark Truth,* Book Two of the WARRIORS FOR THE LIGHT miniseries! I love exploring mysticism (the paranormal) in all of its various expressions as a footpath or road within ourselves. Everyone, of course, has psychic talents. The Sixth Sense is there for a reason! And we possess wonderful, perhaps unknown talents in this area of our makeup. What makes the WARRIORS FOR THE LIGHT different is that they utilize and hone their psychic skill(s) every day. I hope you take your own journey to discover what gifts you have.

One of the many fun things I can do as a writer is share what I know about the "real" world and put it into a fictional format. Stories are teachers. In my Native American tradition, I can remember my father telling us a story nearly every night before bedtime. They were stories with a beginning, middle and end. And, most important, the story was instructive about how to behave as a human being who has strong morals and values, who knows right from wrong, and who walks with compassion on Mother Earth and is of service to others. These stories were powerful and often changed me and my thinking. So we can never pooh-pooh a book, because each one has a life and a heart of its own. I hope in some small, positive way my stories touch you in a similar fashion.

Please let me know how *Dark Truth* touches you! Find me at www.lindsaymckenna.com or at my blog, www.talesfromechocanyon.blogspot.com. I always love to hear from you and find out what's on your mind and in your heart.

Happy summer reading!

Lindsay McKenna

All you WARRIORS FOR THE LIGHT readers out
there who make a difference in bringing peace,
first, within yourselves, and as a result of that
you automatically radiate peace throughout
our war-torn world. Keep on truckin'...
you're doing a fine job!

and to

Dan Millman, Peaceful Warrior, who said,
"Process transforms any journey into a series of
small steps, taken one by one, to reach any goal.
Process transcends time, teaches patience, rests
on a solid foundation of careful preparation and
embodies trust in our unfolding potential."
The Laws of Spirit. Thank you for being who you
are and leading the way from your heart.

and to

Yolande Grille, shamanic facilitator, homeopath
and friend. Thank you from the bottom
of my heart for your compassion, wisdom
and support. No one could ask for a better
companion than you with whom to go through
a "dark night of the soul" episode.

The Legend of the Warriors for the Light

Mystics of the Incan Empire saw the end coming, and created the Emerald Key necklace to help battle the *Tupay,* or Dark Forces on the planet. The seven emerald spheres that composed the necklace were then scattered around the world, until the prophesied "end of time as we know it" period should begin. That time is now.

The *Taqe,* or Warriors for the Light, must find the seven spheres before the *Tupay* do. They must recreate the necklace and wear it if they are to help stave off the thousand years of darkness now taking hold on the planet. It is a life-or-death battle.

Three couples, destined to play major roles in finding the first three spheres, must meet and create the Vesica

Piscis Foundation. The center they establish will be a place where all who wear this symbol—usually as a birthmark on the back of their neck—can come to be educated, to serve and to fight for a thousand years of peace.

Each sphere is inscribed with a special word from an ancient language—one of the Seven Virtues of Peace. The first sphere, discovered in *Unforgiven,* was *forgiveness.* Now, the next sphere will be sought. What will be inscribed upon it? Puzzle pieces in a great cosmic scheme, segments of the Emerald Key necklace are up for grabs. Who will discover the next sphere? Will the world be plunged into darkness or lifted into light?

Prologue

Ana Elena Rafael's heart thudded heavily in her breast. She was surrounded by fog so thick she almost felt as if cotton balls were pressing against her, humid and clammy. Because she had no idea *where* she was, anxiety coursed through her. Looking down at her feet, Ana saw she stood on ground covered in rotting brown, yellow and orange leaves, with bare and twisted roots exposed here and there.

"Help me! I'm lost!" she yelled, then jerkily spun around. Her voice seemed to be absorbed instantly by that wall of white moving sluggishly about her. Her call for help went unanswered.

Cupping her hands to her mouth, her panic growing, Ana shouted even more loudly, "Help! Help me!"

It wasn't like her to cry out for rescue, or even ask for it. No, she knew better. As an orphan, Ana had learned early on to take care of herself, because no help was coming.

Swallowing hard, she felt as if her heart was about to leap out of her chest, and she wrestled with the anxiety flooding through her.

A wildlife biologist, she found herself thinking of her beloved jaguars as she sought an answer to her present dilemma. Jaguars hunted with their ears. *Noise. Sounds.* Yes, that was it. Forcing herself to breathe deeply, Ana waited until the loud drumming of her heart eased. Closing her eyes, she made herself be patient, and waited.

Quietness descended upon her. Calmness replaced her stress. Her anxiety dissipated as bands of fog continued to move around her. Focusing her ears, Ana heard for the first time the distinct bubbling and gurgling of water. Where *was* she?

A jaguar would never panic, she sternly told herself. She'd spent years watching and studying them in the jungles of Belize. Jaguars were the animals she most strongly identified with. The mighty cats had helped her live with the fact that she was orphaned. Whether they knew it or not, jaguars had healed her.

"Welcome, child."

Eyes snapping open, Ana gasped. Somehow, the fog had suddenly disappeared in those few moments she'd had her eyes closed. In front of her, standing on a wooden bridge that spanned a small creek, was a tall, thin woman with silvery-white hair that hung in braids. The look in the woman's green eyes soothed Ana. Her full mouth held a gentle smile that told her this was someone familiar, someone who knew her.

The old woman was dressed in a long turquoise robe, with a dark blue shawl around her shoulders. Her oval face had high cheekbones; her thin hands were long and graceful looking. The sturdy leather sandals she wore suggested that she worked in the fields.

"I… Who are you?" Ana asked.

The woman's smile widened. "You called for me. My name is Grandmother Alaria. And you are Ana Elena Rafael. Welcome home, my child. We've been waiting a long time to see you."

As the fog continued to dissipate, Ana looked around. On the other side of the wooden bridge a village of thatch-roofed huts appeared. She could see many people in simple farming garb wandering about.

But then Alaria's words registered. Ana gazed intently at the older women, who now stood in front of her. "Home? What are you talking about? I've never been here before. I'm sorry, but I don't know you." Ana wished she did. A wonderful warmth and maternal quality radiated from the woman, seeming to envelope Ana, much as a mother might embrace a beloved child.

Wishful thinking, of course. As she tried to shake off the nurturing feeling, Ana realized she didn't really want to.

Nodding, Alaria lifted her hand. "You will know all in good time, child. Come, walk with me. Welcome to the Village of the Clouds…."

It seemed so natural for Ana to reach out and clasp the old woman's frail-looking fingers. To her surprise, her grip was warm, firm and strong despite her obvious age. Grandmother Alaria seemed incredibly resilient with that ruddy glow in her cheeks, that merry twinkle in her large eyes. Ana tried to guess the elder's age and decided she had to be in her eighties. Alaria's silver hair was streaked with shades of gray, as well as coppery strands that hinted she'd once had red hair. The braids were not unbecoming, and gave her the aura of a wise sage from a bygone time. Ana imagined the woman must look like a druid from Britain. Perhaps some powerful priestess, because of her air of quiet authority.

Leading Ana across the bridge, Alaria said, "Does it not feel good here to you, Ana? You have the instincts of your beloved jaguars. How does it seem to you?"

Ana purposely matched her stride to the elder's. "I feel very much at peace now that I know I'm not lost."

The wooden, well-worn bridge was very old and gray with age. The surrounding jungle fell away to reveal many thatched huts in the industrious village. Ana saw men and women of all skin colors, ages and races there. Some carried farm implements—a hoe, a rake, a shovel.

A number of iron cooking pots hung from tripods throughout the village. Women and children tended fires beneath them, and the air was fragrant with a scent like roasting nuts. Ana recognized it as quinoa, one of the most high-protein grains in the world.

Bright yellow-and-blue parrots flew in and landed on gnarled trees at the other end of the bridge. The village, carved out of the jungle, stood on a flat expanse of hard-packed earth. Beyond, farm fields extended as far as Ana could see. The crops, carefully tended in neat, weeded rows, stopped at the foothills of what she recognized to be the mighty Andes. From there, dark purple and sheer gray granite slopes swept upward toward jagged, snow-capped peaks. It was a beautiful sight.

Ana stepped off the bridge and released Alaria's warm, comforting hand. Turning, she glanced back to where they'd come from. The fog was in place once again—a thick, impenetrable barrier stopping outsiders from ever finding this incredibly peaceful village. Stymied, Ana shook her head.

"It is our protection, child," the older woman murmured. "Only those who are supposed to find us do. If you are meant to come here, the fog will disappear to reveal this bridge. And once you walk across it, to our village, the fog once more provides a blanket of protection, for all who come here to live and study."

Alaria had read her mind. Ana compressed her lips, not sure she felt comfortable with the knowledge. Once again, she appraised this old woman with the look of the ancients in her eyes. Around her throat lay a gold necklace that somehow seemed familiar to Ana, though she couldn't place it. The design was of the pendant was of two interlocking circles. Why was she drawn to the symbol?

"Are you thirsty? Hungry?"

Ana tensed. "Are you going to read my mind and find out?"

Alaria chuckled. "No, child. On most occasions, we don't barge into other people's thoughts without their permission."

"You did just now."

Shaking her head, she gave Ana a look of good humor. "The question was written all over your face. It was easy for me to see as you glanced back across the bridge at the fog." Alaria beckoned her toward a stand of tall, thick-trunked trees at the edge of the village, and the wooden bench beneath them. "In fact, one of the questions first-time visitors always have is about the fog and why it is there."

Feeling embarrassed, Ana again fell in step with the elder. "I'm sorry. I assumed you were reading my mind."

Alaria smiled enigmatically. "You were fortunate to be adopted by two very loving people when you were quite young. They protected you and gave you a place to feel safe. Before that, your life was always in jeopardy."

Ana halted briefly at her words, then hurried to catch up. "How can you know that about me?"

"Oh, I know much about you, child. Here, come and sit down."

The sun was barely peeking above the jungle canopy around the village, sending slanting fingers of light into the clearing. The bench where Ana sat was a deep, rich brown, the wood worn smooth with age. She watched as Alaria took a thin, crooked stick and began to draw in the sand in front of them.

"You see, child, people of all races, belief systems, colors, genders and ages come here to study with us." Alaria settled on the bench, then looked at Ana, who rested her elbows on her thighs.

"To study what?"

The woman smiled gently. "They come to study about life in its fullest expression. Look at this...." She pointed to the circle she'd drawn in the sand. "Now, tell me about this symbol. What does it remind you of?"

Ana laughed shortly. "It's a circle, of course."

"Very good. What else?"

Raising her brows, Ana said, "It's round. It's whole."

"Excellent. And how would you equate that circle to a human being? You see, symbols are a language. And not just a silent one." Alaria tapped her stick beside the circle she'd drawn. "You need to understand that this has energy. As soon as I drew it in the sand here before us, it began to emanate a signal, or frequency, just as surely as I'd turned the dial on a radio and tuned in a particular station."

Sitting up, Ana said, "Oh, that's fascinating. I didn't know that."

"Symbols are living beings." Alaria kept pointing to the circle at their feet. "In fact, before humans spoke languages, they used symbols. Every symbol a human devised could be interpreted." She smiled briefly. "Over time, as verbal skills were acquired, the information and knowledge of the symbols—our old, first language—was forgotten and cast aside."

"So," Ana said, struggling to grasp the surprising information, "symbols were our *first* language here on earth?"

Alaria nodded. "You could say that. And that's an excellent connection you've made."

The praise warmed Ana. The air was cool without being chilly. She heard howler monkeys screeching, welcoming the rising sun. The sky was pale blue, with streaks of fog moving across it like elusive ballet dancers. Around her, she saw people with wooden bowls standing in line at the cooking pots. The children and women serving breakfast were spooning in some type of cereal.

Returning her attention to Alaria, Ana whispered, "You're right. There's something about your village that feels like...home. I can't explain it."

Patting her hand, Alaria said, "The longer you stay here, the more it will feel that way. Let's get back to the circle I've drawn here, Ana. There are some important things I must show you before it's time for you to leave."

Just the thought of leaving filled Ana with sudden, unexplained despair. Alaria's nurturing energy continued to reach out and enclose her in a wonderful, maternal way. And like the hungry jaguar Ana often imagined herself to be, she felt like a thief lapping up that warmth and care. She couldn't help it. She knew there was a huge hole in her heart because she'd been abandoned at birth. Oh, she had no memory of being left behind. No memory of anything until, at four years of age, she'd been brought by a farmer from a small town in Peru to a Catholic orphanage in Cuzco, one of the major cities in that country.

"A circle is about containment," Alaria started, breaking into Ana's thoughts. "Do you know what psychiatrists say about that?"

"That would be our ego, wouldn't it?"

With a pleased smile, Alaria said, "You are very astute. Yes. What have you been told about the ego?"

Shrugging, Ana said, "I took a couple of classes in psychology at university when I was getting my degree in biology. Ego is necessary. It's the container that holds our personality. And if your ego is weak, then you have weak boundaries and may have low self-esteem or, even worse, very little self-identity."

"Excellent," Alaria said, holding Ana's gaze. "However, a healthy ego is not a circle."

"Oh?"

"It is a U-shape. A cup." Alaria stood up and drew a curving line in the dust, next to the circle. "A healthy ego allows the give and take of energy, a sharing of our feelings with others." She tapped the circle. "Those who have an unhealthy ego are self-contained. They can't receive and send. All they can do is take. So people with a circular ego are narcissistic and self-serving. They are greedy beggars of a sort, absorbing other people's care, concern, and feelings and hoarding it within themselves."

Ana intently studied the drawing, her chin resting on her clasped hands. "You know, that makes sense." She looked up at Alaria. "Obviously, you have a U-shaped ego."

Laughing delightedly, she said, "And you are also U-shaped."

"That's good to know," Ana murmured, relieved. "I was worried for a moment." She met Alaria's twinkling glance.

"Let's do this…." The old woman drew a dot in the middle of the circle. "Now what do you think, Ana? How does that feel to you?"

"Well, if a circle is symbolic of an unhealthy ego, then a dot in the center of it…maybe represents a person's sense of self?" She tried to put it together. "It's as if the dot represents an individual surrounded and closed off by the circle around them."

"And knowing what you know about energy...?" Alaria prodded, leaning on the stick and gazing down at her.

Ana loved puzzles like this, and found herself becoming animated. Alaria was warm and thoughtful, and would not make fun of her if she was wrong, Ana knew. "This would be a person who is extremely self-centered, selfish and perhaps, in the extreme, really out of balance emotionally. Someone who would likely behave in an obsessive or compulsive manner?"

"Very good!" Alaria again tapped the drawing with her stick. "Did you know that to astrologers this symbol stands for the sun in our solar system? Remember, everything has many layers to it, much like an onion. We can look at any symbol from many levels, many different points of view, for each person incarnates into his or her lifetime with a unique take on reality. An astrologer would see this symbol and say it represents the sun in the person's natal chart. The sun stands for the self in astrology."

"So," Ana repeated, thinking out loud, "The sun represents the self to the astrologer. Not the ego?"

"Oh, yes, an astrologer would tell you that the sun *is* our ego. But they don't see other constructs or possibilities of what this symbol could mean. They are not wrong. They are right within the context of how they perceive it."

"But you see it at this level," Ana murmured.

"Yes, and now so do you."

Ana frowned. "But what level are you talking about?"

Alaria sat back down as a young girl came over with two bowls of cereal. Alaria took one and thanked the black-haired child.

Ana thanked her in turn and took her own bowl of fragrant, steaming cereal. The girl giggled and raced away toward the cooking fire in the distance.

"We'll eat and talk," Alaria instructed.

Ana noticed that someone had generously sprinkled brown sugar and slices of guava across the top of her cereal. The nutlike scent of the red quinoa enhanced the sweet fragrance of the guava, and she eagerly started to eat.

"The level I want to teach you about is the paranormal, or metaphysical, one. It is about pure, invisible energy. Energy is everywhere, Ana. It surrounds us, moves through us. We consist of energy even though we are in a physical body—dense energy that can be seen with our two eyes." She ate a few bites of her cereal and then continued. "You must understand energy, because your life will depend upon it shortly."

The grave warning startled Ana. She halted abruptly, her spoon halfway to her mouth. "How?"

"You are here for a reason," Alaria told her softly. "And we don't have a lot of time. You came here of your own free will, and that was vitally important. We weren't sure you would come at all, but you did, and that creates hope for us, for you and for our worlds."

Ana's confusion grew as she tried to grasp what the old woman was telling her. "I don't know how I got here."

"You came in your dream to us," Alaria said. "Many do so while they sleep." She waved her hand toward the village. "Many people journey to the Village of the Clouds as their body rests at night. Their astral body, or emotional energy body, travels the other dimensions while they're sleeping. Those of many individuals come here for training and healing."

Shaking her head, Ana whispered, "This sounds so strange to me, Alaria, and yet so exciting. My adoptive parents are Native American, and they put great stock in dreams and dreaming. I've heard my mother say that everything is energy, too, but the way you're explaining it makes more sense to me."

"And that is why you have come, child. You are embarking upon a life-and-death mission to find out who you really are. And you have many, many choices to make. By coming here, you've proved that you want to know certain things. I will share with you as much knowledge as I can in a short time. It will help you not only survive, but make some serious decisions—choices that will affect not only yourself, but all of us."

"You speak in riddles, Grandmother."

Laughing, the old woman nodded and went back to eating, as quiet stole around them once more. The children had settled on logs near the fires, eagerly eating their breakfast. Adults had gathered, as well, their friendly banter broken occasionally by a hearty laugh.

For Ana, the place felt like heaven. There was something so simple and rich about this quiet rural life. A profound sense of healing and peace infused her.

"I love this place. It fills me. It feeds me."

"Yes, the energy of the Village of the Clouds is food for your spirit and your soul, Ana. Anytime you come here, it is like getting your spiritual batteries recharged." Alaria smiled. "It's a place of healing and learning."

Putting her empty bowl aside, the elder stood up. "Time to continue with our lesson." Reaching for her stick, she drew two overlapping circles. "What does this symbol mean to you, Ana?"

"Two circles joined? Two egos?"

"Well, yes and no. Does it remind you of anything?"

Ana compared this drawing to the symbol Alaria had sketched before. "I prefer the double circles."

The elder studied her intently. Tapping the circle with the dot in the center, she said, "You don't like this one?"

"It doesn't feel good." Ana pointed to the second drawing. "This one feels right to me, but I can't explain why."

"Here's why it feels good to you," Alaria said. "This is the Vesica Piscis symbol. Quilters call it the wedding ring design." Alaria smiled. "Early Christians called this the symbol of Christ, because the overlapping area looks like a fish. Yet back in ancient history, this was the symbol of the Great Mother Goddess. You see, like all symbols, the Vesica Piscis can connect to the level of your belief, your consciousness in this lifetime, as well as the reality you experience during your present incarnation. The Egyptians used it, also. And so did the ancient cultures of Mesopotamia, long before Egypt rose to power."

"You're saying that the Vesica Piscis symbol is so old that every civilization has used its energy in some way?"

Alaria grinned broadly. "You are very sharp, Ana. It is, in fact, so ancient that the finest archeologists of today have no idea when it first appeared in human civilization. Each time they unearth a new culture, there it is."

Leaning forward, Ana studied the simple drawing. "Why is it so important?"

"Symbols, remember, are our first human language. And our first experience with energy." Alaria tapped the drawing with her stick. "You have two circles conjoined. Most cultures recognize that we have duality—for example, male and female. Two of everything exists here on earth. The circles speak to this point. One circle is male energy, the other female. And—" the elder leaned forward and tapped the oval area where the circles overlapped "—this is a joining of that energy. One circle by itself is alone and out of balance. Yet when you put two together, integrating male and female energy they become one. That integration becomes very powerful, healing, stabilizing and profoundly nourishing for the spirit." Alaria gestured toward the sky. "In reality, we are not separate. We have never lost oneness with the Great Mother Goddess. But so many religions have brainwashed people over the ages, making them believe they are separate from spirit, when they really are not. I believe this is why the Vesica Piscis was given to us—to let us know in our first language that spirit resides within us. We are spirit and are not separated from it—ever."

"I like the idea of being one," Ana confided. "That gives me hope."

Alaria nodded. "Yes, and a sense that spirit is within us, around us, and that all things are connected. If people of this earth would realize that, the world would not be embroiled in so much chaos and war. But enough of that." Alaria tapped the center of the Vesica Piscis. "We call this third component the eye, child. And it's very important that you use this symbol from now on to help yourself."

"How can I use it?"

"Come stand up over here," Alaria instructed with a wave of her hand.

Ana eagerly left the bench and walked over to where the elder stood.

"First, step into one circle of the Vesica Piscis. When you do, I want you to stand with your knees slightly bent, your eyes closed. I want you to imagine beautiful silver tree roots gently twining around your ankles, with the tip of each root going down through the center of your foot and deep into Mother Earth. Keep your body relaxed, your arms loose, your hands at your side."

Ana did as she was instructed. She stood there for at least five minutes, though nothing seemed to happen.

"All right," Alaria said at last, "open your eyes, Ana, and step out."

She followed the old woman's directions.

"Now enter the eye," Alaria stated. "You are already grounded. Just step in there, close your eyes and draw a deep breath into your nose, down into your abdomen, and release it out of your mouth. Do this three times."

Ana gingerly stepped forward. Within a minute, an invisible energy seemed to be gripping her by the shoulders and pulling her forward. Giving a yelp of surprise, she opened her eyes and took a step to keep her balance. "What happened?" she gasped.

Grinning, Alaria said, "Nothing that will harm you.

It is the energy of oneness with spirit touching you. Now, reposition yourself, Ana. Close your eyes and wait. This time, if the energy pulls you a certain way, don't allow it to unbalance you."

This time, when the energy came, Ana leaned forward with it, but so far that she lost her balance. To her surprise, the energy pushed her back. It pulled her to her right side, and then her left. After five minutes, she could feel it becoming less and less strong. Finally, it stopped, and she was standing quietly upright in the eye.

"Open your eyes and step out," Alaria said.

Ana did so. She turned and looked back. "What did I just feel?"

Alaria walked to the bench and sat down. "You experienced the ancient energy of healing and balance that the Vesica Piscis gifts to us, child. You can draw this symbol in the dirt, in the sand, or create it with string or rope. No matter how you make it, just stand in the eye, and you will receive a healing. It will rebalance your aura, the energy that surrounds your body. When you get readjusted, your health remains good, you can think better, you sleep profoundly, you remember your dreams and you become much less stressed."

"Amazing," Ana remarked. "There was no energy in the single circle outside the eye."

"That's right. I wanted you to experience both, because now you see for yourself where the power is. And you know how to use it."

"Wow..." Ana whispered, giving the Vesica Piscis an admiring glance. Then she looked at Alaria and pointed to the necklace she wore. "You even wear the symbol."

Fingering it, Alaria said, "Oh, yes. Right over my heart chakra." She touched the area between her breasts. "It helps me stay in balance emotionally. The symbol on another level inspires compassion, service to others and a sense of oneness with all beings on our planet. Such is its power and gift to all of us wise enough to utilize it."

"What a wonderful teaching," Ana exclaimed, excited by the possibilities. "I can draw this circle and just step into it anytime I feel out of balance?"

"Oh, yes. Or carry sixteen-foot lengths of string or colored yarn and lay them out in a double circle. It will work that way, as well."

"This is such a gift, Alaria. Thank you."

Rising, the elder came over to Ana. "My child," she said, becoming very serious, "it is nearly time for you to go. I need you to recall two things. The single circle with the dot is of the *Tupay,* or heavy, dark energy. The double circle is of the *Taqe,* or light energy expression. Remember this."

"Okay," Ana said. She felt Alaria's hand come to rest on her shoulder, and warmth flowed through her.

"Your mother—" Alaria's eyes filled with tears "—there is not much I can say, for you must find this on your journey, but your mother was *born* here, Ana."

Eyes widening, she whispered, "My birth mother?" A knot formed in her throat and tears flooded her own eyes. She felt Alaria's long, thin fingers tighten on her shoulder before releasing her.

"Yes, my child. Your mother was born here and I trained her for eighteen years."

Ana was startled. "You knew my mother." The tears started burning her throat. "For so long, I've tried to find her, to discover who she was and where she came from." Ana sobbed, pressing her fist against her lips as she stared at Alaria's kind features.

The woman had given her so much valuable information and Ana felt overwhelming gratitude. She had more questions about her heritage, about her mother. But before she felt able to speak, a jolting rumble coursed through the village. It was palpable, threatening, as if a minor earthquake was happening.

"You must go," Alaria said. "Just know your mother was very special, Ana. Come, you must walk back across the bridge. Your time with us is at an end for now."

Ana didn't want to leave, not before asking a hundred questions about her mother. She'd spent half her life trying to find her. But Ana did as instructed. She sensed she would return someday to this sacred place.

Moving across the wooden bridge, she looked back. Alaria had stopped on the other side. "When will I see you again?" Ana called.

"When the time is right," the elder said, lifting her hand in farewell. "Don't forget the lesson. Use the Vesica Piscis every day, child. We love you."

As Ana stepped off the bridge, she was once more surrounded by swirling mists, and felt a bump and jarring. The quiet calm was left behind; a deep, spiraling sensation came over her. A moment ago, she'd felt light as a feather, and now the heaviness was overwhelming.

The vibrating continued. She recognized the sound

of jet engines roaring. And then a voice came over the intercom, jolting her fully awake.

"Ladies and gentlemen, we have just landed in Lima. We hope you've enjoyed your flight on Condor 917. Welcome to Peru. Have a pleasant stay in our country…."

Chapter 1

"Get outta my way! Move! Move!" a young Peruvian boy barked, pushing aggressively against her.

Ana Elena Rafael gave a small cry of surprise as she fought the grogginess of her dream and tried to disembark from the airliner. The aisle was jammed with a crush of restless passengers. The child shoved against her hip and then wriggled past. Ana had been patiently waiting to deplane at the Cuzco airport, when the abrupt attack occurred.

Stunned, she didn't have time to think or move. She'd been standing in the aisle of the first-class section when the pushy child launched himself into her. The boy and his father had sat right behind her during the Lima to Cuzco flight, the child shrieking and pummeling her chair.

Nerves raw, she threw out her hands now, completely off balance. To her dismay, she realized she was going to fall right into the arms of a passenger sitting on the opposite side of the aisle.

Ana saw the man turn and look up as she cried out, a surprised expression in his alert blue eyes. Everything seemed to move in slow motion as she awkwardly pitched forward and he caught her.

She had been vaguely aware of the thirtysomething man when he'd boarded the plane in Lima. It was a one-hour flight up and over the mighty Andes to Cuzco, nearly thirteen thousand feet above sea level. He'd gotten up once to go to the restroom, which was located near the cockpit door.

Bothered by the constant hammering on the back of her seat, Ana hadn't take much notice of any other passengers. She recalled that when the man had come out of the restroom, his blue eyes had focused on her like a laser. Or maybe more aptly, because she was a wildlife biologist who studied jaguars, he reminded her of a big cat focused on its prey. A frisson of warning, of danger, snaked through Ana. It was as if death were stalking her.

She tried to shake off the premonition. She had enough to think about, especially the dream she'd had during the previous flight. The calmness and peace of the Village of the Clouds had been abruptly shattered by the real world, plus her irritation toward the overly permissive father of the rude child.

As the blue-eyed man helped her regain her balance, Ana studied him more closely. He was darkly tanned and ruggedly handsome, with black hair trimmed in a short military style. And those eyes... Mesmerizing. Like the eyes of the beautiful jaguars she cared for back in Arizona at the Wildlife Institute near Camp Verde.

All of those impressions shimmered through her in the brief moments he held her. In his casual jeans and white shirt, he seemed like an everyday workman. So how could such an ordinary man seem so extraordinary? Something told Ana that he had a lot of power beneath his simple facade. *He hides it,* her intuition whispered. He wanted to blend in and vanish. Much like the jaguar, Ana thought. The cat's gold coat was spotted with black crescents, perfect camouflage in the dim, dappled light of the jungle. A jaguar could literally disappear among the shadows cast by trees and sun. This man was like that. She knew it.

And now she was in his arms. The look in his wide eyes was one of worry, shock and concern. Ana's intuition—which her adoptive mother, Mary Rafael, had often told her resembled that of her beloved jaguars—absorbed all his feelings like a sponge. That was how Ana read people. How she knew what they were feeling, instead of what they projected.

Ana could feel his hands. With thick calluses across his palms, long, strong fingers and short nails, they were a worker's hands. This was a man who labored outdoors, no doubt. And now those hands were wrapped around her shoulders.

Cushioning her.

Saving her.

The stranger had stopped her from striking her head on the seat in front of them, or possibly worse. As Ana steadied her breathing, she managed to grip one of his arms. The man was like a rock. His shoulders were broad beneath that thin cotton shirt. Ana felt the thickness and strength of his muscles as she tried to recapture her balance.

She heard the Peruvian boy's father mutter a rebuke to his child, then walk on by without stopping to apologize or help her straighten up.

Something gave way in her ankle; pain shot up her right calf. The blue-eyed man grunted as he took her full weight, his hands gripping her shoulders as he held her upright.

More passengers were pushing past her as she clumsily regained her balance. They were in a hurry. It was 6:00 a.m., and they wanted to get into the city.

Ana felt the man gently settle her into a seat.

"Welcome to Cuzco." He smiled wryly. "I call this one the stampede flight. It's the first plane out of Lima in the morning, and most of the businessmen are on it. Are you okay, *señorita?*"

Ana felt embarrassment tunneling through her. Strands of her hair caught against her lips and she brushed them away. "Thank you…I wasn't expecting to get trampled."

He gave her an understanding look and held out his hand. "I'm Mason Ridfort. My friends call me Mace."

Ana gripped his outstretched palm, feeling her thumping heart responding to his slow smile. His square face showed off his high cheekbones, solid jaw and cleft chin…and a sensual male mouth. "I'm Ana Rafael. From Sedona, Arizona. Thanks for saving me."

The moment their fingers touched, a shock of energy raced up her arm and straight into her chest. The warmth of Mace's hand contrasted with hers, which was cool and moist.

Coming here to Peru scared her. Given her clash with the child and her encounter with this interesting stranger, it wasn't hard to figure out why. But this journey was something she had to do. The dream called to her. Haunted her.

Ana had to find out the truth. Who was she? The orphanage where she'd lived before she'd been adopted was here in Cuzco. And that was her reason to be in Cuzco to investigate that lead. The dream she'd just had was something new. Ana wasn't going to be detoured from her only lead to her young life before being adopted. She would find out what she could at the orphanage and then try to find out later about the mysterious Village of the Clouds from her dream. Maybe the officials at the orphanage had heard of it. Ana made a note to ask. Alaria had said her birth mother had been born in the Village of the Clouds. Where was the village located? Somewhere in Peru? Many times, Ana's dreams were precognitive and came true. She hoped the peaceful village—and the people inhabiting it—were real and would provide answers.

Releasing Mace's hand, she saw that crowd in the plane had thinned to a trickle. Giving him a tense, fatigued smile, she whispered, "I'm sorry. I'm not the best of company right now. I've just had a long flight from Arizona to Florida to here."

"Umm, jet lag. I understand." Her rescuer looked up

and checked the aisle, empty now except for the flight crew. "Are you ready? I think we can disembark without getting trampled this time around."

Ana felt incredibly cocooned by the warmth and security of Mason Ridfort's wonderful auric energy. His care and protecticn embraced her like sunlight. If she hadn't been so distracted, so raw from the child's hammering on her seat for an hour, or the haunting terror of coming back to the orphanage, Ana would have liked to spend time with this man. But right now, her focus wasn't on him. She glanced down at the gold Rolex on her left wrist.

"I'm late," she said. "I can't be late." She quickly shoved herself to her feet. The jab of pain in her right ankle made her wince.

Mace rose in turn. "Twist an ankle or your back?"

Testing her right leg, Ana opened the overhead bin, retrieved her suitcase on wheels and placed it in the aisle. "A little pain in my ankle is all. I'll be okay, thanks." Her hair had fallen forward, a curtain around her face. It swung back as she looked up into his warm blue eyes. "I wish I had time to thank you properly, Mace, but I have an appointment to get to. It's really important. Thanks so much for catching me. I could have hurt myself."

"No problem, Ms. Rafael."

"Call me Ana." She lifted her hand in farewell and hobbled down the aisle. "See you…."

"You just might," Mace called as she exited the plane.

Ana hurried down the empty corridor. By the time she reached the main terminal, her ankle was beginning to burn. Perhaps she'd strained it more than she thought. It didn't matter. The pain in her heart was twenty times worse than that in her ankle.

It turned out that the crowd of passengers leaving the airliner had been nothing compared to those in the airport terminal. She was shocked by the numbers of milling bodies, mostly men in dark business suits. The hustle and bustle was tremendous, the noise setting her even more on edge, along with the elbowing and pushing, the aggressive energy that abounded throughout the area.

She had to get a taxi. As Ana moved toward the glass doors of the airport, it seemed a thousand other passengers had the exact same idea. Again and again she was jostled and pushed. Frustrated, Ana began to elbow these disrespectful men back. Who did they think they were, anyway?

By the time she got out the door, her ankle was hurting in earnest. There were thirty or forty taxis lined up, the drivers gesturing and calling to potential patrons. Ana felt like she was in the middle of a male stampede, with no one caring that she was in the way. Obviously, the number of people was greater than the number of taxis, and the rush to get to one overwhelmed her.

All too quickly, the taxis were gone and she was left standing on the curb. Looking at her watch, she felt frustration and more terror. She had an appointment with Mother Bernadette at St. Mary's Orphanage on Plaza de Armas in less than an hour.

And it was one appointment Ana didn't dare miss. This was the orphanage she'd come from.

So far, nothing in Peru looked familiar to her. But she was twenty-seven years old. How much would she recall of being here as a young child? Only snatches, brief flashes—and nightmares that continued to plague her to this day. Nightmares that had unsettled Ana to the point that they had driven her back here, back to her last home in Peru.

Was she Peruvian by birth? Were her real parents citizens of this country? In a letter to Ana, Mother Bernadette had told her that she recalled her being brought to their orphanage as a four-year-old. The nun said she'd taken notes about Ana's arrival on the day of her induction. Clearly, she had precious information Ana wanted.

The desire to find out *who* she was had eaten at her daily since she was young enough to know they were not her real parents. At age fourteen, her adoptive parents had told her all they knew at that time—Cuzco was a connection to her mysterious past. They had tried to find out more, but had come to a dead end. Now, it was up to Ana to continue the investigation. John and Mary Rafael loved her like the daughter they'd always wanted and couldn't have. And love her they did. Ana loved them just as fiercely in return. No one could have asked for better parents than John and Mary.

As Ana grew older, the nightmares increased in frequency and intensity until she was having them three or four times a week. Often she saw a jaguar. Sometimes she would change into one, and then morph back into human form. At times, a dark hunter stalked her dreams, intent on killing her.

Ana was losing so much sleep, her adoptive parents

had urged her to go to Cuzco. They'd coaxed her into making the journey in order to find out who she was. Then, they felt, her nightmares would cease, and she could live in the present, unfettered by the puzzles of her past.

Ana knew it was the right thing to do. She had so many questions. Why had her mother given her to an orphanage? What circumstances had made her abandon Ana? And what about her father? If her dream on the plane was true—and her mother had been born in the Village of the Clouds—Ana was confounded even more. If her biological mother had been born in that magical place of love and caring, why would she abandon Ana? The village seemed so beautiful and tranquil. It seemed impossible that one of the inhabitants could carry out such a heinous act.

As she stood before the airport terminal on the chilly, gray March morning, waiting for a taxi, she hoped all the mysteries of her origins would be solved during this trip.

The breeze was cool. It was the dry season in this part of the world. Ana wore a beige linen pantsuit and a pale pink silk blouse beneath. The black leather briefcase in her hand contained all her vital information—what there'd been of it when John and Mary Rafael had stumbled upon the orphanage and fallen in love with Ana.

Looking up at the moody sky, Ana thought it might rain. She gazed toward the city skyline, where the spires of many Catholic cathedrals reached above the two- and three-story gray stone buildings. Founded by the Incas, Cuzco lay in a bowl-shaped valley crisscrossed with a network of cobblestone roads and highways.

Before the Spanish arrived, this city was where the Inca had lived for most of each year.

As she'd seen it from the plane window, the road system had reminded Ana of a spiderweb. Grandmother Alaria's words about the ancients using symbols had come back to her.

"Looks like you're stranded."

Mace Ridfort's low, modulated voice came from behind Ana. She turned around abruptly and nodded. With a large duffel bag balanced on one broad shoulder, he stood out starkly against the next wave of dark-suited businessmen. In his other hand he held a badly scarred brown briefcase. Her gaze settled on his hands—strong hands that had grasped and held her. Never had Ana felt so safe, so secure as when this man had caught her, protecting her from injury. What was it about Mace Ridfort?

Noting the glimmer of a smile in his dark blue eyes, she felt as if the clouds had parted and the sun was shining down on her. Jolted, she realized Ridfort's eyes were the same color as Grandmother Alaria's. Was it just a coincidence? Right now, Ana was so out of sorts that her normal intuitive sense wasn't functioning.

Unaccountably, her bruised spirits lifted. When his mouth began to curve in a smile, Ana found herself returning his grin. "This has to be the Dodge City of South America, and I'm in the middle of a longhorn stampede. At least that's what it feels like."

Mace glanced around. "Yes, a good analogy. That's why I take my time getting off the plane and picking up my luggage. It's not worth trying to fight with these guys. They'll eat you up for breakfast and spit you out for lunch if you get in their way." He chuckled at his own joke.

"This is all so *loco,*" Ana muttered. "I'm going to be late for my appointment." She searched his face. "Do you know where I could find a taxi, Mace?"

He shook his head. "They're all heading into the city. You'll probably have to wait twenty to thirty minutes before they return to pick up the next wave of passengers. Cuzco isn't a big place and taxis aren't plentiful." He cocked his head. "But maybe I can be of help." Lifting his briefcase, he pointed to a large parking lot filled with cars. "I'm going to my office in Cuzco. It's right downtown. My Land Rover is over there in short-term parking. Maybe I can give you a lift. Where are you heading?"

"To the St. Mary's Catholic Orphanage. I'd pay you for your time and gas."

Shrugging, Mace said, "Not to worry. Matter of fact, my engineering company has an office overlooking Plaza de Armas, so it won't be out of my way at all. I know exactly where the orphanage is located."

Relieved, Ana felt tears threatened, and fought them back. She put down her briefcase, reached out and squeezed Mace's arm. "Thank you so much. You don't know how important it is for me to get there on time."

Mace's smile widened. "*No problemo, señorita.* Is your ankle okay or do you need some help with your luggage?"

Ana picked up her bag. "No, it's a bit tender, but fine. I'm ready." What was a little sprain compared to the pain she'd carried in her heart all her life, wondering who she was?

Sudden excitement gripped her as they walked toward the parking lot. She was on her way! Beginning an adventure of discovery.

As they drove closer to the center of Cuzco, beautifully manicured lawns and sidewalks landscaped with trees, flowers and bushes began to spring up along the uninspiring highway. Stone statues of historical military figures, as well as an impressive stone obelisk, marked the entrance to the city.

Ana's throat began to close with anxiety, and once again fear wove through her. She sat in Mace Ridfort's beat-up, rusted Land Rover, hands gripped together in her lap. As she looked around the streets, nothing seemed familiar to her.

"You're going to the orphanage," Mace said casually as he drove. "Are you adopting a child?"

"No, I'm adopted. I lived here when I was four to six years old. I'm coming back to try and find out who I really am." Nervously, Ana continued, "And I'm afraid of what I might find. Or not find."

Mace glanced over at her. "No wonder you looked pale and stressed. When I saw you come onto the plane, I was wondering if you were sick or something."

Giving him a wry look, Ana said, "Sick of not knowing who I really am…."

Nodding, he steered the Land Rover deftly through the heavy morning traffic. "We share a common background. I was adopted, too. I know what you mean about not knowing who you really are."

Ana was amazed at the synchronicity. But things like

this happened to her all the time, so why should she be so surprised?

"Do you know who your biological parents are?" she asked.

Mace nodded and concentrated on traffic. "Yes, I finally found out. When I was eighteen, my mother came forward. She told me everything."

"And you're Peruvian?"

"My mother's Quero Indian from Peru, and my biological father, who's dead now, was from France. So I'm a mix. I was adopted by a couple in Lima as an infant. Pablo and Manuela Vargas, who own a copper mine business. They gave me the best education money could buy. I learned four foreign languages and was sent to a nearby private school. I was very lucky and I see them as my second set of parents to this day." Mace added, "You'll be glad you did this. Any information is better than none. After I found out about my biological parents, I went to France to be with my father and get a degree in hydrology and engineering. I came back here after that and reconnected with my real mother."

"You're right, Mace. I know that. But it's scary for me." Taking a deep, ragged breath, Ana saw that they'd reached the Plaza de Armas. Photos she'd seen earlier did not do it justice. It was a magnificent rectangular space with buildings rising around all four sides—one of them an Incan temple. Her stomach knotted even more. She clutched her hands until her fingers ached.

The orphanage looked vaguely familiar to her. Its foundations were part of an Incan temple that had once stood here. The gray rocks were smooth, hand cut and seamlessly fitted together. The red-tiled roof stood out, and the cross on top announced it was Catholic.

Mace pulled up in front of the imposing wooden door and put the car in Park. "We're here." He pointed. "That's the main entrance to the orphanage. And over here—" he said, pointing to a different part of the plaza "—in that yellow stucco building, up on the second floor, is my office. We're not so far away from one another."

"No, we aren't." Ana couldn't tear her eyes away from the door to the orphanage. Somehow, the wrought-iron door handle seemed familiar to her. She'd seen this door in her many nightmares. The door would yawn open like a serpent's mouth ready to devour her—and she'd wake up screaming.

"Here," Mace said, digging into his jeans pocket. "My business card." Handing it to Ana, he murmured, "Since you're new here, so to speak." He grinned. "And if you don't have a friend or someone to help you get a hotel, or want to know a good place to eat, call me up when you're finished here. I'll try to be a good host and erase that bad experience you had at the airport. Cuzco residents are very nice and warmhearted. Most will give you the shirt off their back. I'd hate you to go away thinking we're nothing but a herd of out-of-control longhorns." He chuckled.

Mace's laughter was soothing to her jittery, edgy nerves. Ana studied the card: Mason Ridfort, Civil Engineer and Hydrologist. "You're a builder?" she asked.

He nodded. "Yeah, I build wells all around the country. Fresh, clean water means babies of the Quero people won't die of dysentery or diarrhea. My biological mother felt this was a cause worthy of me. I work with several international aid groups who donate the money so we can build wells for various villages." Mace smiled. "It keeps me real busy."

Tucking the card into her pocket, Ana said, "I've seen the same problem in Belize. Your work is important. You're saving lives."

"Just think of me a modern day knight on a white horse," he joked. With both hands on the wheel, he said, "Remember, I can help you if you need it, *señorita.*"

"Call me Ana. And thank you, Mace. You truly have been a knight in shining armor to me." She gripped the door handle. "Thanks again."

"You're welcome. And I hope everything goes well for you in there. It is scary, coming home to retrace your roots and find out who you really are. Good luck."

Suddenly, Ana felt cold and filled with terror. She had to walk through that door. She had to ask questions. Such trepidation built within her that she wanted to remain in Mace's sunny presence just a few moments longer. But she forced herself to climb out of the Land Rover and wave goodbye.

A cool breeze moved by her, giving her goose bumps. Heaving an inner sigh, the knots in her stomach now fist size, Ana stared at the daunting wooden door that held all the secrets of her young life behind it. Was she ready for this?

Mouth dry, her heart pounding in her chest, she gripped her briefcase and luggage and stepped forward.

Chapter 2

Victor Carancho Guerra cooed softly as his wife, Fidelia, handed him their one-month-old daughter, Abegail. Spanish names had meaning, and his newborn's meant "father rejoices." Indeed, Victor did rejoice when his second daughter was born.

"Look at you, my precious baby girl," he murmured, pressing a soft kiss to her smooth forehead. He turned to give his wife a warm look as he sat behind the counter of his curio shop in Aguas Calientes.

"Abegail has the eyes of an eagle," he said.

His young wife grinned and blushed. Fidelia was a local beauty who had come from a very poor background. It had been easy to court her. She went from abject poverty to riches simply by saying, "I do." Yet

Victor knew she truly did love him as much as she admired him. He was a great man, widely known and respected by all. And Victor liked the fact his wife's name meant "faithful." It carried full weight with him, because his first marriage had ended tragically for all concerned. Victor demanded loyalty from those who wanted the powerful, world-altering secrets he carried.

"We live only to bring a smile to your face, my dear husband." Fidelia folded the soft pink alpaca blanket around the tiny bundle in Victor's arms. "I've got to continue getting *desayuno* ready for us," she whispered, placing a chaste kiss on Victor's bearded cheek.

Lifting his nose to sniff the air, Victor nodded. "Smells good," he said. "I'll take care of our little one here in the meantime."

"Papa…Papa…"

Victor looked down to see his son tugging on his shirt. Marcial was ten years old, Victor's first child with Fidelia. He had named the boy after the Roman god of war. The child was tall and gangly like Victor, his thick black hair bowl shaped around his long, lean face.

"Eh, Marcial?"

Abegail cooed, her tiny hands reaching up to tangle in Victor's neatly trimmed black-and-silver beard.

"Papa, may I help put the price tags on the dolls that arrived yesterday?" Marcial pointed to a new shipment of handmade Peruvian dolls.

"Of course, son. You know where the black felt-tip pen is." Victor gestured to a small drawer behind the glass counter. "They are each twenty dollars U.S."

The boy grinned happily and charged down the

counter, his shoes thunking on the aging wooden floors. The massive glass-encased display case stretched like a fat anaconda from the door of the shop to the back wall, a good thirty feet long and chock-full of items tourists drooled over.

Victor chuckled and returned his attention to their newest addition. Abegail had her mother's beautiful full features, he thought. But all babies were round and plump-cheeked at first. Gently, he stroked a finger through his daughter's thin black hair. Abegail was only a month old and already the pride of his life. Cradling her on one arm, Victor rocked her and made cooing sounds. Soon Abegail's bow shaped mouth stretched into a wide smile.

Her fingers were so precious, so tiny. Victor always marveled at the birthing process and how innocent and beautiful a baby was when it came out of its mother. Abegail's eyes were lively, and he knew they would take on a cinnamon color in time. They were slightly slanted, and again reminded Victor that she took strongly after her mother, who also had slightly tilted eyes. They gave her an exotic look that Victor loved. He glanced over at his hyperactive son, then took a moment to look fondly around the quiet shop. In a couple hours he would open the doors of El Condor Curio Shoppe, which sat at the top of the hill on Aguas Calientes's main street. The tourists would bustle off the Cuzco train and scurry into town to buy his special curios for friends and family. Victor expected a busy day in his store. He'd chanted a money spell earlier to attract much energy and monetary exchange.

To ensure good business, Victor regularly used his paranormal knowledge. Daily he would cast a spell that would quite literally draw people into his shop. Tourists would need to come to El Condor and not know why.

Laughing softly, he tickled Abegail's tiny neck with the end of his goatee. The baby gurgled pleasantly, her hands opening and closing with delight. Victor had nothing but love for his new daughter. How long he'd pined for a little girl! Frowning, he recalled his unhappy past—a painful, terrible memory. He'd been duped by his first wife, who had lied to him about everything. Even now, twenty-eight years later, he felt rage, along with a pain in his chest.

"Papa? Can I put a spell on each doll now? I put the price tags on them already." Marcial held up one of the handmade dolls. It was of a Peruvian girl with a black felt bowler hat on her head. The doll wore a typical highlands costume consisting of a long, colorful skirt and white blouse.

"Of course," Victor exclaimed. "I've taught you how to sit quietly. You know how to cast a circle of salt, place the doll within it and then send in your intent—that it be bought by a *turista*."

Marcial giggled. "This is so much fun, Papa!" He bent over a lower drawer and opened it. The boy took out a large piece of brown paper and carefully laid it on the clean floor behind the counter. He then removed a plastic bag containing sea salt.

"Now, slow down," Victor advised. "Slow down, take your time and focus, Marcial. Focus is everything in our business."

"Yes, Papa." The boy drew three deep breaths in succession and gave his father a winning smile. Then he placed all the dolls on the floor next to the paper, which stretched from the wall to the counter. Victor watched as his son knelt down upon it, opened the plastic bag and, in a clockwise direction, dribbled salt from his closed hand. In no time he had created a circle a little larger than each doll.

"Excellent," Victor declared. Marcial glowed at the praise. The boy set the bag of salt aside and gently placed the first doll within the circle. He then took his wand, which Victor had made for him from the branch of a mahogany tree, and began to trace the outer circle while he mumbled the spell that would cause a shopper to spontaneously buy the doll.

Victor was pleased to see his son's attention to detail. To work in the metaphysical arts, one had to be grounded, intent and focused. At ten years old, Marcial was finally realizing all these things must be in place to create the proper energy around a thing he wished to change.

And of course, the boy received a bit of money with each enchanted object that sold. Victor knew money was the ultimate power in this three-dimensional world, routinely turning would-be saints into sinners. Victor could prove it over and over again. Marcial should learn about the power and effects of money not only on himself, but how it influenced others. To learn sorcery was to be aware of each human being's weaknesses, as well as his or her strengths. A good sorcerer knew how to exploit both. And his son would begin to see how money itself could be used as a spell of sorts, manipulating a person to do what he wanted.

Sunlight was just beginning to peek into the large picture windows at the front of his store. Victor always enjoyed the weak rays that found their way through the perennial clouds hovering over the forested valley. He loved this place, loved the power and majesty of the tall peaks that towered like kindly guardians above Aguas Calientes. Yes, life was good. Because of the spells he placed on all the goods in his shop, they sold briskly and quickly. He was the richest man in town and that made him feel warm in his heart. He would always have money to provide for his growing family, and that was important to him. In two years, he would send Marcial away for special military schooling in Lima, to a boys' academy, so that his son would get the very best and most disciplined education possible.

Victor saw one of his students, Ramiro, walk up to the door of his shop and knock. Victor liked what his name stood for: wise and famous. It gave the lad something to aspire to.

"Come in," Victor called.

The bell over the door tinkled as Ramiro entered and then closed it behind him.

"Good morning, *maestro*," the twenty-year-old murmured as he walked to the counter. He lifted his hand and said hello to Marcial, who did not respond, as he was focused on his spells.

Victor smiled at the short, heavily muscled young man. Ramiro came from a poor family in Aguas Calientes. He worked carrying tourists' baggage from the train, across the deadly Urubamba tributary to the fancy hotels on the other side. Every day, Ramiro risked his life. He had come to Victor many years ago asking for a safety amulet to keep him from falling and drowning in the angry rapids. Ten young men had lost their lives so far, and he didn't want to be another one. His wages kept his parents and five siblings from starving to death. He could not afford to die, for they, too, would certainly die from lack of food. There was a bridge that tourists used and hired help was not allowed to access it. They were forced to take the bags across the rapids, instead.

Victor had cast a spell into a black river stone the young Quero carried on his person. It ensured that Ramiro could safely cross on the wet, slippery boulders, avoiding the cold, swiftly moving waters that spilled down the slope to the mighty Urubamba River. One slip and Ramiro could be swept away, since he didn't know how to swim. As well, the glacier-fed waters that roared unchecked down from the Andes were so cold that a person would freeze within minutes of falling in.

Victor met the young man's dark brown eyes. "And how are you this morning, my boy? You look very happy. What has happened?"

Ramiro's smile revealed his upper front teeth were missing, because of a nasty fight years earlier. "I'm *very* happy, *maestro!* I just had to come and tell you that the spell you gave me to get the attention of Lucinda is working!" He rubbed his hands together, his voice rising in excitement. "I know you are truly a master of the metaphysical arts, *maestro,* and I have studied many years with you. But when Lucinda came from Cuzco to teach at the local school here, I fell blindly in love with her. She would not have much to do with me, a poor man from Aguas Calientes." He shook his head. "But the spell you gave me last week, it has worked, *maestro!* I am floating above the clouds."

Victor grinned. "Indeed? That is very good news, Ramiro." He saw the happiness shining in the man's dark brown eyes. Ramiro was plain looking and his hair needed trimming. His clothes mirrored his station in life: the white peasant shirt he wore was thin with age, though spotless; the brown wool trousers had patches sewn here and there. Still, Ramiro was clean shaven and washed nightly. One of the many things Victor instilled in his students was a sense of pride and neatness in their appearance. A positive presentation was vital if they were to be successful when they went out on their own and opened up their own metaphysical business.

Under ordinary circumstances, an educated woman such as Lucinda would snub a country bumpkin like Ramiro, Victor knew. But he had tricks that could turn the tide.

Laughing almost giddily, Ramiro said, "I sneaked the crystal amulet to Lucinda. I hung it on a silver chain and presented it to her as a gift—a pretty pendant she could wear." His eyes widened in wonder. "The very next day, she met me at the plaza while I was buying vegetables for my poor, sick mother. She invited *me* to have tea with her this afternoon."

"And was she wearing the crystal necklace at that time?" Victor asked.

"Yes, yes, she was." Ramiro reached across the counter and gripped his mentor's shoulder. "I have so much to thank you for, *maestro.* Truly, you are the magician of the world, as they say you are. Long ago, before I became your student, I had heard that you made and sold spells, but now I see that your power is incredible. Thank you so much. This woman holds my heart in her hands. I love her, and you have helped make my dream come true, *señor.*"

"Ah, you see, Ramiro, when one's intent is harnessed with one's desire, it always yields such possibilities. Well, go to tea with the beautiful Lucinda this afternoon. You might bring her flowers, eh? Women always like flowers. And perhaps, a little box of chocolates? You will impress her with your continued thoughtfulness. It sends the right message, that you care about her and want to forge a continuing relationship with her. Flowers and candies cast a magical spell of their own."

"Yes, *maestro.*" Ramiro laughed again and stuck his hands into the pockets of his baggy trousers. "You are such a wise person. I am humbled to remain your loyal servant and student."

"As I am humbled that you wish to learn from me," Victor murmured. He kissed his daughter's head, her fine, dark hair tickling his nose. Straightening, he said, "And don't forget, two days from now we will have another class. There will be about one hundred of my students from Peru, some from *Norteamérica* and others from Europe and Asia who come for their next training session with me. We will meet up on Machu Picchu, as usual, where magic lives even on our three-dimensional plane."

Rubbing his hands together once more, Ramiro said, "I have my calendar marked, *maestro.* I would *never* miss one of your wonderful classes. I wish you held them more often than every three months. But I am in a hurry, and you have always said that learning the metaphysical arts is not for the impatient, but for the plodding." He lifted his hand. "I must go to work. I just wanted to come by and thank you from my heart for all your help and kindness."

Victor smiled. "You're welcome, my young friend. I will see you in a few days."

The door closed. Fidelia poked her head out from behind the dark blue curtain between the shop and their living quarters. "*Mi querido, desayuno* is ready," she sang out.

What a sweet voice his wife possessed. Victor nodded and gazed at their daughter. "My joy, it is time for your father to eat. Are you not happy?" He smiled down at his child. Abegail gurgled contentedly and waved her arms in response.

Lifting his daughter, Victor felt pleasure ripple through him as he saw the chocolate colored birthmark that represented the *Tupay* symbol on her. She had a circle with a dot in the center on the back of her tiny, wrinkled neck. Yes, one day his daughter would learn all about the metaphysical arts. He was already passing on his knowledge to his son, and when she was seven years old, Abegail would start training, just as Marcial had.

"Coming," he called to his wife.

But just as Victor placed his daughter in the bassinet near the table, he felt a powerful disturbance in the energy within the room. He tucked the blanket around his daughter and straightened. What had happened? Everything looked normal. Fidelia was placing pink linen napkins beside their plates and preparing to sit down.

And yet, the power of the unseen wave felt like a shattering tsunami. He gasped in surprise.

"What, darling?" Fidelia asked as she poured them coffee. "What's wrong?"

"Nothing," Victor muttered. He suddenly moved past the table. "I'm going to my office, *querida.* I don't know when I'll be back. I just sensed something and need to check it out right away."

Fidelia seemed alarmed but said nothing. "Of course, my husband."

Of all things! Victor hurried to the rear of the two-story building and down the steps to his inner sanctum, the place where he practiced his metaphysical arts. With his key, the only one that existed, he opened the heavy wooden door, quietly shut and locked it behind him and switched on the light. Victor felt a thrumming sense of urgency he hadn't felt in a long time. But he clearly recognized what the energy was all about.

He sat down in the overstuffed chair at his desk and quickly closed his eyes. Grounding himself, he relaxed and folded his hands in his lap. He knew he had to get a steely control over his stunned emotions.

She was *here!* His estranged daughter, born twenty-seven years ago, was somewhere in Peru. Victor couldn't believe it. Suddenly, he felt both giddy and anxious. His long-lost daughter had finally come home. Ana. That was the name his wife had given the baby she'd carried before she died. It was a name he would always remember.

Victor had to be careful what he chose to do now. Being a master sorcerer, he knew that not all energies or spirit beings in the other dimensions were necessarily friendly toward him.

Those who traveled in what was commonly known as the Other Worlds, and who knew what they were doing, always cloaked the "light"—the aura—that emanated around them. Denizens of the lower realms were always interested in light, since they had so little of their own. Once these roving astral entities found an uncloaked being, they would try and latch on to the aura, much like sucker fish attach themselves to the underbelly of a shark. Though Victor considered them garbage, they were very real and could drain anyone ignorantly traveling through the Other Worlds. And right now, he needed to do that. His long-lost daughter by his first marriage had just arrived unexpectedly in Peru. She might come looking for him.

Victor didn't know if she was trained in the metaphysical arts or not. If she was, he didn't want to give away his presence just yet, and cloaking was an essential defense against a possible enemy.

Controlling his breathing, he quickly shifted into what shamans and sorcerers referred to as "nonordinary reality." Being a master sorcerer, he could accomplish the same thing any well-trained shaman could: easily shift into the Other Worlds.

Instantly, Victor found himself hovering above his body. Turning, he saw his force of spirit guides waiting for orders from him.

Let's track down the source of my daughter's energy, he told them via mental telepathy. His black stallion, a mighty spirit being from the other dimensions, leaped forward, ready for Victor to alight upon his wide, massive back. Once astride, Victor gripped the fiery animal's mane and clapped his heels to the horse's flanks. Instantly, they flew through the darkness of the fourth dimension, no longer constrained by the physical laws of the third. Time and space did not exist here. Instead, he would find his estranged daughter's location in the blink of an eye.

There was a feeling of movement as Victor narrowed his eyes and followed the golden trail of energy left by his daughter. She obviously had never trained in the paranormal arts or she would not have left herself uncloaked, her trail easy for anyone to follow.

Victor knew his daughter was coming home. *Home.* It left a bittersweet feeling within him. What was Ana like? Had she grown to look more like him or his dead wife? Was she interested in learning from him? As his spirit horse sailed through sparkling fields of stars and galaxies, Victor wished mightily that he could know the answer. Ana was his only wound, the one thing his heart pined over, because he was her father and had lost all contact with her after birth.

Twisting to look over his shoulder, Victor made sure his other eleven guides were following behind. Each of his helpers played a powerful role. And at any given time, he could shape-shift into one of them by asking them to cover his human form.

His ebony raven croaked loudly and flapped its wings. He was Victor's first choice for shape-shifting when he had to traverse the third dimensional plane in disguise.

His daughter Ana... What had life been like for her since she'd been gone? Victor had so many questions. Before now, her energy had been cloaked, and he could not find her no matter how much he searched the Other Worlds for a trace of her signature. If she knew about cloaking, why had she revealed herself now? Perhaps because she was coming home to Peru to meet with him? Victor was uneasy.

Ana's arrival was an unexpected gift and a possible problem for him. Still, in his heart, Victor hoped that he and his daughter could become friends and he could teach the paranormal arts. Would Ana side with him and the *Tupay* way of living?

A hundred thoughts collided in his head when he saw the golden energy leading to the Lima airport. The golden, sparkling trail came from a plane in its final descent, with Condor Airlines written on the fuselage. The great silver bird landed with a screech upon the long, black, asphalt runway. Bluish smoke rose briefly from the rubber tires as the pilot slowed down the aircraft.

Because he was in fourth dimensional space, Victor could see through any third dimensional object, whether a building, an animal...or an airplane. He pulled his spirit stallion to a halt and hovered just above the airliner.

Eyes narrowing, Victor quickly followed the golden

thread of energy into the plane. There, in the first-class section, he saw his daughter for the first time in many years. Tears crowded his eyes unexpectedly and Victor quickly wiped them away. She was so beautiful! And sleepy-looking. Victor felt a pang of disappointment as he noticed Ana was nearly the spitting image of his dead wife. She looked nothing like him.

And yet, as he eased ever closer, he saw the birthmark beneath her shining black hair. His heart sang. Ana was just like him. She wore the same mark as he. His first daughter was *Tupay,* after all! Elated, Victor eased away from the airliner now crawling toward the terminal.

Victor twisted to address another of his spirit guides, a beautiful red-and-yellow parrot.

I want you to follow my daughter at a distance. Remain cloaked. Do not allow her to know you are watching her. You will tell me where she goes and keep me filled in. At some point, I must meet with her in the third dimension. For now, let us just watch and learn why she has returned home.

The parrot flapped her wings. *Master, I live to do your bidding. I will remain cloaked and follow your daughter's movements. I will be in touch.*

Nodding, Victor thanked the guide and ordered his horse to turn around. Time to get back to his third-dimensional form and home. As they sped back to Aguas Calientes, Victor's heart overflowed with joy, and at the same time filled with worry. Ana's return was unexpected. Shocking. Wonderful. Perhaps an incredible gift.

As they returned, the great spirit horse alighted in Victor's office, where his human form sat in the chair.

Victor patted his stalwart mount, thanked him and rose above the horse's broad, sleek back. He aimed his energy body feetfirst through an opening in the top of his human head. Easing gently down until his astral feet locked back into place with his physical feet, he felt heavy once more. Once reentry was accomplished, Victor felt the opening at the top of his head close.

Looking about with his human eyes, he reoriented himself for a few minutes. The room was quiet. His heart pounded heavily in his chest. He lifted his hand and rubbed the area, his red polo shirt soft beneath his palm. *Ana is here.*

Frowning, Victor stroked his goatee, deep in thought. As if struck by a lightning bolt, his life had been upended. And it left him shaken. He had to plan quickly and thoroughly.

His stomach grumbled. Fidelia would be upset that he was not sharing *desayuno* with the family, so he got to his feet and made his way to the staircase. After flipping off the light, Victor left his metaphysical lair, where he'd taught so many students over the past fifty-five years of his life. As he trudged up the stairs, his heart expanded with hope. The universe was giving him a second chance with his daughter. How he wanted that chance! And yet he would have to be very careful how he reentered her life. One mistake and she could turn against him.

And that was the last thing Victor wanted.

Chapter 3

Why do I feel like I'm going to my death? The question hung unanswered, like a sword suspended above Ana's head. She wrapped her fingers around the wrought-iron ring that would open the massive door to St. Mary's Orphanage. Casting a glance over her shoulder, she realized that Mason Ridfort was gone; he had disappeared back into the heavy morning traffic around Plaza de Armas. Off to work…

I'm off to my life….

All the honking horns and roar of cars zipping by became muted. Ana's entire being focused on her hand resting on that door latch. The metal felt cool and clammy, just like her flesh. She should be happy this moment had finally arrived. Anxious, yes. Of course.

The details of how she'd ended up at this orphanage would finally be revealed.

What had happened to her before that? Did the nun on duty the day Ana had been brought to them remember anything about the occasion? That was twenty-three years ago. Closing her eyes, she trembled inside, her stomach shaking like Jell-O.

Not known for being a coward, Ana found herself afraid to move forward. Okay, she *had* to do this. She'd waited all her life to find out the truth. No time like the present. As she pulled open the door, it creaked loudly and yawned like a snake's mouth.

Morning sunlight spilled into a courtyard inside. Ana could see the light blue sky framed by the rectangular building. As she ventured farther, she found herself walking on stone tiles toward a garden with a fountain. In the center of the small cobblestone plaza, a granite statue of Mother Mary held out her hands. Flowers were planted in colorful profusion around the ancient stone fountain, which had surely been built by the Incas.

In her research, Ana had learned that the statue had been added much later, after the Spanish conquest and the drive to convert the populace from their Incan beliefs to the Catholic religion. Ana found irony that as one civilization was destroyed, another one came to build upon it. Here, the Spaniards had constructed an orphanage on the foundations of the Incan temple.

Reminders of the Incas incredible stonework were everywhere she looked, so the Spanish hadn't been able to wipe out the civilization as thoroughly as they may have wanted to.

Shutting the door, Ana turned. A smiling young nun, hardly out of her teens came toward her. She was obviously Quero, with high cheekbones, sparkling brown eyes and a sturdy build beneath her blue-and-white robes.

"May I help you, *señorita?*"

"Yes," Ana said, finding her voice raspy with strain. "I've got an appointment with your abbess, Mother Bernadette?" Ana gave her name to the young nun. In the distance, beyond some gray stone walls, she could hear the joyful sounds of children playing. They were probably at recess here at the orphanage school, Ana thought. Had she played on that same playground?

"Of course," the nun said sweetly. "I'm Sister Isadore. This way, Señorita Rafael." She gestured toward a portico covered with red Spanish tiles. "She is expecting you."

Ana looked around, this time through different eyes. She had been an orphan here for two years of her life, yet had so few memories of this place.... And then there were the nightmares that had plagued her ever since she could remember. Fragments of faces. Fragments of conversations. Often, Ana would see the head of a jaguar. Or hear the mew of a jaguar cub. The jungle in her dreams was filled with trees, vines and perfumed orchids. Running through it on bare feet, she could often breathe in the humid, fecund odors of life and death. Ana always saw the face of a woman—one with beautiful green eyes and an angelic smile. Then there was the monstrous-looking face of a man. With a black beard and fathomless dark eyes that drilled through her like laser beams, he scared her to death. Often he stalked and hunted her. Pleasant dreams would turn into terror-filled nightmares as she continued to hide from him.

Ana walked across the well-worn granite stones and seemed to vaguely recall the statue of the Virgin. Perhaps a memory of this fountain? Unsure, Ana followed the nun down another quiet, empty stone corridor. A slight breeze made it cooler here. They stopped at another dark wooden door that said Abbess. Opening it, the nun said, "Go right in, Señorita Rafael. Mother Bernadette is expecting you."

After thanking Sister Isadore, Ana stepped fearfully through the doorway. She felt as if she were entering a torture chamber. Why was she reacting like this? Now Ana wished she'd asked Mace about his adoption. Had he felt similar when he'd found out who his parents were? What had his journey of discovery been like? The knowledge might have helped her come to grips with her own findings.

Straight ahead of her was a huge antique desk made out of some heavy, reddish jungle wood, perhaps mahogany. The light was weak, but drove back the shadows in the rectangular office. The nun sitting behind the desk had short silver hair and wore round wire-rim glasses at the end of her fine, long nose. The glasses emphasized her watery hazel eyes. Her triangular face, just visible above the tacks of papers on the desk, was pinched and lined with age.

Ana introduced herself.

"Ah, Señorita Rafael. Welcome! I'm Mother Bernadette. Please, please, sit down." The nun stood up and gestured toward a large, heavy wooden chair in front of the cluttered desk.

Ana did as she was instructed, keeping her gaze on the abbess. Her dark blue and white robes hid her figure, but she was clearly a frail and tiny woman.

Within moments, a young nun glided silently into the room with hot tea and biscuits. After clearing a spot, she placed the silver tray on the desk. Mother Bernadette thanked her and she quickly left, closing the door behind her.

"You must be worn out from your travels, *señorita*. Have some tea and we'll chat about your time here with us so long ago." With a smile, she picked up a folder from one of the leaning stacks. Mother Bernadette said, "Everything about you is in here."

Fear zigzagged through Ana as she reached for her tea. Gripping the cup and saucer, she leaned back and crossed her legs, her heart hammering. "Thank you for seeing me, Mother. I—I'm on a quest—a journey to find out who I really am."

Chuckling, the abbess nodded sagely and pushed aside the papers she'd been working on. "Oh, yes, my dear child, I understand." Looking up, she smiled kindly across the desk. "The fact is we're all on the same journey. Did you realize that? Oh, we might know who our parents were, our background, but there's still an inner journey to one's soul which must be taken by each of us. *That* is the important part, and something you have within you. No one can ever take it away from you, and that's a blessing."

Ana tasted the delightful hint of bergamot in her tea. "Still, knowing where you came from is so important, Mother."

"Of course it is, Señorita Rafael. I don't mean to suggest that it is not. Now, let me see here...." She opened the dog-eared, yellowing file. "I was a nun here at the orphanage and on duty the day you were brought to us."

Mother Bernadette squinted and moved the file away, then closer, trying to focus on the scribbled words on the entrance form. "Hold on. I need my magnifying glass." She searched for it beneath a sheaf of papers to her left. Finding it, she smiled. "Old eyes, you know. I'm eighty-five years old. The good Lord has allowed me to live a long time, but he sure didn't give me eyes that could keep up with the rest of me."

Sitting tensely, her shoulders tight with anticipation, Ana waited. It seemed that each breath she took rocked her entire reality and then shredded it. What would be in that file? What had Mother Bernadette written about whoever had brought her to this orphanage?

"The man who brought you here was named Juan Sanchez," the abbess murmured, barely lifting her chin to look across at Ana. "It was October thirty-first when he came here to the orphanage. Interesting. That is when the Day of the Dead is celebrated. Did you know that?"

"Yes, in your correspondence you told me the date I was brought in."

"Ah, I see. Very good." She squinted down at the folder in her hands. "I have here in my notes that Señor Sanchez was a farmer who worked a small plot of land about two miles south of Aguas Calientes." She lifted her head. "Do you know where that is?"

Ana shook her head.

"Actually, it's very close. You can take the train from

Cuzco. Aguas Calientes is a frontier town at the base of the beautiful Incan temple complex of Machu Picchu."

"Oh, I see." Ana had heard of Machu Picchu.

"Señor Sanchez said the following about you. "'Child found beneath a dead female jaguar that was shot by an unknown hunter.' Apparently, Sanchez was going to his field one last time before the seasonal rains came, when he heard the shot and saw a man fleeing with a gun. A poacher. And in the corner, near the jungle, he spotted the dead jaguar. When he walked over to it, he saw the arm of a child sticking out from beneath the body of the cat."

Heart pounding, Ana sat up straight. "That was me?" The words came out hoarsely.

"Yes. At first, Señor Sanchez thought you had been shot, too, there was so much blood on you. Apparently you were knocked unconscious. He pulled you from beneath the dead jaguar and carried you to his home, a mile away. He and his wife cleaned you up, and by that time you had regained consciousness."

Mother Bernadette looked up and frowned. She set the magnifying glass on the old, crinkled folder. "I vaguely recall this story, *señorita.* Señor Sanchez was very frightened. His wife saw a mark, a birthmark, on the back of your neck, and she made him take you here, to us. She didn't want you in their home. She felt threatened."

Sitting up, Ana whispered, "Why was she threatened?" And then she recalled her adoptive mother, Mary, telling her that she had a birthmark high on the back of her neck, a circle with a dot in the center. Ana had never paid any attention to it because her adoptive parents had disregarded its significance. Her long black hair always covered it up, so no one else knew it was there.

And then the dream she'd had on the plane, about Grandmother Alaria, slammed back into Ana's memory. The elder had told her of the symbol of a circle with a dot in the center. She had not given Ana any information about it.

Mother Bernadette pointed a gnarled finger at the file. "I drew it. It's a circle with a dot inside."

"That's what scared Señor Sanchez's wife?"

"Oh, yes, my dear." The abbess chuckled. "The Quero people are a very superstitious lot, you know. Everything is a symbol and means something good or bad to them."

Ana placed the empty teacup on the desk in front of her. "So I was found beneath a dead jaguar. This farmer rescued me and brought me to his home. And his wife saw my birthmark and told him to get rid of me." A feeling of abandonment surged through Ana and she tried to swallow the pain.

"Yes, that is so. Señor Sanchez had you bundled in a very old, frayed alpaca blanket when you came here. He had wrapped you cocoonlike so that your arms and legs were not free to move."

Startled, Ana whispered, "But why?"

"Do you have *any* memories of being a youngster here, my dear?"

"Just fragments. The statue at the fountain feels familiar to me. I have dreams, nightmares, but I see only bits of scenes, like pieces of a jigsaw puzzle."

"Do you remember me?"

Shaking her head, Ana whispered, "No, I'm sorry, I don't. I've went through many therapy sessions trying to unlock huge chunks of time, years that I can't remember to this day. My therapist said my brain might be holding memories that it felt would overwhelm me, and that's why I can't recall them. She said one day, when they weren't so upsetting to me, I might remember."

"Well, I must say, you have changed remarkably since you lived here, and what a beautiful young woman you have grown into." Pulling off her glasses, Mother Bernadette pinched the bridge of her nose. "You were a wild little animal when you first arrived, Ana. You could not speak Spanish or any other language. Your hair had been all chopped off. Señor Sanchez said it had been long, filthy, terribly matted, and appeared never to have been combed. His wife cut off your hair and bathed you before he brought you here. You were, for all intents and purposes, a wild animal that had been accidentally captured when that female jaguar was shot and killed."

Ana frowned in confusion. "A wild animal? Me? I didn't speak Spanish? Is that why I was wrapped in that blanket so tightly? Did I want to escape?"

"Yes, that's why Señor Sanchez wrapped you up. You see—" the nun leaned forward on her elbows "—he told me a fascinating story. It's not one I'm sure I believe, but I must tell you about it. He said there was a legend of a young girl-child who ran with a family of jaguars, that the jaguar mother had saved her from death and raised her as her own. This child had suckled the milk of the jaguar, and was seen from time to time at the edges of the jungle by different farmers in that region. They all thought the child was a spirit, of course. They said the jaguar would shape-shift into this young child to lure them into the jungle and kill them."

Shrugging her shoulders, Mother Bernadette said, "Of course, none of this could be true. But you were wild, distrustful and knew no human language." She held up her hand, which had prominent veins running across it. "The first thing you did when I took you from Señor Sanchez was to bite me!" She laughed. "But of course, you were frightened to death. I thanked Señor Sanchez for bringing you and I took you to our laundry room to begin your cleanup process."

Ana shook her head. "I remember *none* of this! I should. It sounds so important."

"Frequently, children do not remember early events. You know," Mother Bernadette said, gently tapping her temple, "our brain protects us from trauma, so that we can get on with our life, survive and thrive."

Rubbing her brow, Ana closed her eyes. "All those fragments, those pieces. I remember seeing a jaguar all the time. Her face. Her beautiful gold eyes."

"Hmm, that's interesting! Jaguars often kill humans. We have two or three farmers a year who are killed by them in the jungles of Peru. I can't imagine the legend of a child living with a jaguar family could be true—that such a thing could actually happen. The child would be eaten for sure." Mother Bernadette gave a cackling laugh. "It could be that you were kept by another farmer's family, got lost, and a hunter saw this jaguar stalking you. That was why the cat was killed, I'm sure. And then Señor Sanchez accidentally happened upon the scene and rescued you."

Shrugging helplessly, Ana said, "There's so much to think about here. I'll have to compare the nightmares and dreams I've had over the years with what you're saying."

"Of course, Ana."

"Señor Sanchez lives near Aguas Calientes, you said?"

"Yes. You might go down there and ask him and his family about that time. He may be able to give you more information than I have here."

"I will. What other records do you have on me, Mother Bernadette?"

Squinting, she held up her magnifying glass and studied them for a few minutes. "We put in the notes that you were untamed. You had no social skills. You did not know how to get along with the other children. The only sounds you would make were hisses, growls, snarls and mewing, and you'd bite anyone who came close to you. I recall that we put you in a room of your own, and it took me about three months to get you to trust me."

"Oh."

"And after you gave me your trust, I began to teach you Spanish. You caught on very quickly, I might add. You were a very sharp student. During the two years you were with us, you learned how to get along with others, to communicate and play without feeling threatened." Mother Bernadette put the magnifying glass aside. "By the time your adoptive parents, John and Mary Rafael, came along, you were a beautiful green-eyed child with shoulder-length hair. You were a voracious reader and had gone through every book in our children's library. You caught up in a hurry in those two years, learning not only how to read, but to write, as well. I loved taking time out of my day, every day, to teach you something new. You were so alert and hungry for information. John and Mary Rafael fell in love with you at first sight. At the time, we did not give adopting parents all the information you are now receiving. Peru's laws have changed since then."

The nun smiled benignly. "I felt glad that you would be leaving the country, to escape the curse that everyone said you carried. Where you were going, myths and legends and symbols were not given such importance in a person's life. I knew this would be good for you. You would not have to carry around the awful knowledge of who the Quero thought you were."

"What do you mean?" Ana asked. She felt the birthmark on her neck heat up. Unconsciously, she rubbed the area.

"I don't want you to become upset by what I'm going to say, Señorita Rafael. Keep in mind, this is a Quero or Incan myth, and that's all it is."

"Please tell me about it."

"It has to do with your birthmark." The nun pointed to her neck. "It is said to be the symbol of the *Tupay,* or Dark Forces."

A chill worked its way up Ana's spine. The dream with Grandmother Alaria came back full force. All that fear she'd felt returned. "What?" The word came out strangled.

"Oh!" Mother Bernadette admonished, "pay no attention to these legends, Ana! They mean *nothing.*"

That isn't true, Ana wanted to scream. Instead, she bit down hard on her lower lip and kept silent.

"The legend goes that the *Tupay* are a group of

people who are considered pure evil," the nun said in a bored tone. "They are sorcerers who learned the dark arts of ensnaring helpless and innocent victims to do their bidding. Those who wear the birthmark are said to be part of a growing army, in this world and the Other Worlds—" she waved her hand in the air "—that will eventually take over the earth and rule through fear, war and violence."

Snorting softly, Mother Bernadette added, "All lies, of course. But you'd be amazed how ingrained this belief is in the Quero people. And that was why Señor Sanchez's wife, when she saw the birthmark of the sun, became crazed with fear and insisted you be given immediately to an orphanage. That was why she wanted you out of their home."

"She did not want me there because I—I represented..." The last work stuck in Ana's throat and made a lump. She touched her neck and rasped, "...evil?"

"I'm afraid so, my child." The old nun gave her a kindly smile. "But listen to me, will you? We believed nothing of that silly stuff! We were *glad* to have you. I do remember my time with you, and you were a challenge to be sure, but not because you had that birthmark. You were a wild little child without social graces or language. But that could—and was—rectified."

Scanning the book-lined office, Ana said, "And was I evil here?"

Laughing, the nun said, "No, of course not! You were like any other normal child we cared for, my dear. You were not mean by nature, nor did you hurt others. Oh, at first you were very wary and would protect yourself from whatever you thought was a threat. But eventually, you stopped being so defensive. By the time your adoptive parents found you, you were a sweet, shy child. So beautiful, as you are now. You are anything but evil, from what I can see."

"My adoptive parents never told me any of this and they tried to find out more so they could let me know at an age when I could handle the information."

"I know, and I made a conscious decision not to tell them any of this. I told them an unnamed farmer brought you to us. I gave them no name. We didn't want you saddled with such superstitious garbage."

"Thank you." Ana dragged in a ragged breath. But she *was evil.* The mark on her neck meant something, after all, and the dream was coming true. She began to realize her dream on the plane was somehow the precognitive type—a dream about the future, one that later became reality. Inwardly, she knew it meant a great deal more than what Mother Bernadette was telling her. Ana searched the nun's face and asked why the abbess hadn't even told her adoptive parents. "What else do you know about the mark of the sun?"

Shrugging, Mother Bernadette closed the file, pressing her hand across it. "Nothing, really."

"Would Señor Sanchez know more?"

"Most likely. He is Quero and it's an Incan legend. We try to erase all those silly notions from the children who come here. We instill a good religious beliefs instead, ones that are not fraught with such ridiculous fears and threats. Here, they learn that Jesus is their savior and that he loves all children. We replace their fears with love. It's a healthier, much more positive belief than the dark, heavy energy, the terror that the Quero believe in."

"Yes." Ana felt it was time to leave, so she stood. "Thank you for your time, Mother."

The abbess rose and shook her hand gently. "I'm glad to have been of help, Ana. Your journey to find out who you are can now truly begin. Try to locate the Sanchez family farm near Aguas Calientes. Perhaps they can give you a lead to whoever was caring for you before that. God bless you...."

Ana staggered out of the orphanage, tears blurring her eyes. With her briefcase in one hand and her luggage in the other, she stood there. The sun was high now, removing the coolness of the damp morning air it. The grassy, tree-filled plaza was just across the busy street. She had to think. Stomach roiling with nausea, she tried to battle the burning tears that leaked from her eyes as she woodenly crossed the road.

Ana saw an empty bench near the center of the plaza. Young people walked across the lawns and older folks traversed the crisscrossing sidewalks. A few mothers with babies in carriages strolled by. Just a normal day.

Ana felt anything but normal. Her legs wobbled and she felt sick. She sank onto the bench beneath the shade of a nearby tree and placed her luggage beside her feet. Pressing one hand to her throat, she bowed her head and gripped her stomach. *She was evil.* Somehow, she knew that. It was why she'd been so afraid to come here, why she'd resisted going into the orphanage.

The dark truth was...she carried evil within her.

Ana's birthmark meant something. The dream on the plane confirmed it, too. Oh, Great Spirit, what was she going to do? Her stomach was a rolling knot of pain now, and sobs tore from her compressed lips. All her life, she had waited for this moment. Dreaded it. And now, to be told she was the spawn of evil was devastating. The knowledge began to eat through her like acid.

The world of honking cars, smelly diesel engines, chatting people and barking dogs all faded away from Ana's consciousness. As she sat there, head bowed, she felt her world fall apart, just as it had so often in her dreams. *Fragments.* Fear entwined with massive confusion within her.

Now that she began to understand the cause of her nightmares, an even deeper sense of foreboding took root in her. She wore the symbol of evil on the back of her neck. And now, she could feel evil release itself within her soul. This frightened her as nothing else ever had, like a time bomb ready to explode.

Ana seemed to have no control over this dark, unnamed thing unraveling deep within her. She was coming back to where she was born, like a salmon returning instinctively to the stream of its birth, where it would spawn and then die.

But her drive to know who she was had turned up such horror that she was shocked beyond belief. *Never* had she expected such a sentence. People in Peru would consider her evil personified if they saw the mark of the sun on her neck. Now more than ever she had to hide it. Keep her hair down and never wear it up. No one could see it!

Behind her tightly shut eyelids, new pictures were

unleashed in Ana's consciousness. She saw a man studying her now, the same man with the black goatee, his eyes glinting like obsidian. This time, his face was lined and his beard silver interspersed with black. Before, she'd only seen glimpses of his face and those disturbing, haunting eyes that frightened her to her soul. Now she saw his face fully and he was even more scary. Somehow, she knew this man.

Daughter? You are of my blood. You and I are one. I come to you in peace. Can we not share an olive branch between us?

Was she going crazy? Ana heard his low, mellow voice inside her head like the echo of a drum. She grabbed at her skull, willing it to stop. Willing him to go away. But he did not. She saw him handing her an olive branch.

"Go away!" she rasped, terror in her voice. "Get out of here! I don't know you! I don't *want* to know you!" She began to breath harshly through contorted lips.

Ana saw pain and hurt on his face the moment she whispered those harsh words to him.

Daughter, I love you so much. I have searched the world over for you. I have just found you once more. Can you not forgive me? Can we not move on and share one heart filled with love toward one another? Surely you want to know me. I am your father. You are of my blood—

"No!" Ana shouted. She jerked upward, her eyes flying open. The day was sunny and real life intruded. There was no man in black standing before her; it was her imagination. It *had* to be. Breathing hard, Ana fell back on the bench and tipped her head backward. Without thinking, she closed her eyes once more.

This time, she saw the angelic face of a woman smiling at her, with such love that all her terror dissolved in an instant. The unknown woman spoke in a language she did not understand. Her voice was soft, filled with warmth and joy. For a moment, it soothed Ana's tumult.

She felt as if she was strung helplessly between these two people, not knowing who to believe. Was she completely losing her mind?

Her stomach clenched as she saw the man in black once more. He was walking away from her, raising his hand in farewell.

I'll be back, my lovely daughter. I will return when I do not cause you so much stress. I love you....

"Ana?"

Ana barely heard the low, male voice calling her. It sounded familiar, but she was so ensnared in her vision that it seemed to be coming from far away. Only when she felt a hand, warm and gentle, settle tentatively upon her shoulder did she realize the voice was real and not a figment of her imagination.

With tears streaming down her face, she lifted her head. Mace Ridfort! Oh, his hand felt so good to her! So comforting, when she felt so horribly vulnerable and at a loss. His touch was stabilizing to her wild, tumbling world.

He stared down at her with genuine concern, those blue eyes filled with care. Ana felt the heated sunlight of his aura, and instantly, his presence brought her a modicum of peace, of sanity.

"Oh..." Ana hiccuped through her tears. "Mace..."

"I was coming out here to eat my lunch and I saw you. What's wrong, Ana?"

Chapter 4

His quarry was literally at arm's length from him. Finally, after all the years of training, of practicing for his mission as a Warrior for the Light, his target was here, right in front of him. *Unbelievable.* In his wildest dreams, Mace Ridfort had never imagined that she'd literally show up and he'd be standing this close to her.

Shaken by the quixotic and unexpected events, Mace forced himself to concentrate on his task. From the time he was nine years old, his job had been to find and destroy the two *Tupay*—the Daughter of Darkness and her father, the Lord of Darkness—who could lead the planet to its ultimate destruction.

And here she was—the daughter herself. Mace's mother and father, both Warriors for the Light who wore the Vesica Piscis symbol on the back of their necks, had trained him relentlessly for two decades to find this duo. Mace had never dreamed that finding either of these sinister beings would be so easy.

As his hand rested on Ana Rafael's shoulder, and she looked up at him through teary green eyes, Mace was torn. He had been told that the Daughter of Darkness would be as evil as her father. But as he gazed into her anguished eyes, he couldn't feel one drop of evil within her. Had his jaguar guide been wrong?

Mace hardly noticed the warm sunlight or the noisy traffic as he quickly thought back to the moment his jaguar guide had woken him out of a sound sleep at his Lima apartment. He'd been there on well-drilling business at his main office. The last thing he had expected was for his jaguar spirit guide to growl and wake him up. His guide had informed him that the Daughter of Darkness was coming to Peru. That Mace had to get to the airport and board a certain flight in order to meet her. That it was time to become the hunter.

His quarry had finally appeared. It was Mace's job to locate her and then use her to find her father, the Lord of Darkness. His guide transmitted a picture of her so he could identify her.

Shaken awake by his guide's unexpected orders, Mace had quickly dressed, left his apartment and taken a taxi to the Lima airport.

And when he'd walked into the first-class section of the Condor Airlines jet, there she was—two seats back and across the aisle from his own seat. When Mace saw her, he didn't feel anything but turmoil around her, certainly not the evil emanation he'd expected. His jaguar guide insisted she was the one, however, and Mace accepted that dictate. His jaguar guide had never been wrong in the past, so he had no reason to distrust the information, even if Ana Rafael looked like an innocent angel.

Shaking himself internally, Mace kept his aura tightly guarded so that Ana wouldn't suspect who he was or why he had suddenly appeared in her life. She could not know he was a hunter-assassin who was going to manipulate her to get to her father.

No one knew where Victor Carancho Guerra was. The Dark Lord was so powerful that he could cloak himself from even the most highly qualified and psychic Warrior for the Light. No one would find him—until he resurfaced. A vibration much like a radar signal would then be sent out, throughout all the dimensions. And only then would Mace be able to locate him.

Now, with his daughter showing up here in Cuzco, Mace knew without a doubt her father would finally unveil himself. And when he did, Mace would be there to kill him before he could claim his daughter and make her queen in his kingdom of chaos.

As he gently gripped Ana's shoulder, Mace felt no guilt about hiding who he really was. He had been born for this task. When they had created him, his parents had known what his mission on earth would be. They'd realized that by coming together in an ultimate act of love, a special child would be conceived. He would be carefully trained and educated by both of them.

Mace was very clear about his destiny. He'd been born to kill the two people who stood in the way of one thousand years of peace unfolding on earth. And no one wanted peace more than Mace.

Still, as he watched Ana's face, he found himself wondering why she didn't *feel* evil to him. With his highly sensitized metaphysical abilities, he sensed only her pain and shock.

"Do you mind if I sit with you?" he asked quietly.

Ana blotted her eyes with a damp tissue that was quickly growing tattered. "Please sit down." Somehow, being around Mace soothed her. His aura was so warm and loving, and Ana was desperate for his nearness. The tenderness and concern in his dark blue eyes was her undoing, and she began to speak in fits and starts.

"I—I went to find out about myself in there."

"The orphanage." He removed his hand from her shoulder. Ana straightened, blotted her eyes again and fought back her tears. Mace removed a linen handkerchief from his back pocket. "Here," he told her, handing it to her, "it looks like you could use a new one."

Their fingers met. Mace felt cool, beautiful green energy flowing up his arm that, surprisingly, slid right into his heart. Of all things! Shocked over this development, he quickly drew back his hand. He hadn't expected that kind of energy from Ana. After all, she was evil personified. Confused, he realized he needed to have time alone to assess what the hell was going on here, because it made no sense, in light of his training.

"Th-thank you," Ana whispered, again blotting her eyes. Her tears were stopping, her stomach began to unknot. She knew it had to do with Mace, with his nurturing, healing presence. She gave him a searching look and almost asked, *Do you know how healing you are?* But she didn't. He was practically a stranger. But he had been an orphan, too. Buoyed by their shared experience, Ana felt she could confide in him.

"Oh, Mace, it was awful!" The words came tearing out of her. She told him the whole story—about having the "evil" birthmark on the back of her neck, about where she came from. When she'd finished her story, she moved her thick black hair aside and turned her back to him. "Do you see that sun birthmark? Here, on my neck?" she asked.

Mace's eyes narrowed speculatively. No question, she had the *Tupay,* the Dark Forces, symbol. "Yes, I see it." He feigned ignorance. "But what does it mean to you? Do you know what it's all about?"

Miserably, Ana allowed her hair to fall back across her shoulders, hiding the chocolate-colored birthmark once more. "No. My adoptive parents thought it might be significant, but they didn't know how. And when Mother Bernadette said it was a symbol of ultimate evil, well, I..." Ana took in a deep, ragged breath. "I couldn't believe it, Mace. I just couldn't."

"What kind of evil?" He opened his sack lunch and pulled out a peanut butter sandwich.

"I don't know. I don't want to believe I'm evil. She said the Quero people have many legends and stories about the sun birthmark." Ana gazed at him intently. "I'm *not* evil. My adoptive parents are kind, good people. They do a lot of charity work. They give half their money away to others, to help them have better lives. They raised me to have strong morals and values.

I know right from wrong. I don't lie, cheat, steal or do things intentionally to hurt others." Ana opened her hands and stared down at them. "I couldn't hurt a fly. I won't even step on a bug or a spider in my home. I capture them in a little glass and release them outside."

Mace offered her half his sandwich. "How long has it been since you last ate?"

Wiping her eyes one more time, Ana said brokenly, "Last night, I guess. In Miami. I stayed at a hotel for a few hours before catching the flight to Lima today."

"You'd better eat then," Mace urged her softly. He intended to make friends with her. The cosmos had designed this meeting, and he was going to take full advantage of it.

Reluctantly, Ana took his proffered half sandwich. She was deeply touched by his compassion toward her, his generosity.

"I don't feel hungry at all. My stomach's been tied in knots the size of a baseball until a few minutes ago."

"It would be upsetting to have someone say you were evil," Mace agreed, chewing his half of the sandwich. Out of the corner of his eye, he studied Ana's profile. She stared down at the food, her lower lip trembling. The energy around her was still that of shock mixed with grief and disbelief. How could she not know she was the Daughter of Darkness? That confounded him, and bothered him. Still, invisible to all but Mace, his jaguar guide sat next to the bench and confirmed that she was the one.

Giving an explosive laugh, more of relief than anything else, Ana said, "No one has *ever* accused me of being evil. Not ever. I've devoted my life to helping Mother Earth. My adoptive parents are Eastern Cherokee. They raised me with a love of our Mother." She swept her hand toward the grass in front of her. "They taught me to honor and revere her. When I finished high school, I went to college and got a master's degree in wildlife biology. My life is about helping to create a jaguar preserve in Belize. I work with other like-minded people and organizations who love these beautiful animals. The jaguars are threatened, and if we don't create safe places for them, they will disappear, too—like so many other animals disappearing right now."

Mace was stunned. "You love jaguars?"

Ana felt his sudden intense interest. How stabilizing Mace's energy was to her. She even felt a little hungry. Biting into the sandwich, she nodded. "I've been jaguar crazy since my adoptive parents brought me home from Cuzco to where they live in Camp Verde, Arizona. The cats are so beautiful, so incredibly wild, natural and graceful. I just can't get enough of them."

Stymied, Mace worked to conceal his reaction to this new, surprising piece of information. The Daughter of Darkness should hate jaguars, not love them. Such was her nature, Mace had been taught. Spiritually speaking, the jaguars of the world were aligned with the Warriors for the Light, and served them on the front lines, helping to battle the evil of the Dark Lord and his hundreds of thousands of other sorcerers.

"My parents raised millions of dollars to create a sanctuary for them in Camp Verde, near Sedona. I work there. We take in jaguars who have been injured, try to restore them to health, and release them back wherever they came from." Ana smiled faintly as she held Mace's intense stare. "We do a lot of research, and I work with many biologists in Central and South America. We try to persuade each country to create wonderful, large preserves for jaguars, such as Belize has. A lot of the work I do is with the cats themselves. I'm not a veterinarian, but I'm often in the surgery room with our vets when they operate on one."

Ana felt better just talking about her other world. "I'm more of a field researcher, Mace. I spent two years in Belize tracking five jaguars. I wrote a book on my experiences called *Jaguar Eden.*" Ana smiled more widely as she felt his keen interest. "My book became an instant bestseller, much to my publisher's surprise. People loved the stories I wrote about the jaguars. It has been reprinted five times and translated into sixteen languages."

Wiping her mouth with the handkerchief Mace had given her, Ana added, "Everyone who reads my book seems to fall in love with jaguars. And every person that does will want to protect and preserve them. I hope every reader writes to their government, or to officials in Latin American countries, and pleads with them to create more preserves for the cats. Jaguars are just too magnificent to lose. I would die, literally die, if they disappeared off the earth. I couldn't stand the thought of that happening."

Not exactly words that Mace had thought he'd ever hear from the Daughter of Darkness. After finishing his sandwich, he pulled out an apple. He reached for the Swiss Army knife clipped onto a belt loop and cut the fruit in half.

Ana had finished her part of the sandwich, too. Mace knew she had to be hungry despite the shock of finding out who she really was. Or, a small voice niggled, was this all a very good act on her part? Did Ana know who he was? That he was setting her up as a decoy to get to her father? Mace knew too well that a master sorcerer could take on a very unassuming personality, cloak his or her aura, and project an entirely different facade—so people never saw evil coming until it was too late.

Ana could be setting him up, too. Mace knew that people aligned with the darkness would kill a Warrior for the Light without a second thought—for they were archenemies.

"Apple?" he asked, holding up half of it. He saw her lips curve slightly. Still, there was so much pain in her eyes. Mace decided Ana had to be one of the best actresses he'd ever met, or she really was in pain. *Impossible,* he decided. He made a mental note to assume she not only knew who she was, but that she was consciously manipulating him until she found a time and place to kill him.

"Thanks," she murmured, taking the apple from his hand. "I guess I was more hungry than I thought. It's very kind of you to share your lunch with me, Mace."

"Hey, that's what orphans do for one another. We take care of each other, because we had no one in the beginning take care of us." Well, that was all lies on his part, because Mace had never been orphaned. But the falsehood gave them something in common. Such a link would create trust with her.

As Mace watched her nibble on the apple, he wondered if Ana was lying about her work, too. It would be easy enough to check out on the Internet what she had told him about the jaguar preserve in Camp Verde. Now that she had revealed herself, Mace would get other Warriors for the Light to find out just how truthful this woman was—or wasn't. He assumed her cover story was a disguise to make him think she was just an ordinary human. Which she was not. She was an interdimensional being with powers well beyond what most people dreamed of, and beyond most Warriors for the Light.

Mace knew he had to tread carefully, remain on constant guard with her. Yet the softness of her face, the vulnerable look in her emerald eyes, all conspired to tell him differently. She had to know who she was no matter what she was projecting right now. Ana was a consummate actress, and damned if she wasn't convincing as hell. Mace found himself wanting to believe her entire story. But it had to be lies. It had to be….

"I need to get to the train station here in Cuzco," Ana told Mace after she'd finished the apple. Wiping her hands, she said, "Do you know where it is? I want to go to Aguas Calientes. Mother Bernadette said Juan Sanchez, the farmer who found me, lives near that town. I need to ask him questions." Ana watched Mace's face. He seemed deep in thought as he placed the apple core in the paper sack and folded it.

"Funny enough," he told her, smiling, "I'm going to Aguas Calientes tomorrow morning. Why don't you let me get us tickets? I can ride with you, show you the ropes, and also get you a hotel reservation for while you're down there." Mace hooked a thumb over his shoulder. "The Liberator Hotel is right here. Best five-star hotel in Cuzco. I'll walk you over there now and you can get a room for the night, get some rest. I know you've got to be exhausted."

Ana felt the weight lifting off her shoulders. She found herself wanting to throw her arms around this helpful, capable man. "That's a wonderful idea, Mace. Yes, I should find a hotel room. I need a shower. I'm so tired, gutted, really. Some downtime to think and sleep would be great." She almost told him about the man she saw in her vision. The one who'd said he was her father. As she darted a glance at her benefactor's ruggedly handsome face, she thought better of saying anything. Mace would probably think she was crazy. She didn't want to risk losing his support right now with such an admittance. Even he would have limits on what he could believe.

But who was that bearded man in black? He seemed so gentle and warm, so sincere about being her father. Was she somehow inventing all this because she was so desperate to know who her parents were? Ana wasn't sure. And she was too exhausted emotionally to make sense of it.

Rising, Mace placed his hand beneath her elbow and helped her stand. "Maybe, if you feel rested by this evening, I'll come over and take you to dinner. There's a nice little restaurant, La Retama, just off the plaza. I'd like to hear more about your jaguar research." By that time, he would have the goods on Ana Rafael. His contacts at a secret company in Chesieres, Switzerland, all Warriors for the Light, would quickly confirm her story, one way or another. The facility had been put in place a century ago to monitor Dark Forces movements. It was the only organization of its type, and one that all Warriors for the Light contacted if they had questions or problems. It was better than nothing, although Mace desperately wished his parents were alive to answer his questions about Ana and her energy signature. He was sure what she'd told him was lies, but at least his contacts in Europe would be able to research her story and confirm what he already knew—that she was the Daughter of Darkness.

Ana fell into step with Mace as they set off across the plaza. More people were spilling from the buildings now. Students from the nearby university lay in the green grass, eating their lunches. Older, retired people strolled by.

Suddenly, Ana felt lighter. Hope filled her and erased some of her initial dismay over the morning's discoveries. She enjoyed walking with Mace, being with him.

Sometimes, by accident, their hands would brush. Each contact soothed her aching heart and hurting soul. Did he realize the power he had to heal her?

Ana looked up at his strong profile. She had to know more. But when she sent out an energy thread to touch his aura, it was met by a hard, unyielding shield.

Though she was mystified, Ana was too tired to ask why he was so protected. Oh, she understood many people "armored up" like this. Particularly sensitive, psychic people, and maybe Mace was like that. His shield was up simply to protect himself from the sounds of the city and the crowds of people. Ana didn't like a city environment, either. She preferred the jungle, where she was alone, except for her beautiful gold-and-black jaguars.

"I have your business card," she told him as they crossed the wide cobblestone avenue and headed toward the multistory hotel. "May I call you around quitting time? If I'm feeling better, I'd love to have dinner with you."

Mace gave her a dazzling smile. "I'd like that, Ana. I think we have a lot more in common than you realize...."

Chapter 5

Victor was unhappy. As he sat in his office, he reflected on what had happened. He'd journeyed to see his estranged daughter, had offered her an olive branch, hoping for peace between them, and she'd rejected it. Well, where did that leave him? She seemed very distraught. Did she remember the past? If so, it meant she remembered everything. No wonder she'd pushed him away.

Moistening his lips, he looked down at his folded hands. The universe was playing a cosmic joke on him. He was the most powerful sorcerer in this world and the Other Worlds, and yet he couldn't forge a connection with Ana, his daughter by his first marriage.

What to do? Stroking his goatee, Victor didn't try to avoid the pain in his heart. Ana was of his loins. She was his daughter even if she looked too much like her mother. The clincher had been when he saw the *Tupay* symbol on her neck, as she sat alone and crying in the Plaza de Armas. He'd seen that she'd just visited the orphanage. What had that old bitch of a nun told her? Victor chided himself for not journeying earlier, when his parrot spirit guide informed him that Ana had reached Cuzco. Fidelia had accidentally burned her hand on the stove while baking him his favorite cake, a chocolate torte, at that very moment.

Victor couldn't just tear downstairs to his inner sanctum and journey when his wife was in tears, her hand blistered and red. It pained him to see his wife in such anguish, and he'd tended her burns gently and thoroughly. Afterward, he'd come down to the office to find Ana.

Rubbing his chest, Victor knew he couldn't give up. She was *his* daughter! And there was no reason for her to be alone. Victor wondered who her adoptive parents were and where they lived. Perhaps now he could find out. Energy trails lasted only so long in the Other Worlds and would disappear within twenty-four hours. He'd only been able to trace her to Miami, Florida.

Shaking his head, he let out a frustrated sigh and stood up. He'd try again later and go into her dreams tonight. Perhaps he could succeed in making peace with her. How could any daughter turn away from her father? Victor found that an unfathomable question. And a thorny dilemma.

Ana tossed and turned restlessly in the strange bed, the sounds of the city intruding. Even as she slept, her dreams were vivid and colorful. She burrowed her head into the feather pillow and found her pleasant dream suddenly fading. In its place was the man she'd seen yesterday, while she was in the plaza, crying.

Moaning, Ana turned onto her back, the sheets tangling around her legs. An alarm sounded deep within her and she went on guard. The man with the black-and-silver beard was dressed in dark clothes. His narrow, lined face became clear as he drew closer; his expression one of hope. In his hand was the olive branch, which he held out to her again.

Dear, sweet daughter of mine, I am your father. Do not be afraid. I love you. I'm so glad you have come to your true home. Can I not stay and just chat with you, my darling girl?

His low, mellow voice filled her head. Ana wanted to scream but couldn't.

Stay where you are! Don't come any closer to me!

Victor nodded and halted. He saw the terror in her glorious green eyes. Jaguar eyes, just like those of her dead mother. *Very well. I'm not here to frighten you, Ana. I only want to reintroduce myself to you. Thank you for allowing me to talk with you.*

Ana couldn't explain why she didn't like him. Her body just froze when he appeared. How could he be her father when he felt so threatening? It didn't make sense.

What do you want? she responded. *And how do I know you're really my father? You could be nothing more than a nightmare. I've seen you so many times before, your face haunting my dreams. I would wake up screaming and crying. A real father doesn't make his daughter feel like that.*

Gently, Victor opened his hand. *Ah, my darling daughter, you perceive my "haunting" you as bad. I only sought to find you. I lost track of you after your mother died. I was beside myself when you suddenly disappeared. I did search for you, Ana. Everywhere in the world, every night in my dreams, I would hunt for you. I would call your name. I would cry in the morning when I awoke because you never answered.* Victor reached out in supplication. *I am your father, dearest. You are my flesh and blood.* He touched his heart and gave her a beseeching look. *I'm so sorry I frightened you. I'm not so adept at dreamtime travel and I probably scared you instead of reassuring you that I loved you, missed you and wanted you back in my life.*

Everything he said made sense to Ana—up to a point. She searched the man's features and saw tears glimmering in his flat, black eyes. Ana could feel his pain, feel that he told the truth. But she had to know more.

Then tell me your name. Let me come to you. I'll decide whether you're really my father or not. And since you know I'm here in Peru, why haven't you visited me in person? I would think if you knew I was here, you'd have met me at the airport.

Victor smiled benignly. *I am called Victor, my daughter. I was not able to go to Lima when you flew in. I have a young family, a newborn daughter called Abegail, and I couldn't leave my wife because of this. But I'm here now and I came as soon as I could. Please forgive my tardiness, for I never meant to make you wait. That is why I came to your dreams, to gently reintroduce myself to you, and I hope, to reenter your life.*

Ana eyed him warily. *I'm going to Aguas Calientes in the morning. Can you meet me there in person?* she demanded firmly.

He nodded. *Of course I can. My dear wife just burned her hand badly on the stove and I must take her to the doctor tomorrow, but I shall come there within a day of your arrival and find where you are staying. Is that all right with you?*

Ana agreed but she didn't feel good about it. She saw Victor lay the branch he held at his feet.

Let this olive branch be the beginning of a new relationship with one another, dear daughter. I will leave you now and see you in two days' time in Aguas Calientes. I love you....

Ana watched as he turned and dissolved into nothingness. The next moment, she jerked awake. Breathing hard, she fumbled for the lamp switch on the bedstand. When she turned it on, she gasped in terror. There, on the foot of her bed, was an olive branch with green leaves on it. Leaping out of bed, her eyes huge, Ana stared at it.

Had Victor been *here?* In her room? Rattled and tense, she looked warily around her. Was he *here* now? Unable to shake off the unsettling energy, she went around the room and turned on every single light.

Shaken to her core, Ana went into the bathroom after searching every possible place a man might be hiding. After gulping some cold water from the faucet, she splashed her sweaty features, then gripped the edge of the sink and stared into the mirror. She looked terrorized and felt that way in every cell of her body. No matter what this man said, she did not trust him. Stomach rolling, she walked back out into the room, picked up the olive branch and threw it in the wastebasket.

Ana knew she wouldn't sleep. She looked at her watch and saw that she had three hours before she had to be at the train station. As she sat on the edge of the bed, she hid her face in her hands. *Oh, Great Spirit, why is this happening?* she wondered. Had she lost her mind? Was she caught in some kind of elaborate dream?

A ragged sigh slipped from her lips. Lifting her head, Ana knew she had to do something to distract herself. She grabbed a novel by one of her favorite Native American writers and settled herself on the bed.

At this point, the only stability she had was Mace Ridfort. And Ana clung to that thread. In three hours, she'd be with him, and that gave her the strength to hold on.

Mace was damned unhappy but he cloaked his personal feelings so that Ana couldn't detect them. They sat in the train heading to Aguas Calientes. Mace had gotten them first-class tickets so they wouldn't have to endure the crowds and noise of the other cars. As the train gently rocked from side to side, climbing up through the Sacred Valley above Cuzco, Mace watched Ana across the linen-covered table.

"How's *desayuno?*" he inquired, pushing his own eggs around on the china plate. Dressed in starched white, long-sleeved cotton shirts and smartly pressed black pants, waiters quietly moved up and down the aisle, tending to the few patrons in this section.

Ana wore a long-sleeved white blouse, the sleeves rolled up to her elbows, and olive-green trousers. Today she looked ready for jungle duty. But then, to Mace's consternation, he'd found out from his Swiss sources last night that everything she'd told him was true. Not one lie came from those provocative lips of hers.

"Delicious," she assured him. She didn't really feel like eating after her disturbing dream last night. She glanced out the window and absorbed the natural beauty of the grassy, flat valley ringed by the snow-capped Andes.

None of it seemed familiar to Ana. She had hoped that being here would stimulate memories. So far, nothing did. Ana saw many adobe huts, and hardworking Quero men out in the fields in the early morning hours. Strips of fog lay across the valley. As the sun rose from behind the peaks, the mist began to dissolve magically before her eyes.

"I'm not convinced. You aren't eating like you mean it," Mace observed wryly. He forced himself to chew his scrambled eggs and rye toast. Ana looked tired this morning. Beneath her tilted green eyes, dark circles revealed disrupted sleep. He could feel her angst, her worry and confusion. If he put himself in her place—an orphan who did not know anything about her past—he could understand her feelings completely.

But Ana was the Daughter of Darkness. Again, Mace had trouble controlling his confusion. She didn't feel like evil!

The worst part was he found himself inexorably drawn to her, man to woman. His entire life had been shaped around destroying two of the most evil *Tupay* in the world. And now he was sitting with one of them, desiring her, his body tightening every time he looked at that full lower lip of hers, the lush curves of her mouth. His heart expanded, then ached. What a hell of a fix Mace found himself in!

"I'm sorry I couldn't meet you for dinner last night," Ana said, forcing herself to eat. If she didn't keep her strength up, she couldn't push forward with her plans for once they arrived in Aguas Calientes. Mace had gotten her a reservation at a hotel next to the India Feliz Restaurant, his favorite haunt when he came to town to dig nearby wells. After checking in, Ana was going to fill up her knapsack with food, water and other essentials, and follow the train track out of town. She would find Juan Sanchez's home and speak with him.

"That's okay," Mace said with a quick smile. He opened the marmalade jar and slathered the orange contents across his rye toast. "I had to work late, anyway. There were a lot of communications I had to catch up on at the office." That wasn't a lie. Ana just didn't know the information concerned her.

"When I got to my room I took a long, hot bath and just soaked." Ana smiled. She enjoyed watching Mace. Today he was dressed casually again, in jeans, a shirt and work boots. He looked as rugged as the Andes. "I called my parents last night and filled them in on everything." She frowned and stabbed at the eggs on her plate.

"And what did they say about that birthmark?" Mace asked her. Last night, he'd initiated a deep investigative search on her stepparents. The Daughter of Darkness was to have been born from two *Tupay*. Even though

John and Mary Rafael were her adoptive parents, that didn't erase the possibility they were *Tupay.* Mace had asked for a search of their medical records to find if any birthmarks had been recorded on either of them. That way, he could further confirm that Ana was who his jaguar spirit guide insisted that she was—adopted or not.

Shrugging, Ana said, "They were upset, naturally. For me. My mom, bless her, said that even if it were true about the symbol, that I was raised in a loving household with strong morals and values. My father added I clearly know right from wrong. They said to ignore the legend, that a person always has choices and that free will can negate the legend."

"I see," Mace murmured.

"They also pointed out that children who come from dysfunctional and broken homes, even homes where parents are on crystal meth, may struggle, but can go on to lead meaningful, healthy lives. They don't have to mirror a bad set of parents or a poor background. They can pick themselves up by their bootstraps and make something good of themselves."

Mace nodded. "That's right. I see it down here all the time." He gestured out the window at a small town where the train was coming to a halt. "The Quero are direct descendants of the ancient Inca people. Many are very poor and have to scramble to feed their families every year. I've seen their children come to Cuzco to go to school, move on to college, then graduate and become doctors, lawyers, accountants—whatever. So it is done all the time."

Brightening beneath his warm gaze, Ana felt hope

start to dispel her worry. Mace had a magical effect on her. How much she wanted to tell him so! But she wasn't sure he'd understand. Just from being around him, she felt her spirits lifting. He helped her feel emotionally stable in her highly chaotic world.

Ana reached for the marmalade and slathered some on her toast. "My parents said to stay focused in my heart, to listen to it and always let it lead me. This morning, I'm working on centering myself, so I can get a different perspective on my journey from what Mother Bernadette told me yesterday."

Mace finished his meal. The waiter, a Quero youth, came by to remove his plate, and Mace thanked him in Quechua. Then he returned his focus to Ana.

Some of the darkness had dissolved from her glorious catlike eyes. She worked with jaguars. She even looked like a jaguar; the shape of her face reminded him of the magnificent animal. And her high cheekbones spoke of her Quero heritage.

Mace knew her bloodline was Incan. But then, according to a legend found written in stone at Machu Picchu years ago, the Daughter of Darkness would be of pure Incan stock. So, how could he continue to feel such innocence around her? She seemed to trust him with incredibly sensitive information. Did he trust her in return? How he wanted to, but he simply could not.

On guard as never before, Mace pondered the situation. Ana must be deeply cloaked, trained in sorcerery to the point of being a chameleon, so that no one—not even him—could pick up on her true purpose. If he trusted her, he might very well step into an elaborate trap. That prospect made Ana ten times more dangerous to him.

Did she have any idea who he was? Mace had lain awake, tossing and turning all night, wondering just that. If she knew he was her would-be assassin, then she was wise to keep him close, where she could watch him.

As he watched Ana enjoy her toast and marmalade, Mace tried to resist her magic. Fascinated with her full, soft mouth, he wondered what it would be like to press his lips against hers. Would she feel so innocent if he kissed her? Mace knew he was becoming mesmerized by this seemingly guileless woman, whose sensuality was beginning to lure him to her like a fish to a baited hook. Angry with himself, he scowled and picked up his coffee cup.

"In Aguas Calientes," Ana said, handing the waiter her empty plate, "is there only one set of railroad tracks in and out of town?"

"Yeah, only one. The community sits at the foot of the mountain, far below Machu Picchu. The tracks that go south follow the Urubamba River. That's where you want to go. The jungle's so thick in that area that you cannot walk through it. Anyone heading south walks the railroad line or hitches a ride on the train. The forest is impenetrable except to jaguars, peccaries and other, smaller animals. You'll see a lot of little paths through the jungle, but they aren't wide enough or high enough for a human to follow."

Mace sipped his black coffee. "You'll see what I mean when we leave the Sacred Valley and start descending to Aguas Calientes. Look at the jungle walls as we pass and you'll get a good idea of what it's like below that little tourist town."

Nodding, Ana picked up her cup after in stirring cream and sugar. "Sound advice." She gave Mace a grateful look. "What would I do if you hadn't walked into my life? I just shake my head and wonder at how we met in the plane. You've been my knight in shining armor ever since, saving me in so many ways." She spontaneously reached out and touched the back of his hand. Her gesture was meant as a thank-you.

His blue eyes flared with surprise, and then narrowed upon her, much like she'd seen a jaguar do when hunting its quarry. Ana was shaken by his sharp, feral look. And just as quickly as it occurred, Mace erased it from his eyes, replacing it with a much warmer, inviting expression. An unwelcome thought flitted across her mind: had she made a mistake in trusting him? Her instincts shouted at her to be cautious. Yet she needed someone she could trust right now.

"I'm always helping tourists out around here," Mace said. "I know what it's like to be in a strange country, and not know the customs, the people. I always appreciate local help when I travel, so I'm just passing it on."

Sure he was. Mace felt his entire hand tingling from Ana's unexpected touch. Her voice was tender with gratitude, and he soaked it up like a thirsty sponge. When Ana trailed her fingers across his hand, shock and heat had bolted up his arm and straight into his heart. Her touch made him tremble with yearning. For the Daughter of Darkness herself.

Mace recalled his parents' warning that a female

sorcerer could seduce a man, even a highly trained Warrior for the Light, because she had a superior power. She could throw sensual energy into the mix and lure the warrior through sweet guile and manipulation. Energetically speaking, the power of a woman was twice that of any man, Mace knew. Only women could create. They could carry and birth a baby. This was why the Lord of Darkness wanted to connect with his daughter: she had the power of the feminine, and he needed that in order to conquer on a global scale.

Even with his heightened awareness, Mace had *never* experienced such conflict as when Ana touched his hand. He worked to keep his disturbed feelings locked away from her. "If the Sanchez home is only two miles from town, that should be an easy walk for you. Plus, you're used to jungle situations, from working in Belize on that jaguar project."

His smile seemed wooden and forced suddenly, and this bothered Ana. She like Mace Ridfort, probably too much. "Yes, I'm okay in jungle situations," she assured him. "It will be a piece of cake, having a railroad bed to walk on."

Surreptitiously she eyed his hand. There was no wedding ring on Mace's finger, but as an engineer out in the field, drilling water wells, he might not wear any jewelry. Maybe she had overstepped her bounds with him. The thought that Mace might be taken by another woman was like rain washing away the sunlight. She had no right to be drawn to him or any man right now. This journey was about finding herself—not getting into a relationship. She had to stop thinking and dreaming about Mace, as she had done last night.

"We'll be in Aguas Calientes soon," Mace noted, pointing out the window. The train began the downward portion of its journey off the high Andean plateau. The brakes were constantly applied as it headed through a seemingly impenetrable jungle that grew up on either side of the raised track bed.

Ana forgot her disappointment over Mace's reaction as she eagerly looked out the window. Aguas Calientes! Her heart beat a little harder. Would she remember any of it? She wanted to recognize something, if just one fragment of her life before the orphanage.

Ana walked off the train platform, carrying her knapsack on her back, a hiking stick in one hand and a small suitcase in the other. She almost expected to find Victor meeting her here, even though he'd said he had to take his wife to the doctor today. Warily, Ana examined everyone at the station. Maybe it had all been a dream and Victor wasn't her father. But she couldn't shake off the haunting feelings she'd had during their supposed conversation last night.

Mace walked casually at her side as they followed a muddy path toward the small Incan town carved out of the surrounding jungles. Ana gasped suddenly to see dark, loaf-shaped mountains rising before her. Their dark, jagged sides were covered with orchids, bromeliads and other jungle plants—a colorful, textured cloak. The sky was foggy, but the sun was quickly burning it off, leaving patches of blue.

Excitement flowed through Ana as she spotted the mighty Urubamba River. The water was a clear sea-green, indicating it was coming from glaciers high in the Andes. Mace had told her that the foaming, splashing river wove like a snake between the three main guardians: Machu Picchu, Huaynu Picchu and Mama Putucusi. These three mountains formed a triangle, with the sacred river winding between them. Mace had said that the Inca emperor Pachacuti had chosen this site because the elements came together in a magical triangle. He had built the most beautiful, otherworldly temple on the male apu, or mountain spirit: Machu Picchu.

Ana craned her neck to see white, wispy clouds still hovering around the top of the mighty dome. She yearned to take one of the many tourist buses up to the top and walk the sacred ground of the Incas. But not today. She had more important business to attend to. Following Mace down the slippery, muddy trail, she finally reached the awakening town.

Aguas Calientes was a conglomeration of structures that ranged from lumber, to pieces of plywood nailed together, to a three-story stone hostel called Gringo Bill's. The India Feliz, a restaurant Mace pointed out as they climbed the road through town, was a two-story redbrick building. More modern hotels farther up the thoroughfare were made of local gray river rock.

It was clearly a tourist town. Ana hiked at Mace's side, gawking like a typical *turista*. Quero Indians already had their wares out on display—handwoven, colorful rugs and knitted alpaca and llama sweaters with beautiful geometric designs. Bushel baskets of fresh produce included peppers, bananas, onions, corn and many types of potatoes—all staples of the local populace. The noise level was high, the vendors looking up in anticipation as tourists began to filter into town from the railroad station above.

"Here we are," Mace said, gesturing to a river-rock archway, the entrance to Hotel Machu Picchu. "I'll get your reservation confirmed and then I'm going to my office, which is right next to the India Feliz, in case you need me."

"Right. You pointed it out earlier." Ana walked across the gray-and-black-flagstone lobby. The reservation desk was mahogany and gleamed reddish-gold in the light of colorful stained-glass lamps. Two female clerks, dressed in dark red blouses and black skirts, seemed more than happy to be of service to them.

Afterward, Mace left Ana and walked to his field office. She understood he had a drilling project going on about half a mile down the railroad track she'd be hiking on shortly. His company had won the bid to put in three new wells for the growing town.

Happiness thrummed through Ana as she went to her room on the third and highest floor. It was clean and welcoming, with teak floors that shone a rich sienna color in the weak sunlight. Setting her suitcase on the bed, she checked out her new accommodations. The walls were white, as if newly painted. A pink bromeliad sat in a red pot on a mahogany stand. And what lovely views. One window faced Machu Picchu, and the other, the wall of jungle. The curtains, dark red with pink and yellow orchids, were pulled back to give visitors the full effect. A mahogany settee, desk and upholstered chair completed the furnishings.

While she could have spent hours luxuriating in these surroundings, Ana was eager to locate the Sanchez homestead. She hurried out of her room, locked the door and slid the key card into her backpack. As she looked up and down the hall, she was unable to shake the feeling that Victor was nearby. But she saw nothing and decided to ignore her misgivings. Taking the stairs, she could feel her heart pounding not from exertion, but anticipation. Soon, she would know more. She just had to keep putting one foot in front of the other.

As Ana walked out of the open lobby and into the crowded street, a weight lifted off her. She strode along, absorbing the contagious and exciting energy of Aguas Calientes. Above the hotel were a set of hot springs, said to bring healing to those who had aches and pains. To her right rose majestic and mysterious Machu Picchu, now completely unveiled.

Ana's senses were engaged by the odor of white corn tortillas frying and ears of fresh corn bubbling in open kettles of boiling water. She heard throaty sounds of panpipes and raspy snare drums filtering out of bars and restaurants. As she passed the yellow stucco building where Mace worked, Ana wondered if he was still there or if he'd already taken off for his well site.

Once she reached the railroad tracks, Ana walked along the wooden ties between the well-worn shiny steel rails. Birds called from above, but she couldn't see them. Howler monkeys screamed in the distance. Sleepy Aguas Calientes was springing awake now that the tourists from Cuzco had arrived on the train.

Sliding her fingers beneath the wide, padded straps of

her pack, Ana was glad to have a baseball cap to shade her eyes from the bright sunlight lancing across the forest canopy on either side of the tracks. The day was very humid, the air nearly dripping with moisture. The wooden ties she gingerly negotiated were covered with mold, an indicator of just how much rain fell in this area.

A helicopter flew by and Ana turned to see it dip out of the clouds and land somewhere north of the town. Another helicopter circled the temple sites. Ana was sure the passengers were wealthy visitors who didn't want to take the train trip, but preferred to shoot a few photos and head back to Cuzco.

The whole world seemed alive and quivering with energy. As she inhaled the clean air into her expanding rib cage, Ana felt a new hope threading through her. Hope of finding out who she was. Who she might be. Would the Sanchez family remember her? The question haunted Ana as she followed the curving track.

The noise and bustle of town were soon left behind, absorbed by the trees, bushes and vines that rose twenty to thirty feet high on either side of her. She was alone and it felt good. This was a scene she was familiar with, thanks to her experience living in the jungles of Belize. This felt familiar. Comforting. And it soothed Ana's jumpy nerves. Towns and cities always made her want to run out of them, screaming. Ana longed to hear the natural sounds of the world, rather than manmade racket. The rustling of leaves and humming of insects healed her, kept her sane and happy.

A squadron of blue-and-yellow macaws suddenly burst from the forest canopy and flew overhead. Smiling, Ana knew that was a good sign. The four parrots were heading the same direction she was: toward the Sanchez farm. Barely able to contain her joy, she lengthened her stride. She was in a hurry. She had a date with destiny.

Chapter 6

"Excuse me," Ana called to a white-haired man wearing a crumpled straw hat. He leaned wearily on his hoe while standing in the furrowed field. "I'm looking for a Señor Juan Sanchez. Do you know where I can find him?"

Ana had hiked two miles down the tracks, and this was the first agricultural field she'd come upon. The old farmer was alone and had been weeding between the rows of knee-high corn. The long, rectangular field stretched between the jungle and the tracks.

Lifting his head, the old man squinted in her direction. "I'm Juan Sanchez. And who are you?" He slowly straightened as he turned toward her.

"Ana Rafael." She smiled and quickly moved into the field. Holding out her hand to him, she added, "I'm a wildlife biologist from the United States, Señor Sanchez. I was told you had a phenomenal story from a long time ago about finding a little child beneath a dead jaguar?"

Brightening, Juan pumped her hand. "Ah, yes. That story." Taking out a well-used cotton rag, he mopped his deeply lined brow and motioned toward the end of the field, where a huge tree with broad, spreading arms provided some shade. "We rarely get visitors out our way. Especially ones wanting to know about a particular story from our parts." He eyed her as if deciding whether or not to speak further with her.

Ana felt her skin prickle, as if he were somehow scanning her energetically. But the look in the old man's twinkling brown eyes made her feel glad, for no apparent reason. She didn't mind his suspicion. There was a sense of safety that emanated from him, of care. His hands were work worn, his knuckles swollen and arthritic. It was evident he had cared for the earth, and that gave her a good feeling.

"I'm sure you are a little distrustful of people coming to you with such a request," Ana said.

Juan shrugged and smiled, as if knowing an inside joke that she did not. "I was told that one day a beautiful young woman from *Norteamérica* would come to me." He pointed to the jungle. "A mother jaguar told me here." He pointed to his skull. "She spoke inside my head and told me to look for this young woman. She said she would have a rainbow of colors around her." Giving Ana a keen glance, Juan waved his hand. "You have such colors. I can trust you, and I trust that you are here for good reason." Patting her shoulder, he said, "I need a rest, anyway, *señorita*. Come, follow me. I have my jug of water over there beneath the tree and we can sit down and chat a bit."

Ana nodded and fell into step with the bent man. His hair was snow-white and stuck out beneath the tattered straw hat. His steps were careful and he used the hoe almost as a makeshift cane. Finally, they reached the spreading tree and its welcome shade. Juan gave Ana a toothless grin and motioned for her to sit down on a stump that would serve as a chair.

Ana wanted to ask him about the colors around herself. He was probably talking about the aura, which everyone possessed. But to talk to a jaguar using mental telepathy? Oh, that intrigued her as nothing else could. Her adoptive mother had taught her that everyone had an energy field around them, which turned different colors depending on their mood and character. She wasn't surprised at the elder's pronouncement of seeing her aura. Her mother could see them, too, and had taught Ana how to do so.

"My wife brings me lunch around 3:00 p.m.," he confided. Gazing up at the sun, he said, "A long time to go before that happens."

Ana sat down and pulled out her notebook and pen. "I have a sandwich I could share with you if you're hungry," she offered.

Holding up his hand, Juan chuckled indulgently. "Oh, no, *señorita*. Thank you for your kindness. Now, how may I be of help to you?"

"I really appreciate your time, Señor Sanchez. As I

said, I heard this story from people in Aguas Calientes, about a little girl found alive beneath a dead jaguar."

After taking several gulps from his bottle, Juan wiped his mouth. "Oh, yes, we are famous, or perhaps infamous, for what happened here in this very field many, many years ago."

Ana wasn't going to tell the farmer that she was that child. After the nun's pronouncement that she came from evil, Ana didn't want to scare the Sanchez family away. Better to be a stranger to them at this point.

"As a wildlife biologist, I study jaguars for a living," she confided. "And when I heard of your story, I had to find you. A year ago, I helped create a sanctuary for jaguars in Belize. I'm interested in protecting them because they are becoming endangered and rare."

Wiping his mouth with the back of his thickly veined hand, Juan nodded. "I feel honored you have come to talk with me. And bless you for helping the jaguar nation. They need protection from poachers who would steal their lives for their beautiful coats. A long time ago, jaguars were honored by the Inca people." Juan pointed to his chest. "I am of Quero heritage, the pure blood of the Incas. I was raised to know that jaguars are sacred, powerful and can speak with us if we were of good heart. My mother taught me to talk with jaguars when I was very young." He squinted at Ana. "And she also taught me to see the colors around a person."

Juan pointed to the east edge of the field, against the wall of jungle. "Over there, *señorita.* That's where it all happened. You can't see it from here, but there's a shallow stream of pure, clean water that flows along between my property and the forest." Juan took off his hat and dropped it near his dusty feet. "For about a year before the jaguar was shot by this hunter, I'd been seeing *la niña,* the little girl, at the edge of the forest there. She'd come out and get down on her hands and knees and drink water from that stream.

"Now, she was wild. Her black hair looked like a messy rat's nest around her head. She was wary, but over time, if she saw me working in this field, she wouldn't run away. Instead, she'd walk over to this tree we're sitting under and watch me."

"A little girl?" Ana gulped. Intuitively, she knew it was her. She wanted to ask a million questions, but held back and allowed Juan to continue his story.

"Yes. The girl was maybe three or four years old. Though I tried many times to call to her, to get her to come over to me, she never would. Yet she was very curious and I think she was fascinated with me, though I don't know why."

"Didn't she belong to someone?" The words came out strangled.

Juan shrugged. "Well, if she did, I never saw her parents. She was completely naked except for her long, tangled black hair. Barefoot, naked and like a little brown ghost appearing and disappearing. When *la niña* first started showing up, I asked my wife, Juanita, if any nearby farming families had a little girl of this description and age. She asked around at the local markets and they all said no. Others had seen her, too, but they could never get near her. She would run off and hide in the jungle."

Gulping, Ana scribbled down the information. Why

didn't she remember any of this? Her brain had completely blocked the first five years of her life, except for a few vignettes that seemed impossible to believe. "Then she was…."

"An orphan, I suppose. My wife thought perhaps her parents had died in an avalanche, and that she was left all alone at a very early age."

"That sounds possible."

Juan twisted his head to look in her direction. "That wasn't it. The first time I saw *la niña* come to the stream she had a big female jaguar at her side. I about died of shock."

"A jaguar was *with* her?"

"Yes, *señorita,* a healthy and beautiful female. I knew she was a female because she had two cubs at her side *and* this young girl."

Eyes widening, Ana stared disbelievingly at the old farmer. "But how could that *be?*"

"Oh, I know, I know, *señorita.* It sounds as if I'm making up this tale, but I am not. Bear with me. Let me tell you what eventually happened."

Her heart pounded in her chest, and Ana could barely focus on the notebook in her lap. The words she scribbled were nearly illegible because her hand was trembling so badly over the information the farmer had just shared with her. Juan Sanchez's face was sun darkened, deeply wrinkled, his chocolate eyes clear, and she found nothing but honesty there. "I—this just sounds so bizarre to me."

"Doesn't it?" He shook his head sadly. "I'll bet you've never seen a jaguar with a human, have you? At least, not eating it?" The corners of his wide, thin mouth curved as he studied her. "You know, in our Incan traditions, we had jaguar warriors—men and women who *trained* with jaguars to become *like* them. They traded spirits with one another in order for it to be so. Shape-shifters, the emperor's soldiers were called. They were under orders from the Inca himself. They were charged with protecting him and the royal family against all enemies. They were the most powerful warriors on earth."

Juan smiled faintly. "They were the Inca's warriors of the night. They were able to pierce the darkness with their trained eyes and attack other kingdoms. The jaguar warriors were well-known for seeing at night." He tapped his deeply creased brow. "All these skills were taught by the jaguar nation. So, in my culture, people have befriended the jaguars over thousands of years, not hunted them. We made friends with them, respected them and learned from them. Truly, they were our highest spiritual teachers. So when I saw this child, I knew in my heart she was not only being taken care of and protected by this mother jaguar, but being trained by her, as well."

"I studied jaguars for two years in Belize, and they usually won't bother humans," Ana told the farmer. She was amazed by what he'd just confided to her. No one had ever told her about humans and jaguars working as a team. And shape-shifters! An eerie familiarity awakened within her. Was that what happened to her from time to time? Did she shape-shift? Ana did not know. Somehow, all this information took her breath away and triggered a deep knowing. Being here with this man, listening to this story, felt right to Ana, and she never questioned her gut instinct.

Ana saw the farmer nod and said, "At least the ones I studied always went for peccary—the wild pigs—or other animals. One farmer got bitten in the hand by a jaguar, but that was it."

"Well," Juan said, gesturing toward the stream, "from that day onward, I saw the four of 'em together at the stream. This is the only water source for about twenty miles in the jungle here. A lot of animals come to get a drink."

"And they didn't run if they saw you in the field?"

"No. At first, when that jaguar arrived with her cubs and that little girl at her side, it shook me. I told my wife about it and she said they were evil, that this must be a sorcerer shape-shifted into a jaguar, who held *la niña* prisoner."

Ana stared at him. "Did you believe that?"

"My second wife is a devout Catholic, *señorita,*" Juan said very seriously. "Anything out of the ordinary for her is automatically blamed on the devil."

"What about you?" Ana tensed inwardly. She was sure the woman would take her *Tupay* birthmark very seriously.

Juan rubbed his stubbled gray beard as he stared at the stream. "As a Quero, I believe in the old ways of my people, the Incas. When I saw that jaguar, I felt there was a special relationship between her and that little girl. I stood here many times watching *la niña* play with the jaguar's growing cubs. Sometimes I'd hear her laughter. The cubs loved her. She loved the cubs. And sometimes I'd see the mother jaguar lick the little girl's face as if she were her cub, also." Juan shook his head. "It was as if the past, our Inca heritage, had come to life before my eyes once more. It is one thing to have the stories passed down to you, and quite another to see them come true before your eyes." He smiled fondly. "I saw them many times, so I know I wasn't making it up. I took it as a sign of the legend coming to life."

Staring down at her notebook, Ana tried to control the onslaught of memories. In those fragments, she would feel soft, warm fur against her face, she'd hear the deep purr of a cat. It hadn't been her imagination, after all. And it was no accident she'd ended up as a biologist studying jaguars....

Ana tore herself from her reverie. "What legend?" she asked Juan.

Rubbing his chin, he said, "There is a legend of a young woman who would carry the mark of the Dark Side, the *Tupay* symbol of the sun, on her body. She was Dark, but in her heart, she carried another symbol." Juan leaned down, took a small stick and drew two overlapping circles in the dry red soil at their feet. "The Incas called this the symbol of the Warriors for the Light. It is *Taqe,* light energy, the path to peace and harmony in our world." He straightened and set the stick aside, then pressed his hand to his chest. "*Taqe* is the way of the heart, *señorita.* The way the Incas knew to create lasting peace among all races, all colors, here on our Mother Earth. And to this day, there is a line of humans who bear this symbol, because they are the children, through blood lineage, of the jaguar warriors of so long ago. Bloodlines never die. They may fade, but are never destroyed." Juan gave her a searching look. "These warriors may not be aware of who they are because there is no longer a jaguar school to call them to training. They may not have the conscious memory of their heritage, but unconsciously, they will follow it. You will always find these people in service to the world in some useful and positive way."

Ana's gut churned. She felt abject terror when Juan mentioned the *Tupay.* Unconsciously, she placed her hand against her stomach. "You mentioned a war between the Light and the Dark?"

"Yes." Juan sighed and looked around. "The legend says this woman of the Dark with the heart of Light will be born and decide whether she will fight for one side or another. They say she has the heart of the jaguar, and it is hoped that the energy of our beautiful, sacred cat will persuade her to turn from her dark desires."

Ana wanted to squirm. It felt as if Juan were talking about *her*. He probably was. The dreams of her past didn't lie. She had them all the time. Her adoptive mother had assured her long ago that the dreams were good. Once, Mary had told her that Ana was shape-shifting in her dream, taking on the spirit of the jaguar over her human form, and turning into the cat.

Mary had considered it normal and told Ana that among her medicine people, some of them had this innate ability. Ana, though, was afraid of that possibility. Losing control scared her more than anything else.

Tearing her attention back to the present, she asked the farmer, "How long did your contact with the mother jaguar and *la niña* go on?"

"Almost six months, throughout the dry season. By that time, the little girl had a burning curiosity about me, I think."

"Why do you say that?"

"Because I used to put some bread or fruit by the stream for her. Juanita, my wife, would wrap a bit of food in a cloth for her every morning. *La niña* was so thin. I could see every rib on her body. I felt sorry for her. I don't know what she was eating and I was worried she'd starved to death."

"That was very generous of you to leave her food." And it was. Juan was very kind looking, and Ana felt her heart go out to the old man. She imagined that food was hard to come by.

"*La niña* got so she looked around for the food," he said, smiling. "Every time she came for water, which was usually at dawn, I would be there. When I started putting a bit of food near the stream bank, well, she really liked that! *La niña* would peek about, looking for that packet of food as soon as she arrived. Over time, she crept closer and closer to me, to watch me for an hour or more. I would smile, wave and say hello to her. And then one day I decided to leave a little bit of candy on a broad rubber tree leaf that I'd pluck off the tree. Only I put it at the edge of my field instead of on the stream bank. I wanted to get her to trust me, so I started doing this every day. And each day I'd put the leaf closer to where I was working. She'd come and get it every time." He chuckled fondly.

"Because of my own Quero training, I was not afraid of the jaguar at her side, *señorita*. The mother cat would always sit at the stream and watch the little girl, much as a mother would watch her child explore. The jaguar never stopped *la niña* from coming into the field where I was working. Eventually, one day, I was able to hand the little girl the candy myself! That was a great day." Juan grinned. "I felt like I was taming a shy, wild animal who didn't know she was a human being. When she was with her jaguar mother, I'd hear her mew, grunt, snarl or hiss, just like the other cubs. I don't think she knew any human language."

Shock rifled through Ana. She kept her face down because she didn't want Juan to suspect her true identity. With her gut in knots, she held her breath as the old man continued.

"My wife was afraid that I was working with the devil," he added. "But I saw the relationship between the girl and the jaguar. There was love between them."

"So, you said the jaguar mother treated the little girl as one of her own?" Ana's voice was thin and strained.

"I did. She often licked her, as if she were one of her cubs. Licked her face, her hair, which was an unholy mess. She would often nudge her to lie down next to the cubs as they suckled. *La niña* suckled from the mother jaguar, as well. I'm sure the girl survived due to the rich milk of the jaguar."

"That seems impossible. What I know as a biologist—"

Juan eyed her. "I know that, *señorita*. But my father was a Quero medicine man. I had seen him with wild animals many times, and they never hurt him. He had a special, spiritual relationship with the jaguar nation."

Turning, Juan looked across the field toward the stream. "I know this little girl had a spiritual relationship with this mama jaguar."

"I understand."

"Anyway, something tragic happened," Juan said, frowning. "I was making good progress with the child, getting her to trust me. I would stop my work when they appeared, and I would gently call her to me. I would speak to her softly about many things. I don't know that she understood the words, but I could tell she knew I would never harm her. Her curiosity grew about us two-leggeds, I'm sure.

"By the beginning of the wet season, when I had to abandoned my farming plot here for the year, *la niña* was no longer afraid of me."

Juan plucked a blade of grass and chewed on it thoughtfully. "I had a plan, *señorita*. My plan was to get her to trust me enough to come home and live with us. The wet season was coming and I was worried for her."

Ana fought back tears and kept on writing. "You said something awful occurred?"

"Yes." Juan straightened, his voice growing sad. "The day before the rains arrived, I came out to my field one last time. I had just put down my hoe, my food pack and water jug, when I saw movement at the far end." Scowling, Juan pointed across the waving corn. "There was a man, a poacher, I'm sure. He carried a big rifle with him. I watched as he leaped off the train tracks and started to look toward where the jaguar and the little girl always appeared at the stream. I didn't know him, but he gave me a bad feeling. I could see the colors around him."

Juan made a circular motion with his hand. "They showed an angry thunderstorm, and I knew him to be an evil person."

"Who was he?"

Holding up his palm, Juan muttered, "You will know shortly, *señorita.* Anyway, I felt as if the little girl was in terrible danger, and so was her jaguar mother. They hadn't arrived yet, but I knew they would. Just as I started to shout at the stranger, to stop him, they appeared out of the jungle. By now, *la niña* was very trusting of me, and she started to run toward me. To get her share of my *desayuno.*"

Juan's mouth tightened and he scratched his furrowed brow with dirt encrusted nails. "I saw the hunter stop in his tracks when he noticed the girl. He raised his rifle *at her,* not the jaguar! I screamed at him, waved my arms to draw his attention. But the little girl didn't see him—she had eyes only for me, *señorita.* She was smiling, her little arms open, hands stretched toward me...."

"Oh, no," Ana choked out as she sat there, her eyes riveted to Juan's suffering features.

"That hunter *was* pure evil. *Tupay.* I felt it. I saw it. He wanted to kill that poor little girl. I screamed at her to stop, and started running toward her, but I was too far away. The next thing I knew, the mother jaguar burst out of the jungle and charged across the stream. She raced at top speed into my field and headed directly for *la niña,* who was running toward me."

Shaking his head, Juan whispered, "Everything slowed down. I saw the hunter draw a bead on the little girl. As I saw the jaguar racing toward her, I kept yelling at the hunter to stop. I felt so helpless." After wiping his watering eyes, the old farmer looked down at his short, jagged fingernails. "I heard the gun go off."

Juan sighed raggedly. "It was a terrible sound, *señorita.* The whole jungle seemed to vibrate from that one shot. And then it was quiet, as if in shock. Just as the hunter fired, the female jaguar made a mighty leap into the sky toward the little girl. The bullet struck the big cat, the shot so powerful that it threw her backward at least six feet. The jaguar hit the little girl and knocked her to the ground. I stumbled and fell myself, gasping in horror. The jaguar was dead and lying on top of the unconscious girl. At that time, I didn't know if they had both been shot or not."

Taking in a ragged breath, Juan said, "I cursed the hunter. He took off running, back down the railroad tracks, back toward Aguas Calientes. I screamed angrily at him as I raced across the field to his victims. My heart was bursting with pain. I was so afraid *la niña* was dead. When I fell to my knees beside the jaguar, I could barely see the girl's ratty black hair sticking out from beneath the cat. There was blood everywhere, and I began to cry and pray to the Inca to spare *la niña*'s life. I pushed the jaguar off her. The little girl was so pale, muddy and lifeless. Her body was covered with warm, red blood. I was afraid to touch her, for fear the bullet had found her, too." Juan wiped his eyes once more. "I pulled her free, gathered her in my arms and ran to the shade of this tree. I stripped off my shirt and started wiping the blood and mud off her. I couldn't find any wounds on her, and soon enough, she became conscious. But she was dazed. She recognized me, so she didn't fight me. I just wrapped her in my shirt, held her to my chest and hurried home."

Tears burned in Ana's eyes as she searched the kindly farmer's wet face. "That poacher," he grated angrily, "has blood on his hands to this day. I have cursed him daily since then, because he *wanted* to kill the girl. I know he did. I don't know why. If I ever see him again—" Juan reached for his sharp-bladed hoe "—I will slice this through his head for what he did. He needlessly killed a beautiful jaguar guardian. Her two cubs died, too. They were too young to survive without their mother. He tried to murder *la niña.* And then he ran like the coward he was."

"Wh-what happened then?" Ana asked, her voice unsteady.

"I took her home. My wife was angry with me. She was alarmed at all the blood on the girl. *La niña* was frightened of her, so I took her to the tub and washed her off with warm water. I dressed her in one of my soft, old cotton shirts and put socks on her feet to keep her warm. My wife calmed and I asked her to cut off the girl's hair because it was so filthy. I could not put a comb through it."

Juan smiled softly. "That little girl sat in my lap, trusting me. Her little hands gripped my big fingers. She was wary of my wife and the scissors she held. We had to cut all her hair off. All of it. There was no way we could save any of it. Then I took her back to the tub and washed her again, with soap and warm water. Her scalp was scabby and had many little bites and swellings all over it.

"As I was drying her little head with a towel, there was a smudge of mud still on her neck, so I took a washcloth and wiped it away. My wife shrieked. She frightened me to death with her scream. *La niña* cried out and clung to me. My wife began sobbing hysterically."

"Why did your wife scream?" Ana asked.

Juan tapped the back of his neck. "She had the sign of the *Tupay* on her neck. The sun symbol. When my wife saw that, she flew into a panic. She said the girl was the devil incarnate. I have never seen her so frightened. I tried to tell her that was not true, that the little girl was sweet and pure. But she wouldn't hear it. She chased me out of the house with a broom and told me not to return until I'd handed *la niña* over to the orphanage in Cuzco. My first wife, Maria, would not, but she died many years ago."

"So, that's what you did?" Ana asked, wiping tears from her eyes.

Juan gave her a unhappy look. "I had to. I had just enough money to travel to Cuzco. By nightfall, I was on the steps of the orphanage, talking with Sister Bernadette, who took the little girl in to care for her."

"You saved her life."

"No, *señorita.* The mother jaguar saved the little girl's life. She deliberately jumped in front of her to save her from the hunter's gun. She took the bullet meant for *la niña.* All I did was give her a chance to go on with her life." Juan seemed to search Ana's face. "I have often wondered what happened to her, if she was adopted. Despite the birthmark on her neck, her green cat eyes held nothing but innocence, never evil."

His trembling, emotional words reached Ana's raw, pounding heart. Again she felt the sun symbol on the back of her neck prickle, as if to remind her of its presence. The birthmark said she was evil. Yet, as she absorbed Juan's compassionate words, Ana started to believe in what he said—that she was not evil. Did she dare hope? "You are a hero in my eyes, Señor Sanchez. You did something very good and kind."

"Who could let a little child starve to death? You tell me," he said, suddenly gruff. "I cannot tell this true story without shedding tears." Once more, he wiped his eyes with his tattered rag.

"It has a happy ending. Maybe that's why." Ana fought back her own tears, and slowly closed the notebook in her lap. The sun had changed position. Perhaps an hour had gone by, but it felt like five minutes to her.

"My wife was happy to have *la niña* gone. But I was not. I am just a poor farmer and Cuzco is a long, long way away. I often wanted to take the train to see if she was still there, and how she was doing, but we are very poor."

Hearing the longing in his voice, Ana reached out and touched Juan's stooped shoulder. "I have to think that your good heart and influence helped her have a positive life."

"I hope so, *señorita*." Juan smiled faintly as he gazed toward the stream.

"Do you have a description of the poacher? Were you close enough to see his face?" Ana asked.

"I was close enough to notice he had a black beard beneath his narrow, thin face. He wore black clothes, but those who hunt the jaguar frequently wear black or dark green to melt into the jungle. And he had dark, lifeless eyes. I'd never seen him before, but I know he's a sorcerer. That's all I need to know. With time and age, my eyes are bad now. I probably wouldn't recognize him unless I was standing within two feet of him."

Ana closed her eyes and felt her heart squeeze violently with fear. Juan was describing Victor, the man who intruded into her dreams. He was the one who had killed the jaguar, who had tried to kill her! This was why she felt as if he was stalking her, hunting her. Her breathing quickened as the danger she was in became clear. Her father wanted her dead.

But she had to keep this from Juan.

"By any chance, do you know a man by the name of Victor?" she asked.

"I do not, *señorita.* Are you all right? You look very pale."

Taking a deep, ragged breath, she forced a smile for the benefit of the worried farmer. "I—I'm fine, really. Just feeling out of sorts. Jet lag, you know? And this altitude I'm sure is bothering me. My body must be adjusting, these first few days being in Peru." Ana hated to lie to this dear old farmer, but she had no choice.

"Ah, then chew coca leaves. That will cure your altitude sickness, *señorita.*" Juan smiled sympathetically. "We Inca have chewed those leaves for centuries, because we live at such high altitudes. That or drink the tea."

Reluctantly, Ana stood up. "I think you're right. I don't want to go, but I have to." It was nearly noon. "I want to thank you for telling me your story, Señor Sanchez. It means so much to me." Her heart felt as if it would tear from her chest. Ana watched as tears glimmered once more in his squinted eyes. Juan's features blurred as hot tears flooded her own eyes. Gulping, she whispered, "I don't want to go, but I have time constraints. The train leaves for Cuzco early this afternoon, and I have to be on it."

Another lie, and Ana felt horrible. But she was barely in control of her fleeing emotions over the revelation of her father's treachery. She needed time to think and to get a handle on herself. Victor had said he would see her in person tomorrow. Oh, Great Spirit, she didn't want anything to do with him! He could be coming to kill her with that same rifle.

Gazing up at her, Juan nodded. "I understand, *señorita*. But drink some coca leaf tea and you will feel better shortly. That I promise you. You have green cat eyes, too. You know, when you walked up, I thought immediately of *la niña* once more. She had the most beautiful green eyes, as you do. And she had the very same rainbow colors around her."

Afraid that he might realize she was that child, Ana smiled brokenly. "I'm sure my colors aren't the same as hers. Though I wish they were." Reaching into her pocket, she drew out six hundred soles. "Here, I want you to take this, Señor Sanchez. Your time is worth money to me. Take this gift, please."

Gasping, Juan stared at the crisp, colorful bills. "You are so generous, *señorita*." He took them gratefully. "Thank you."

Ana pulled the baseball cap a little lower over her eyes after she shrugged into her knapsack. It was time to walk the two miles back to town. She needed to think and read over her notes on Juan's story. "You're welcome," she told the farmer. Lifting her hand, she whispered tremulously, "And someday, Juan, I'll be back, I promise you."

Smiling, Juan waved. "You are kindhearted, *señorita.* I will look forward to your next visit. Come whenever you like. We will share a good cup of coffee at our home the next time you come, eh? Juanita will love you! I can tell you more jaguar stories if you like."

Ana gave him a long, fierce hug. Juan smelled of sweat, of the earth and the damp fragrance of the jungle. "Thank you, I will. I love coffee. Farewell for now, my good friend."

The old farmer clasped her to him, as if he were not going to let her go. Ana felt his love toward her, felt his strong, arthritic fingers gripping her upper arms. "You are more than a friend, *señorita*. You have touched my heart, my grieving spirit. I feel as if *la niña* has somehow returned to me in a way I cannot explain." And he released her.

Ana would have loved to go home with Juan right now, to get to know this dear old man and his wife. Wiping her eyes, she gave him an unsteady smile. "I will come back."

As she hurried toward the tracks, Ana experienced a jumble of emotions, one of them fear. As she hiked back to town, it escalated steadily, until she felt suffocated with dread. Of her own death coming to meet her. The sorcerer, Victor, had not finished off what he'd started when she was four years old, and now he was coming again. This time, Ana knew he wouldn't miss.

Chapter 7

"And that's the whole, incredible story," Ana told Mace over a late dinner at the India Feliz. Well, she'd shared *most* of the story with him. Ana hadn't had the heart to tell him about Victor, the father who had tried to kill her. When she could find a working phone, she would talk to her adoptive parents. They would know how to comfort her, as well as counsel her on her next step. For now, as much as she was bursting to confide in him she needed to be cautious with Mace. At the same time he understood her experience more than most, and she was hoping he'd give her some feedback.

It was Ana's nature to trust people she'd known a short time. All her life, she'd been a decent judge of character. She had always chalked it up to gut instinct, but with Juan's explanation, she wondered if the mother jaguar might have given her something extra, a deep instinctual knowing. With Mace, she certainly felt an inexplicable connection that defied all logic. Sitting and sharing with him felt natural. Her heart told her he could be trusted with anything she ever revealed to him. But Ana wasn't sure she should surrender all her secrets. He was terribly handsome and she was drawn to him like a proverbial magnet. What woman wouldn't be? He was intelligent, compassionate and apparently single.

Right now, however, she needed a friend, someone with whom she could discuss these surprising developments. She sensed Mace wanted to be her friend. Deep down, she had to admit she wanted to be more.

This isn't the time for a relationship, she scolded herself. Her father was coming to see her tomorrow. This was life and death. Leaning on Mace any further would only put him in danger. So many times in the last hour, she'd nearly spilled the truth about Victor. She knew Mace would want to protect her, would insist upon it. He had rescued her a few times already.

But Ana had to handle Victor alone. She didn't want to, but she had to. All the close calls out in the jungles of Belize had taught her that she could take care of herself even in highly dangerous situations.

Here, she was staying in a hotel. People would be around and she could call for help. Of course, because he was a sorcerer, he could trap her when she was at her most vulnerable. He could always find her….

Ana took a deep breath and focused on the present, on Mace. The restaurant was crowded, and since Mace knew the owner, he had requested a quiet table alone on the second floor. Ana nudged the bones of her fresh trout, wishing she had more of an appetite.

"What an unbelievable story, Ana," Mace murmured as she finished her tale. He was tired after a long day out in the field, traveling between two sites by helicopter. A day in mud and water, plus problems with the drill rig, had taken its toll on him. But no matter how drained he was, being with Ana reinvigorated him. In the low light, with her hair soft around her face, Ana looked enticing, more so than he wanted to admit. She wore casual pants and a white shirt, with a purple-and-fuschia silk scarf draped around her neck. Her small gold earrings accented the golden tones of her skin and shining eyes.

There was nothing he didn't like about Ana, he realized. On one level, Mace felt utterly defeated. No one had trained him to deny his male needs in a confrontation with the Daughter of Darkness. How could they have?

It was up to him to rein in his hormones. But what about his stupid heart, which had been pining away all day for just a look at Ana? And what about his feverish dreams of making love with her?

With a sigh, she said, "I can't believe I was living so close to a jaguar."

"I can't believe that, either," Mace growled. Staring down at his half-eaten trout, he recalled from his training that jaguar guardians were powerful spirit guides *only* for Warriors for the Light. *Never* would a jaguar work for the Dark Forces. So what the *hell* had Ana been doing with a jaguar at her side? Quite literally, living with one? Frowning, he forced himself to finish his meal.

"I've studied jaguars for years," Ana said softly, sitting back in the chair. "There are few incidents in Belize where they have harmed a human. But…to live with one?"

"Surely you had someone looking after you during that time, even if Señor Sanchez or his wife didn't know about it."

"I had dreams, Mace, right after I was adopted. I dreamed of turning from a human being into a jaguar, and back into human form again." Ana glanced at him to see if he believed her. Mace's eyes were narrowed on her speculatively.

"Go on. What happened?" he urged, his voice low.

"This is going to sound crazy, I know, but these dreams, or whatever you want to call them, continued. They continue to this day, Mace. I see myself shape-shifting. That's what my adoptive mother called this magical process. She said that, with time and training, the medicine people of her nation can do this sort of thing." Ana splayed her hands. "And one time, well, the dream became a reality. I have never told anyone this, not even my parents. I was too scared."

Frowning, Mace stared at her long, beautifully formed hands held over the table. "What happened?"

"Well, the first time occurred when I was in Belize, watching the jaguars for scientific purposes. I was on the jungle floor, tracking one of my jags, when I saw a poacher stalking him." Ana pulled back her hands and tucked them beneath the tablecloth. Looking down, she whispered, "I felt such terror, such rage that this hunter might kill one of my jaguars that I..." Her voice died away.

Ana risked a look at Mace. She found his eyes focused on her, as intensely as a jaguar's would be when hunting a quarry. Again, she felt a moment of distrust. Perhaps he was only showing interest, she decided. That thought gave her the courage to go on.

"Something so weird happened," she admitted, holding his sharp gaze. Leaning forward, she lowered her voice even further. "I remember feeling a whirling sensation.... I felt such protection toward the jaguar and such anger toward the hunter who was going to kill him. I felt heat and dizziness overtaking me, Mace."

Ana pointed to the top of her head. "It was as if some invisible weight or energy other than my own was slipping *around* me, like you would pull a glove over your hand. As this happened, I lost my balance and nearly fell to the ground. I remember gripping a nearby tree to steady myself. And I felt this downward, anchoring sensation as this...thing, this energy...slipped around me. My rib cage became longer and wider, I saw my vision shifting, my sense of smell increased a hundredfold. And—" Ana held out her hand and stared down at it "—my hand was no longer my own. Instead, I saw a beautiful gold paw with black spots, and the claws of a jaguar."

"And then what happened?" Mace's mind was tumbling in shock. A select few knew the process of shape-shifting—it was secret and sacred information. Ana could not fabricate her experience. It had really happened to her; she had morphed from human to jaguar form in a moment of great danger and stress. If a person had not been trained, the change would happen automatically, and there was no control over the process. Mace had been trained, and could stop himself from morphing, but Ana had no such background.

As he stared at her in utter disbelief, Mace realized she was not *Tupay* at least. No *Tupay* could ever shape-shift into jaguar form. They certainly had the ability to change into other animals or beings, but never this cat. The jaguar nation worked only with Warriors for the Light. How he wanted to believe she was destined for good and not what he had to destroy. The skeptic in him had to keep a distance, stay alert. The sad fact was that, properly trained, *Tupay* could also possess another person's body. They could slip their astral energy into an unsuspecting human and share the space with them, one of their favorite ploys. And when a *Tupay* exited the possessed body, the person instantly died.

Would Ana do such a thing? Why? Mace wanted desperately to ask, but didn't dare give himself away.

"What else?" he demanded in a choked tone.

"You're looking at me like I'm loco." Her expression was one of anxiety mixed with confusion.

Shrugging, Mace lied, "No. That's not it. Among the Incas, shape-shifting was a skill. They revered the jaguar as sacred, as being from the Light. I don't think you're crazy, Ana. You may be from that bloodline and not know it. You may have that skill through genetic inheritance. Who knows?"

Mace really didn't know. His confusion was deep as hers, but for other reasons.

Relief flowed through Ana and she sighed. "I'm so glad you don't think I've lost it, Mace. And thank you for that information. Juan Sanchez said the Incas revered the jaguar as sacred. He told me that the Inca's jaguar warriors were specially trained so that they could shape-shift." Ana smiled with uncertainty. "I guess I'm learning one puzzle piece at a time about myself."

"What did you do when you became a jaguar?" Mace asked.

"I felt myself hurtling toward the hunter at a gallop. I heard myself growling deep in my throat. I startled the hunter and he screamed. He dropped his rifle and ran away. At the same time, the jaguar he'd been stalking ran off in another direction, because of the sudden commotion."

"And what did you do afterward?"

Shrugging, Ana said, "I stood there panting. The next thing I knew, I felt that same dizziness, that spiraling feeling. Seconds later, things changed, I changed. I could actually feel whatever it was coming off me, like peeling off a tight glove. It was such an odd feeling." Ana gave him a searching look. "You seem to know a lot about shape-shifting."

Mace tried to sound casual. "Not really. I'm familiar with the local legends about it."

"You know more than I do," Ana murmured.

"Did it ever occur after that?"

Taking a deep breath, Ana said, "It has triggered four times, Mace. And every time it does, it scares the hell out of me. I don't know what's happening or why. And I can't control the process. I feel so helpless when it occurs."

Stymied, Mace wanted to tell Ana everything, but he couldn't. Not until he figured out what was going on and why a *Tupay* such as Ana could shape-shift into a jaguar. No one had educated him on this nuance, and it was a damned important one. He had no one to ask, either. "I—I don't know of anyone around here who can help you with this." Another lie. He caught the distraught look on Ana's lovely face and his heart tore. "But I'll keep a lookout for a Quero priest or priestess. I know they have jaguar shape-shifters among them. If I find one, I'll let you know."

Ana brightened. "That would be wonderful. Thank you. I've been too scared to share this with anyone, Mace. I guess I'm entrusting you with my deepest, darkest secret. Thanks for listening and not judging me."

Mace was getting sucked in deeper, with no hope of escape—and no answers, either. "You can tell me anything, Ana. I'm your friend. I won't ever laugh at you. Over the years that I've been down here, I've discovered that life is pretty mystical for many people in South America. The Indians on this continent never gave their magical world away, unlike others who think the rational and logical mind is the answer to all of life's experiences. No, magic exists, Ana, and you've stepped squarely into it. I believe what you've told me."

The look she gave him flooded him with heat and stirred his lower body to life. Her emerald, slightly tilted eyes were the eyes of the jaguar, no question. And he hungered to make Ana his mate, as only a jaguar could.

Yet Mace had to suspect that she was adroitly luring him into her web of danger, then death. It was a game, he warned himself. A deadly one. As much as he was drawn to Ana, there was no way he could see her as the woman of his dreams.

Through his parents, Mace had received the finest training known to the Warriors for the Light. He had purpose here. Somehow, he had to find answers to these troubling issues by remaining close to Ana.

"I know you believe me," she whispered. "As Juan told me the story, I felt like I was in the middle of a fairy tale, not real life. But it was *my* life he was talking about, Mace. I must have lived with that mother jaguar, been cared for by her."

"It *was* real," Mace agreed. Tomorrow, he'd find Señor Sanchez and look into the old farmer's story. The field was close enough to the drilling project that it would take only an hour or two out of his day to check it out.

Stifling a yawn, Ana straightened. "Listen, I'm really tired. It's been a long, emotional day for me. Thanks for dinner, Mace, but I've got to go to bed before I fall over." She placed her napkin on the table and gave him a sleepy smile. His dark expression brightened as she did so.

It was so easy to like Mace. More and more, Ana wanted to snuggle into his arms and find out how strong he was, and how well he kissed.

That mouth of his was a beacon to her, and she didn't try to fight her growing attraction. She'd found out earlier from talking casually with the woman owner of the restaurant that Mace was single and had no present relationship. She'd volunteered the information to Ana. Relieved, Ana allowed herself the private pleasure of simply absorbing Mace's sunny energy, which throbbed so vitally around him. And unaccountably, his energy lifted her spirits.

Mace rose to his feet. "Let me walk you to your hotel." He glanced down at his watch; it was 9:00 p.m. "This time of night, it's wise to have an escort if you're a woman," he confided, pulling out enough soles to pay for their meal.

"Sure," Ana said, hitching her knapsack over her left shoulder and heading for the wooden stairs.

As they walked up the street, past bars loud with music and filled with tourists, Ana absorbed Mace's closeness. With the thought of Victor around somewhere, the feeling that he was near, she was glad to have Mace's company on the way to her hotel.

The clouds had lowered and lamplight from the merrymaking reflected from them. Clouds were a common nighttime phenomenon in a jungle. Yet she ached to see stars. In Arizona, the night sky was alive with their sparkling beauty.

"What are you doing tomorrow?" Mace asked her.

"I don't know. I thought I might nose around town here and ask about this hunter. Maybe some locals know of him." Ana didn't like lying to Mace, but she had to. Her stomach clenched in terror just thinking about Victor showing up. And the possibility that he might try to kill her. She wanted to talk to Mace about that, but compressed her lips. For now, Ana forced herself to enjoy these precious moments of peace.

Mace saw how the humidity was curling tendrils of Ana's hair around her oval face. Her hair was long and nearly covered her full breasts beneath her snug shirt. If she was aware of her femininity, how beautiful she looked, she didn't seem to realize its effect on him. But

Mace did. Too much so. "The tourist traps would be a good place to hit." He motioned to both sides of the street. "The people who run them have been here forever. I'll bet they would know about this hunter, if anyone would."

"Good suggestion," Ana responded. Halting at the doorway of the hotel, she turned and gazed up at him. "Thanks for everything, Mace. In my eyes and heart, you are truly a knight in shining armor." And following her heart, she lifted her hand and slid her palm along his jaw. The dark stubble made him seem dangerous. Ana saw surprise and then heat flare in his shadowed blue eyes, and her breath hitched in her chest.

As she caressed his cheek, Ana felt more than saw his hands lift and curl around her upper arms. She was completely unprepared for what happened next: he lowered his head toward hers.

Automatically, without thinking, Ana tilted her face upward, her lips parting. Mace was going to kiss her. It felt so right, so needed. How did he know? All thought skittered like dappled sunlight dancing across water as Ana's lashes closed.

The moment Mace's strong, searching mouth met and melded with hers, golden light burst behind her closed lids. A moan moved up from her heart and into her throat as he caressed her tenderly. His fingers dug firmly into her arms, his body strong and unyielding, and she flowed effortlessly against him. The jagged heat of his breathing danced across her cheek. His mouth searched hers with a hunger that stunned and pleased her. Mace *wanted* her. All of her. Ana knew this on every level of herself. As she pressed her hands against his broad chest, she could feel the heavy thudding of his heart.

His scorching, exploring kiss made her mind melt, and an intense pleasure built within her. The fire that ignited incited Ana's physical response, increasing her yearning for him. For all of Mace, not just his cajoling, coaxing lips. So many glittering sensations filtered through Ana in those seconds that it was impossible to process all of them. For an instant, she felt as if a bolt of invisible, white-hot lightning had struck them. Her mind exploded in a shower of golden light. She saw her body expand and become a billion starry particles, along with his. Then Ana felt them combine and become one. There was an anchoring, breathtaking sense of unity with Mace.

Their mouths clung hotly, and his arms and hard male chest were all she was aware of. Yet something else, something incredible, had occurred the instant they'd come together in this unexpected kiss. Ana wasn't sure what it was, or why. She just wanted to show him how much she desired him.

She ached to be fulfilled by this man who had such a vital life force shining within him. She wanted to share that vigor, that bubbling joy with him, for she had a similar energy. A meeting of two *equal* beings, physically and in spirit… That was the fleeting thought moving through her spinning brain.

Slowly, so slowly, Ana felt Mace retreating from her. Finally, their lips, which had clung so hungrily, reluctantly parted. Gripping his arms for stability, Ana found herself breathing raggedly. She lifted her head and almost drowned in his hooded, burning gaze.

Once again that sense that he was a hunter came over her. She tried to explain it away. No one who kissed the way he did could be cold and calculating. She woozily told herself that he was a man hunting the woman he wanted to have in his arms, in his bed. A sweet, burning ache filled her then. It was the need for Mace, Ana realized.

She gave him a wobbly smile. "I didn't see that coming, Mace…."

"Neither did I."

"I liked it, though." She saw the dark confusion in his eyes. Why? The longer she probed his expression, the more she could feel his inner state. Before, he'd hidden himself and she couldn't access his feelings.

Had that bright light she'd experienced melded them together in a new, energetic connection? Ana didn't know. She *was* sure of how her lips had throbbed with the potent power of his mouth covering hers, dominating and hungry. Her gaze rested on that male mouth of his. "You're a great kisser, Mace." She chuckled, feeling giddy.

As Mace released Ana, his hands burned. He wanted her, dammit. In every possible, carnal manner a man could want a woman. But he couldn't go there! And what the hell was that explosion of light that had fused them that way? Mace had a lot of trouble hiding his consternation. What could all of this possibly mean?

"Thanks. You're not so bad at kissing yourself." He tried to crook the corners of his mouth. That was such an understatement. And as he gazed like a pauper at the richness of Ana's parted lips, he groaned internally. Mace had been considered the epitome of a Warrior for the Light. A guardian dedicated to protecting people against the coming darkness. And here, tonight, just now, he'd found he had feet of clay. Ana could be a spider just waiting for the right time to entrap him. She could know everything about him. As much as he wanted to surrender to this new connection, he couldn't.

Lifting her hand, Ana whispered, "Thanks for everything Mace. Can we have dinner tomorrow night? Maybe I'll have found out something more by then." If she was still alive… Ana felt torn as she stood there, wanting so badly to tell Mace about the threat Victor presented. Yet she couldn't see him believing such a story, no matter how open-minded he seemed.

"I'll be here, Ana. Dinner sounds good. Same time and place?"

He watched as she pushed her dark hair across her shoulder. Just that one graceful movement made his body feel desperately raw and needy. What would it be like to have her hand gliding over his flesh like that? Before he got himself into trouble, Mace took a step back, lifted his hand and told Ana good-night.

"Yes, good night, Mace." She gave him a brief smile and hurried into the hotel.

Turning on his heel, scowling, Mace thrust his hands into the pockets of his jeans. Dammit! He knew the legendary warning: if a person of the Light and a person of the Dark met in oneness, the outcome for dominance was never assured. And if the Dark won, the spirit of the warrior would be forever entrapped. In Mace's mind, it was not a risk worth taking. He felt very unsure about how things were turning out. Ana had shape-shifted into a jaguar four times. How was *that* possible? Shuffling down the quiet, darkened street, he glumly headed back to his own hotel.

Ana *must* be leading him into her lair. She, too, would know the house rules when it came to war between the Dark and the Light. She would know that to bed him, to get him inside her, she'd be escalating a personal battle for complete domination. If she won, it would forever neutralize him, ruin his chance of overcoming her and her father. And if that happened, the Warriors for the Light would have lost. And what a terrible loss it would be....

He cursed himself. Like a lamb to the slaughter, he was being drawn to her. Mace found himself incapable of keeping his hands off Ana. Or his mouth, in this case. Even now, his fingers itched to move up her arms, thread through her thick, luxurious black hair, caressed her face and body.... Were her dreams going to be as hot and fevered tonight as his? Or was she lying awake, smiling, because she had nearly destroyed his defenses?

Chapter 8

Ana moaned as she worked to understand the images before her. Her dreams were more vivid than usual tonight. So much had happened in one day. And she had even more to fear.

The cotton covers were light, but she tossed them aside to expose her bare legs. She always slept naked. The fan slowly turning overhead kept her cool in the high jungle humidity.

In her mind's eye, a face kept appearing in front of her. A woman's old and weathered face coming out of the darkness. She wore a purple scarf in her hair, white wisps escaping. When she smiled, Ana could see that many of her teeth had gold fillings.

"Come to me, Ana Rafael. I have something for you.

You are being hunted and you will be killed. You must come to me very, very soon." The woman gestured toward her with a thin, bony hand.

Ana struggled to see where the woman was standing. As the scene came into sharper focus, she recognized Aguas Calientes. There was a building painted light blue. A sign overhead read Parrot's Haven.

The woman cackled. "Come at ten tomorrow morning. Meet me here. I have information for you that could save your life. You are being hunted. You will be killed if you do not come."

And then a dark shadow erased the woman's face and Ana felt her heart cringe in abject terror. It was *him!* It was Victor, the sorcerer who had tried to kill her as a young child in Juan Sanchez's field. Her father was hooded and moving toward her, the edges of his cape flying as if he were a dark owl skimming the night sky in utter silence. Closer and closer he came. Ana wanted to scream, but she could not. She wanted to run, but was anchored in place, as if she had concrete weights on each foot. Hearing his laughter sent a chilling wave up her spine. Every hair on her body stood up in terror.

And then he swooped down upon her. The black hood over his head vanished. She was looking into flat black eyes that had no depth, no light in them. And he was smiling, but the frightening grin didn't reach those empty, dark eyes. She could smell him and it made her feel sick. Gagging, Ana tried to back away, but she was paralyzed.

"Daughter, do not run from me," he murmured in a sweet, cajoling tone. "I have much to teach you. And you do want to be taught, don't you?"

Gulping, Ana held up her hands to protect herself from his nearness. He seemed to realize he was too close, and floated back a few feet. "Go away!" she told him, her voice trembling.

His expression grew sad. "Ah, Daughter, you and I are much alike, but you do not know it yet. I can give you all the answers you are seeking. Isn't that what you want? Don't you want to know who you *really* are? You are my blood. We are alike."

Ana saw his eyes widen and she soon was enveloped in warmth. It surprised her. Sparkling pink energy came toward her and something deep inside her wanted to slap it away.

She couldn't. His black, penetrating eyes robbed her of control over her actions.

"I—yes, I want answers. But not from you. Get out of here!"

The dark figure seemed hurt by her sharp rebuff, and his eyes filled with mist. For a moment, Ana felt terrible that she'd said that. Yet her gut told her not to trust this man of darkness. "I mean, you scare me. You startled me."

"Ah, I see. Well, then, I am sorry, Daughter. I did not mean to frighten you. I am a man of magic, as you can see." He lifted his black cape, which hung to his knees. "I become a bat to fly at night. A raven during the day. That is what frightened you. I won't do that again. May I visit you in person tomorrow? I promise I won't come like a thunderstorm. I do want to teach you, and you have much to learn. Wouldn't you like that?"

Ana nodded and gulped, her heart racing. She felt

danger, and yet, also a desire to know more about this dark man. "What is your full name? Where do you live?"

"My students call me *maestro*. You may call me Father, because you are my long-lost daughter, dearest Ana. I am so happy you have come home. Home to me."

Her world tilted. Ana stared at him. His face, once so tense and controlling, seemed very gentle and open right now. He stood like an ordinary man in front of her, dressed in black from head to foot, the cape swirling about his narrow form.

"You are the one who tried to kill me in the field, aren't you?" she demanded. Ana saw his eyes narrow with sudden rage.

"You have me confused with someone else, Daughter. I would *never* hurt anyone or anything." He lifted his hand. "Do not go to this woman you saw earlier in your dream state. Only I can give you the answers you seek. You must give me permission to visit your dreams."

Ana was torn. "I—I don't know. I need time to think about this."

"I am your *father,* Victor Carancho Guerra. You will do as I tell you! I am the greatest master sorcerer in this world and any other. I can give you power, Ana. Real power. You can rule at my side, as the legend foretells."

Shock bolted through Ana. "You tried to murder me in Juan Sanchez's field when I was very young! Don't deny it!"

For a long time, Victor studied her. Finally, he rasped, "Yes, I did try to take your life."

"But why?" she cried. She didn't want this man to

be her father. Every cell in her body screamed against it. And then Ana remembered the symbol of the *Tupay:* the sun. And the evil that went with it. She carried that very symbol on the back of her neck.

As if reading her frantic thoughts, he gave a mirthless laugh and turned to lift his hair. She could see the *Tupay* birthmark on the back of his own neck.

"See this, Daughter? Ah, yes, I can tell you do recognize our symbol, after all. You have one, too." He allowed his hair to fall back around his shoulders. As he loomed closer, his voice echoed like thunder around Ana. "You're my seed. You carry my symbol. You are just like me."

Ana breathed raggedly. "I'll *never* be like you! I'm not evil! I may carry that birthmark, but that doesn't mean I have to be like you!" She Ana tasted death in her mouth. She had a connection with her father whether she wanted it or not. She felt him preparing to kill her, and knew there was no escape. They were alone, and she was going to die. Suddenly, she wanted to live as never before.

"Give me your answer, Ana. Do you want to become my daughter once more? To work with me? I will give you power, riches and fame beyond your wildest dreams. I will teach you the paranormal arts and you will have world dominion at my side. Think of it!"

"No!" she shrieked. And as she did, she saw Victor's eyes narrow with a deadly hatred. She felt it ooze over her like a suffocating slime. "I'll *never* be your daughter. I'll *never* work with you. We're enemies. Don't *ever* come to meet me, and stay the hell out of my dreams!"

This last she screamed at the top of her lungs, hunching over and raising her fists to defend herself.

Ana heard the snarling of a jaguar. Blinking, she looked around, and saw a huge gold-and-black-spotted female jaguar just above where she stood.

"What is that?" Victor roared, pointing angrily at the spirit jaguar. "What is *she* doing *here?*"

Ana heard the incredulity in her father's dark, deep voice. His eyes were wide with shock as he stared at the cat hovering just above her. "This is impossible. You can't have a jaguar as a spirit guide!" Victor yelled. He backed off as the cat floated down to Ana's side, mouth open and snarling a warning at the sorcerer.

Glancing at the jaguar, Ana remembered Mace's words. At last she understood that somehow this spirit cat was hers, and she was here to defend her. In the next moment, the jaguar sprang toward the sorcerer. She saw Victor leap back, give a yelp of real terror then fade away. The sleek animal landed on the spot where the sorcerer had stood seconds before.

Gone. Victor was gone. The jaguar panted heavily, ears twitching. She turned and looked toward Ana.

You are safe for now, mistress. I will always be here to try and protect you, but he is the most powerful sorcerer in your world. I will always be with you, and if I need to, I shall give my life for you. Fear not. He is gone and you are safe....

Ana gasped. She jerked into a sitting position, her heart thrashing in her chest. As she pressed her hand against her breast, she stared warily around the room.

All was quiet. The curtains were drawn. A little light

from the streetlamps leaked in around the edges. The fan moved the sluggish, humid air above her, silently doing its job.

Gulping, Ana felt the alarm rooted deep within her. Now she was sure Victor was her father.

She reached for the notepad and pen that she always kept nearby. Her dreams were many and colorful, from the earliest she could remember, Ana had written them down. They provided a doorway to information, even if she couldn't put the puzzle pieces together right away.

After scribbling out her latest dream, Ana poured herself a glass of water, drank it and lay back again. Her heart was finally settling down.

She felt a soft, heavy weight nearby on the bed. Looking to her left, she couldn't see anything, and yet she felt warm fur. Instinctively, Ana realized it was her guardian jaguar, the one who had chased off her estranged father.

"I don't know what's going on," she whispered raggedly, "but thank you for being here. I was so scared. I still am. I'm glad you're with me…."

Ana supposed she should feel foolish, talking into the darkness, but she didn't. Whatever had happened in her dream was real. And she could feel her guardian lying on the bed next to her, alertly watching out for her continued safety.

Mace had said South America was a place of magic. Well, now she was fully immersed in it.

Within minutes, she had spiraled into a deep, healing sleep.

* * *

At 10:00 a.m., with the sun struggling to burn its way through the foglike clouds over Aguas Calientes, Ana stood in front of a two-story, blue stucco building. The sign said Parrot's Haven, just as in her dream. Ana could feel her invisible jaguar guardian at her side, her strong, warm body occasionally brushing against her left thigh. She was with her. And that was comforting as nothing else could be right now.

Ana waited for some kind of sign. The cobalt-colored door was rectangular. A chain with a padlock was wrapped around the massive brass handle. About her, the town was gearing up to welcome the next train-load of tourists arriving from Cuzco. Vendors opened buildings, put colorful wares out in hopes of a sale. The air was filled with scents of breakfast: frying eggs, bacon, refried beans and tortillas. Ana started to become impatient.

And then she heard sounds. Movement. The door creaked opened. The same woman she'd seen in her dream peeked out from behind it. She gave Ana a wide grin as she fiddled with the padlock. With painful slowness, she pulled the chain off the door handle.

"Come in," she invited in a croaking, aged voice.

Ana hesitated, remaining on guard. Victor's warning screamed in her mind. The woman pushed the door wide and put an Open sign outside. She was dressed in a dark blue cotton blouse, a multicolored skirt that hung to her thin ankles. She wore no shoes and her feet looked hard and callused. Her white, stringy hair was gathered up and tied with a purple scarf.

"Coming?" the woman called cheerily, slowly turning to look back at Ana.

Abruptly, Ana stepped inside. The windows were small and in need of a good washing. The place was airless and filled to overflowing with antiques of all kinds. Blue and yellow macaw feathers hung like a shield from the high ceiling. The old woman hobbled along, leaning on a curved cane. With a trembling hand, she flipped a series of switches. Naked lightbulbs flashed on to reveal what could only be described as an attic full of old, dusty things one might find in an abandoned house.

The old woman cackled. "I can give you a duster if you want. You can clean everything for me."

Startled, Ana realized she had read her mind. "Uh, no, thanks."

Gesturing, the woman said, "My name is Vidonia. And you are Ana Rafael, yes?"

"Yes, but how do you know my name?"

Pushing aside a faded, lavender print curtain, Vidonia chuckled. "Come have morning coffee with me, and I will tell you what you want to know."

Again, as Ana made her way carefully through the crowded antiques, terror nearly overwhelmed her. She reminded herself that she had to find out who she was. No matter where the journey took her, she had to go.

"Sit, sit," Vidonia invited, smiling. A percolator was bubbling away on a gas stove. The fragrance of coffee filled the air.

Ana sat at the small, round mahogany table with a beautifully crocheted lace cloth on top. Two chairs had been placed strategically across from one another. The cream and sugar and spoons were already on the table. Vidonia had obviously expected her to show up. Ana watched as the old woman poured coffee into two large pottery mugs that had Incan designs of the sun painted on them.

"Best coffee in the world," Vidonia told her, handing her a mug.

"Thank you," Ana said as her hostess slowly sat down. Her face was square and deeply wrinkled from age. She looked as if she'd descended from the Incas, with her tobacco-brown skin, her lively, dark umber eyes, her full mouth encircled with vertical lines of advanced age. Ana wondered how old she was.

"I don't know," Vidonia said with a chuckle. "I was born when the Queen's Moon briefly put out the light of the Inca's Sun. I heard later that it was called an eclipse. I was born during an eclipse." She took her spoon and with great effort, sprinkled a bit of the sugar into the mug of steaming coffee. "But never mind me." Her eyes shifted and narrowed. "I felt you coming. They said you would one day. And they were right."

Sipping her coffee, but not tasting it, Ana whispered, "Who are 'they'?"

"Don't matter, my dear." Sipping her own coffee with great relish, Vidonia said, "Isn't having a cup of coffee with a good friend just the best? What else is there in life but this moment, eh?"

Struggling to stop the torrent of questions begging to be asked, Ana sat quietly. Inwardly, she squirmed. "You're right, of course."

"A long time ago, my mother, who was a fourth-level Incan priestess in the service to the Inca and his queen, told me that one day I would meet a woman who could change our world."

Ana's stomach knotted. She tried to steel herself for the inevitable: to hear that she was *Tupay* and therefore evil personified. "I know the story," she told Vidonia in a husky voice, her brow furrowed.

Cackling with delight, Vidonia smacked her lips and took a another drink of her coffee, her arthritic hands wrapped around the mug. "There are *many* stories around, my dear. You have been told only one of them. My mother was a great and famous jaguar priestess. A kind, good woman in service to others her whole life. A healer of great repute. People came from far and near for her help. She never turned anyone away. She served her community from her first breath to her last."

Vidonia waved a skeletal finger at Ana. "When I was in training with her as a child, she told me that one day a woman would come to our town, and that I was to give her a message from the Inca's queen herself."

Frowning, Ana said, "And I'm that woman?"

"Of course you are! Are you so asleep you do not know your own power? Who you are? Tsk-tsk…" Vidonia gestured toward the side of Ana's chair. "I am a jaguar priestess. I have sight in my third eye, here in the middle of my brow. I can see into unseen realms. You sit with a mighty jaguar guardian next to you. She is there for your protection, your education and support. Surely that tells you who you are?"

Ana couldn't see the jaguar herself, but she felt the

comfort of the large cat's fur against her left thigh. It wasn't her imagination, after all.

Relief funneled through her. Gulping, she searched Vidonia's kindly face. "I really don't know who I am." She went on to explain what she had found out about being an orphan and adopted. As well, about Juan Sanchez's story.

Vidonia sat there, head cocked her narrowed eyes focused on Ana. When she had completed her story, the woman stroked her narrow chin. She took a long drink of her coffee and set it on the table between them.

"Hmm. Well, if you really don't know who you are, no wonder my mother gave me this message to tell you. She must have seen with her far sight and known that other choices would be invoked by the players involved. And she knew there would be changes to the legend we all know."

Barely able to contain herself, Ana asked, "What legend are you talking about, Vidonia?"

"The legend about *you*...."

Chapter 9

Mace was wearily walking back into Aguas Calientes along the railroad tracks, rain drizzling around him, when, all of a sudden, a sensation he'd been waiting a lifetime to experience hit him. A wave of evil, of turmoil and savage hatred, rolled over him like an invisible tsunami. Seconds earlier, he'd been near exhaustion from working all day in the hot jungle with cranky drilling equipment. Jerking to a halt on the tracks, he snapped his head up as he digested the energy wave. Instantly, everything changed.

It was the signature of the Dark Lord! Mace had been trained from youth to identify it. Looking up through the rain, he turned toward Machu Picchu, to find it swathed in mysterious clouds. The Dark Lord was *here.* He'd unveiled himself!

Heart pounding, Mace knew he might have only one chance to find and kill him.

His mind spun with questions. Where was Ana? Had she contacted her father today? Was this why he'd unveiled himself? Unsure, Mace hurried to his hotel, which wasn't far away.

"Mr. Ridfort?" the clerk sang out, waving at him. "There's a message here for you. From a lovely young lady. She was in a hurry, breathless, and said to give this to you as soon as you came in, *señor.*"

Scowling, Mace thanked the young clerk and rapidly read the message.

> Mace, I'm on a quest to Huaynu Picchu tonight. The jaguar priestess called Vidonia told me to go to the top. That I'd receive an important initiation there. I won't be meeting you for dinner tonight. Take care. You're in my heart...Ana.

Mystified, Mace hurried up the stairs to his room. After shimmying out of his sweaty, muddy clothes, he dived into the shower, washed and hurried out of the stall, quickly pulling on clean clothes. The vibration of the Dark Lord continued unabated, like a five-alarm fire shrieking nonstop. And Mace knew where the bastard was at: on Machu Picchu.

It was nearly dark when Mace trotted out of town and down the railroad tracks to the tourist bus center. Everything was quiet. No one was around. The tours had stopped running hours earlier. Spotting an older man sweeping the cobbled stones in front of the ticket office,

Mace went over to him and pulled out a photo he'd taken of Ana in Cuzco.

"*Señor?* Did you see this young woman with black hair and green jaguar eyes here earlier? Did she take a red bus up to the top of the mountain?" he demanded, pointing toward the temples wreathed in clouds and misting rain.

"Oh, yes, she was here." He pointed to Machu Picchu. "And she was in a hurry. She caught the last bus to the top."

"Did you see her come back down?" Mace felt a terrible urgency, and a great deal of fear for Ana.

"No, I did not see her return." He shrugged and started to sweep once more. "She could have, but I may have missed seeing her come off the bus with the last of the tourists."

Mace knew what had to be done. Jogging down the tracks, away from civilization, he turned and moved into the jungle. There was a secret way up to the temple area, one created by the Incas to get up and down the mountain in one hell of a hurry. Once hidden among the trees, where no one could see him, Mace halted.

It was time to shape-shift into a jaguar. He closed his eyes and grounded himself. Breathing raggedly from the exertion, Mace geared his entire focus toward the transformation. Instantly, he felt the shift not only within himself, but outside. The male jaguar spirit guide came over him, slid over his head, shoulders, and enclosed the rest of his body. It was a long fifteen seconds for Mace. His teeth elongated, his neck thickened, his arms changed, hands and fingers disappearing, replaced by pads and long, curved claws.

As he opened his eyes, Mace dropped to all fours. Now he was in his jaguar form. Looking around, he felt his guide's primal side. The jungle now appeared much brighter with glowing colors around every plant, tree and vine. Sniffing the air, Mace picked up the scent of Ana. He'd recognize her feminine fragrance anywhere. And with it, he smelled something cadaverous on her trail. It was the Dark Lord's signature scent. The sorcerer was stalking her.

Turning on his hind legs, Mace galloped up the hand-carved stone steps that wound all the way to the top of the mountain. From there, he would be able to track Ana's movements by scent alone. A brooding storm above opened up and thick drops began to pelt his fur. A slash of lightning blazed across the turgid sky.

The only way to get to Huaynu Picchu was via Machu Picchu. A rocky, narrow trail led from one mountain to the other. Mace was familiar with it. As he ran, growling with each labored breath, taking the steps three or four at a time, he felt urgency as never before. Instinctively, he knew Ana was in danger. But this didn't make any sense at all! Her father, the Dark Lord, would be happy to see her and meet with her.

If only Mace could get there in time! Ana was leading him, just as the legend had said she would, to a final confrontation with the Dark Lord.

Mace knew that to kill the most powerful sorcerer in the world, he'd have to rip out his heart. Without his black heart, Victor Carancho Guerra would be banished from the earth. He could never set up shop here or in the invisible dimensions surrounding it. Guerra could not create the chaos that would bring the world into a millennium of darkness.

As Mace raced closer and closer to the top of the mountain, the rain continued. Lightning sizzled above him. Thunder rolled and pounded noisily. His coat was soaked, but he was impervious to the elements and the dropping temperature. His entire strength, his entire being, was focused on finally confronting the Lord of Darkness.

Mace didn't want to look at what else had to be done. He had to kill the father…and then the daughter. His pumping heart kept the blood pounding through his cat body. Mace didn't want to kill Ana, but he had to.

And somewhere in the darkness, he knew, he would either live or die this night….

Ana gasped and nearly tripped on the narrow granite steps that led up to the Temple of the Moon. She was shivering, cold and wet—and terrified. The wind shrieked around her, pulling and tugging wildly at her clothing. The Temple of the Moon, Vidonia had told her, was where she needed to go. It stood on the west side of Apu Huaynu Picchu, the young mountain, which was sacred to the Incas.

Around her neck, on a leather thong, swung a jaguar's claw. Vidonia had told Ana that once she climbed the thousand hand-carved steps to the lunar temple, she must find a wide, triangular rock facing south. Once there, she should search for a small hole carved into it—and insert the claw into the hole. When she'd done so, the old woman had said, Ana's path would be revealed to her. She would receive her initiation and more information about her parents.

With the rain running off her face in rivulets, she found it almost impossible to see. Ana kept her small flashlight trained on the stairs ahead of her. If she slipped, she would fall off the side of the mountain—and likely plunge to her death. There was no guardrail, nothing to hold on to except the next slippery step. This was no time to lose focus. Carefully, she placed each boot tip, then slowly pushed herself upward, keeping the front of her body pressed close to the steps. The stairs were so steep that mounting them upright was impossible.

Despite the storm, the torrents of rain, Ana grimly persisted. She wanted to learn about her parents. She *had* to! And she understood that the elements were testing her.

Ana suddenly froze on the steps. She could feel it. Taste it. Nostrils flaring, she detected the scent of dead, rotted meat, and she gasped again, with repugnance. Someone was following her.

He was close. And evil.

Rigid with fear, she blinked water from her eyes and twisted around to look down the steep steps she'd just climbed. She flashed her light, but the weak beam couldn't penetrate the darkness or the rain. Ana saw no one, and yet she felt him coming after her.

Mind churning, she turned back around and put the flashlight in her mouth, grasping the steps with both hands. Was it the hunter? The man in black? Ana didn't know.

With every crawling, crucial step she took, she drew closer to the temple. The next time lightning flashed,

Ana could see she had only about ten more steps to the top. One thousand steps. It felt like an eternity.

The wind screamed and tore at her. Ana groaned and flattened her belly against the stones to keep from being blown off the mountain by one especially violent gust. Bowing her head, she dug her fingers into the muddy, soaked ground and pulled herself up the last steps as the wind roared like a banshee around her.

The rain fell nonstop, pelting her. It was cold up here, much colder than Ana had expected. She hadn't dressed for such a climb.

Staggering forward on hands and knees, she threw herself into the temple and lay there, panting. As soon as she could she gripped one of the hand-hewn stone columns and dragged herself upright, bracing against the furious blast of wind. Gripping the column with one hand, her flashlight in the other, Ana wiped her face with her sleeve and tried to clear her eyes. The hat she'd worn had long ago had been ripped off by the storm.

Again she felt that strange, paralyzing terror. Breathing hard, she peered around, to no avail. It was impossible to see anything. Her skin crawled and the back of her neck, where her *Tupay* symbol lay, felt as if it were on fire. Ana couldn't understand where the threat came from. Yes, she was scared, but it was only a storm. The front would pass and then she could find the slab of stone where she had to insert the claw. So why was she feeling as if she was going to die?

Shaking her head, she cringed as yet another bolt of lightning ripped across the sky just above her.

In those split seconds, she saw him.

A scream tore from her lips.

There, just thirty feet below her on the narrow steps, was the man in black. He had a rifle in his hand—aimed at her.

Frozen in place, Ana gripped the column with desperation.

The wind roared around her.

The thunder banged and pummeled her. The ground shook beneath her feet.

The hunter! He was here!

Daughter, do not be fearful. I am here to help you....

Ana couldn't think, couldn't move. She heard the hunter's words clearly in her mind. He was hooded, his face hidden, yet, she knew him from her dream last night.

Be at ease, Daughter. It is slippery. I have come to help you make the last steps easier.

Something screamed *no* in her mind. Ana hesitated, torn between allowing the man in black to come up to where she stood, wavering at the temple entrance, or running away from him.

A sudden dizziness struck her. Instantly, Ana recognized the sensation. *Oh, no!* She was turning into a jaguar again! As much as she tried to fight the feeling, she couldn't concentrate enough to stop it; the energy came over her.

In the next flash of lightning, she saw the hunter lift his rifle and fix it on her. How could this man, who claimed to be her father, want to help her? He was going to shoot her!

Everything slowed down to single frame, as if Ana were watching stills of a movie. She saw a jaguar come out of the darkness and land on the man's back, knocking him forward. The gun roared. Ana felt a bullet whiz dangerously close to her head. She cringed and watched the rifle fly out of the hunter's hand. The weapon spun into the night, lost in the chasm far below.

Mace lunged forward, the stinging rain slashing at his face. Luckily, the thick lashes around his eyes protected them somewhat from the deluge. As he raced up the steep, slippery stone steps, his night vision kept the *Tupay* sorcerer in sight. The fear of arriving too late sizzled through him as lightning danced overhead. The wind slapped his powerful feline body. And then Mace saw the sorcerer lift his rifle and aim it directly at Ana. How could that be?

His primitive jaguar mind warred with his human mind as he tried to make sense of what he was seeing. Why would this man kill his daughter? Hadn't the Lord of Darkness waited all this time to find her?

None of Mace's questions could be answered as he slipped and slid on the narrow steps. With claws fully extended, his large, padded feet barely fit on each one. Mace was in a precarious situation. These steps were enough to test anyone, man or animal. He wondered how Ana had gotten this far in such a terrible storm.

Automatically, his body arced and tensed as he approached his quarry. Shifting all the power to his hind legs, he lifted his front paws upward. As he did so, a gust of wind slammed into him. Slipping sideways, Mace felt himself hurtling toward the Lord of Darkness in a twisted position. He tried to straighten out, but it was impossible. Mace heard the sorcerer shriek as his claws landed powerfully in the folds of the man's cloak.

The rifle went off. Mace felt the blast very close to his face. The sorcerer shouted a curse and dropped the weapon as he tried to evade the attack.

Satisfaction thrummed through Mace as his claws sank into flesh. The sorcerer was real, after all. He was in a physical body, and that meant he was vulnerable. Opening his jaws, Mace lunged for the terrified man's face.

The sorcerer lashed out as he fell. Mace grunted and felt himself falling, falling, falling…and then, amazingly, he landed on all fours on a rocky ledge next to the narrow stairs. Whirling around, he heard the sorcerer land behind him.

Before he could react, Mace felt a huge rock strike his left shoulder. Pain shattered through him and he fell sideways onto the slippery stones.

"I'll kill you!" Guerra screamed, picking up another rock and throwing it at the cat. To his surprise, the jaguar did not run away. Instead, the animal gave a deep growl, scrambled to his feet and evaded the second boulder. Then he turned and gazed at Guerra with huge green eyes. He hurled yet another heavy rock, but the jaguar just stared at him.

The sorcerer breathed harshly and backed up. Only when lightning flashed could he see the massive, threatening male cat. Reaching down for another hefty stone, Guerra wished he hadn't lost his rifle. Or had he? Desperately, during the next lightning flash he looked around. His weapon lay no more than five feet away from him, near the steps!

But as he lunged for it, Guerra heard movement. He knew the jaguar was coming for him. Fingers stretched outward, he clawed for his rifle before it was too late. There! Jerking the weapon up, he settled his finger around the trigger.

With all his might, Mace hurtled toward the sorcerer, not needing the flash of lightning to sight his quarry. The man had found the dropped weapon, and was going to aim it and shoot—shoot to kill. It couldn't be! Mace's left shoulder ached. It slowed him slightly, but not enough to prevent him leaping again at the Lord of Darkness.

Guerra screamed and automatically raised the rifle in self-defense. The jaguar came out of the night, claws extended, mouth open and those glistening fangs aimed right at his throat. Because he couldn't pull off a shot fast enough, Guerra swung the rifle and hit the cat in the head as hard as he could. The animal groaned and slammed into the stone staircase.

As Guerra scrambled to his feet, rifle in hand, he understood very clearly this was not a normal jaguar. Without a doubt, this was a shape-shifter—a Warrior for the Light. And Guerra knew the risks of one of the hunter-warriors finding him. They were raised from infancy to track him down and kill him. This was the first one to find him.

Grimly, the sorcerer pointed the rifle toward where the cat lay. Though stunned, he knew he had only seconds to train his weapon and shoot. But the night was black. He needed lightning to flash, but the weather wouldn't cooperate.

Rain flooded his eyes and the winds dragged at his

cloak. Frightened, Guerra cursed the heavens. Where was that jaguar? Knowing of the cat's excellent night vision, he understood he was at a disadvantage. As he heard the jaguar scrambling to his feet, the sorcerer made a decision.

Throwing the rifle down, Guerra leaped upon the stone steps. He had to gather his wits, his focus around him in order to do this—fly like a bird and escape this unstoppable jaguar. He grabbed the edges of his cloak and gripped them tightly. He willed the black raven over him, and as he waited, dizziness assailed him. Would he be able to shape-shift soon enough?

Mace shook himself, his head ringing. Pain flashed through his skull and he panted. As he drew himself upright, he heard the sorcerer above him on the steps. Mace scrambled to all fours and hurled himself up the wet stairs once more. The pain in his left shoulder was tremendous, but the will to kill the evil one was greater.

Guerra spread his cloak, the wind catching it and ballooning each side outward like wedge-shaped wings. No! The Dark Lord was in the middle of a shape-shift. Without thought to his own safety, Mace pounced once more. This time, his hind feet found purchase and he sprang directly at the sorcerer. As Mace closed in, he saw his prey change into a black raven. Within seconds, the big bird flew off the steps and into the night.

Mace landed on the stairs with a thud. He found himself suddenly alone in the middle of the frightful, furious storm. The Dark Lord had escaped. Disappointment, sharp and keen, sizzled through Mace as he stood looking into the night, tail twitching. He had failed, and he wouldn't be surprised if Guerra had created this storm in the first place to hide his ominous presence from Ana.

Glancing upward, he realized that Ana was above him in the temple. She had escaped Guerra's attack, and now Mace wanted to go to her. But he couldn't. There was so much confusion in his mind that he turned and padded slowly back down the narrow stone steps. He had to get down off the mountain and make for his room in Aguas Calientes. At the edge of the jungle, near the railroad tracks, he would change again from jaguar to man. But not until then, because he didn't trust Guerra.

Ravens didn't fly at night, and Mace was sure he'd land on the nearest tree, remaining until daylight. When anyone shape-shifted into a physical form they were bound by those strengths and weaknesses of the individuals they became. And ravens did not fly at night. Guerra would have to wait until dawn. And then what would he do? Mace might, if he was lucky, have a second chance of killing the sorcerer.

Mace kept up his guard as he padded down the steps. His heart centered on Ana. How was she doing?

The lightning ceased and the night grew dark once more. Ana heard a shriek, accompanied by the familiar growl of a jaguar who had trapped his quarry. Dizzily, she sank to her knees on the floor of the temple. The shape-shifting sensation seemed to be gone. She was still human! But who was that jaguar who had leaped upon the hunter?

Escape! I have to escape!

Blindly, Ana scrambled forward on her hands and knees. She didn't see the rock wall coming toward her, and was knocked unconscious.

As she came to, she noticed the downpour was even heavier. Torrents of gurgling water rushed past where she lay. But she heard no more growling, no more commotion. No one was assaulting her mind without her permission.

By luck, Ana discovered a sheltered niche and crawled into it. Though barely able to fit into the hollow, she found it was surprisingly dry and removed from the fury of the storm. Wiping her face, she shut off her flashlight. She didn't want to be found by the hunter. He hadn't come to help her get to the top of the mountain. He'd been about to kill her.

Until the jaguar leaped at him, Ana reminded herself. Rubbing her face, she lay on her belly, heart pounding. Had this all been her imagination? Mace had warned her that magic still existed in South America.

Ana knew what she'd witnessed had really happened. Confused, she rested her forehead on her folded hands. The storm continued unabated around her, but here in this crevice, she was relatively dry and safe. Oddly, as the storm began to let up, Ana no longer felt the stalking terror she'd experience before.

Had the jaguar killed the hunter? Was that why she felt safe now? Wiping her face, she waited.

Vidonia had said she must fit the claw into the stone no later than 3:00 a.m. It was a jaguar moon, the time in the lunar phase when there was no light. Vidonia had warned that evil walked the land under a jaguar moon, but she'd also said that the claw she'd given Ana would protect her, so that she could finish her test and receive the initiation she wanted.

Exhausted, Ana closed her eyes. The hands on her watch read 11:00 p.m. Feeling tiredness pulling at her, she stretched out in the temple atop Huaynu Picchu, and fell asleep.

Ana jerked awake in total darkness. But she could hear crickets and frogs chorusing outside her hiding place. The storm had moved on.

Groggily, she crawled out of the hole on her hands and knees. The air was damp, and she could smell the honeyed scent of nearby orchids. Yet even out here it was dark.

The priestess, Vidonia, had appeared in her dream. She had told Ana to wake up and go to the triangular stone.

Turning, Ana listened intently. While she felt no threat, no sense of danger now, she wondered if the hunter lay in wait for her somewhere.

No. He was gone.

What about the jaguar? Was he still around? If he'd killed the hunter, chances were he was eating the body. Shivering at that thought, Ana ran her hands up and down her arms.

Something internal drove her to shrug on her knapsack, turn on her small flashlight and make her way through the temple.

Glancing down at her watch, Ana saw it was two-thirty. She had half an hour to locate the triangular rock. As quickly as possible Ana climbed about, slipping in the puddles, the clay sucking and sticking like glue as she shone her light over the jumbled rocks.

When at last she exited the temple, Ana found in front of her a huge triangular rock, just as Vidonia had described. Moving quickly up a set of wider stone steps, she stopped before the megalith, which was at least fifteen feet high and twenty feet in width.

Ana felt all kinds of energy striking the flat surface of the stone and pinging back out. It reminded her of a big radar screen of sorts, sending and receiving signals. Mystified, but knowing she had to find the hole, Ana quickly ran her palm across the surface, trying to locate it. Finally, after a lot of searching, her index finger dipped into a hollow. Immediately, Ana focused her light on the area. And there it was.

Heart pounding with dread and excitement, Ana lifted the jaguar claw that hung around her neck. Vidonia had told her to keep it on, but insert the claw and then flatten her body against the stone and wait. The hole she had found was head high, and Ana positioned herself against the stone. It felt oddly warm, considering how cold and wet the night had been earlier.

Fully pressed against the stone, her left cheek tilted, Ana lifted the claw and inserted it into the hole. A perfect fit.

In an instant a flash of light went off around her. There was a sense of swift motion, but her eyes were tightly shut and she clung to the stone, her palms flattened against it. Fear mingled with hope, and dizziness assailed her. Her knees weakened. No! She had to stay against the stone! She had to know the truth. She had to find her parents. A whirling sensation began in earnest, and soon every particle of her essence seemed as if it were being drawn *into* the great megalith. Ana felt the rock, felt its spirit and sheer power. The light continued to dance in front of her tightly closed eyes. Warmth replaced cold. Dryness replaced the wet clothes that clung to her trembling body. Before she could even think about moving she heard a slight popping sound. It didn't go on for long, and when it stopped, Ana felt at peace. Gone was her fear. Her longing. Her terror. Her questions.

Slowly, other sounds came alive. The gurgling of a nearby brook. The squawk of parrots. The light continued to embrace her, and Ana opened her eyes. She was still pressed against the triangular stone, but things were different—very different. Lifting her head, she looked up. The dawn sky held shreds of low-hanging clouds just above the mountain where she stood. Monkeys called back and forth in the jungle canopy. The world was awakening for a new day.

How could that be? Seconds ago, it had been pitch dark. Ana pushed away from the stone, but kept her hands flat against it for a moment more. The ground beneath her now was covered with thick, lush grass, not mud. Where was she? What had happened?

"Welcome once again, child."

The familiar voice made Ana jump, and she spun around in surprise. Grandmother Alaria stood less than six feet away, smiling at her. The tall, regal, white-haired woman extended her thin hand toward Ana. A dark blue robe covered her lean body, and she wore simple leather sandals on her feet. Ana's eyes honed in on the leather thong holding three jaguar claws around her neck, along with the Vesica Piscis necklace.

"Grandmother?" she croaked, unsure of how she'd gotten to the Village of the Clouds once again. Before, she'd visited the elder in her dream state. This was different, and Ana felt completely unsettled. She wasn't dreaming this time.

"Welcome back to the Village of the Clouds, my child. I was expecting you, so do not be frightened. You are safe here, Ana. Completely safe."

Drinking in the soft, glowing light around the elder, Ana could only stare openmouthed. "But how did I get here, Grandmother? Where is this place?" Ana looked around. The Village of the Clouds appeared to be like any other community she'd seen in the jungles of South America. Only the feeling was different there. She felt incredibly at peace and in harmony with all beings.

The saintly glow around Alaria's head reminded her of the halos she'd seen in Italian Renaissance paintings of Mother Mary. The woman seemed ageless and unearthly. Perhaps it was her gentle smile and her sincere welcome.

Abruptly, Ana realized she had not seen the elder's lips move. She had heard the woman's low, warm voice in her head. Once more, Ana was experiencing telepathy, but it wasn't harsh or invasive as with Victor.

"My dear child, there is not much time. On another visit, perhaps I can answer more of your questions. You're here because you just passed one of your initiations. The jaguar priestess, Vidonia, gave you something that belongs to you. And that is why you are here with us."

Frowning, Ana clutched the jaguar claw that hung down between her breasts. "This? It belongs to me?"

Nodding, Alaria said, "Never be without it from now on, my child. It is your ultimate protection. You have been sent here for a reason. You will undergo another initiation shortly. That is your path and that is how you will come to understand who you really are."

There was a sensation of heat on the back of her neck, and Ana ruefully rubbed the area where she knew the *Tupay* symbol resided. "I know who I am now, Grandmother. And it's not good."

Alaria gave her a look of compassion. "No, you do not know fully who you are, Ana. Things are not what they seem to be, my child. Some call you evil. Others see you as someone to be controlled. And if you cannot be controlled, they will try to destroy you, instead." Alaria lifted a thin finger and pointed to the pendant Ana clutched in her hand. "That claw contains the truth. And in the next few days, all will be revealed to you. Do you see where it hangs? Over your heart!"

Ana let it fall between her breasts. "Yes."

"Remember this—everything you do in these coming days must come from your heart. You have the capacity to allow your love to transcend any fear you carry within you. Love can change the world, Ana, but you must have faith and know that it can. When you think all is lost, my child, focus on the love in your heart. Focus on it with every breath you take and it will save you. It will change the dynamic that is loose in our world right now. You can help us so much. But you must begin by following your heart."

Stymied, Ana murmured, "I've found out Victor is my father and he's a horrible sorcerer. He tried to kill me again on the steps of the temple, until a jaguar came out of nowhere and attacked him. I want to know who my mother is. Vidonia said I would find out. I *have* to know, Grandmother Alaria. I've waited my whole life to discover who I am. Can't you tell me *something* about her? Even just a name?" Ana's voice cracked with emotion. Tears burned in her eyes as she pleaded hoarsely with the elder.

Alaria moved forward until there was barely a foot separating them. "You have carried the weight of the worlds upon your young shoulders, Ana. You are stronger than you realize, and that is what you must now connect with—your strength. Your path is through your heart, the path of love and compassion. To do this is to know who you are. The information you seek will come to you within days. That I promise you. What you must do now is go back to your world and play out an event that you have agreed to take part in." Alaria lifted her hand and tenderly brushed the tears from Ana's cheek.

Ana gulped back a sob. She had never experienced such incredible peace as she did at this moment. The elder's touch was like that of a butterfly grazing her flesh, and Ana felt her neediness dissolve.

"Your mother's name was Magdalena. And she was the opposite of your father. Hold on to that knowing, child. Call upon her when you feel all is lost. It is time now for you to return to your world. Know that we love you, and that we will meet again when the moment is right."

And with that, Grandmother Alaria vanished, leaving Ana with more questions than ever before.

Chapter 10

Mace gritted his teeth as he stood beneath the hot stream of water in the shower. He'd injured his left shoulder when the Lord of Darkness had struck him with that rock. The heat took the ache out of his badly bruised muscles, but his disappointment overwhelmed him. He'd missed his target!

As he'd lunged up the steep, slippery steps, he had miscalculated distance. Instead of landing squarely on the Lord of Darkness's back, his outstretched claws had ripped into the man's cloak.

Mace felt some satisfaction that the sorcerer had had to drop his rifle. The shot he'd fired had missed Ana, who'd been crouching on the mountaintop above them.

His mind hazy from exhaustion, Mace had morphed

back into human form at the edge of the jungle near town. His green eyes changed back to blue. Once the change was complete, he'd felt the full impact of his shoulder injury. Plus, being struck in the head by the sorcerer's rifle had given him an ongoing headache. After getting back to his room, Mace had taken a couple of aspirin to dull the pain.

He scrubbed his face now beneath the pummeling jets of water. He'd been damn lucky, he knew. The sorcerer had been knocked off the stairs, but Mace had not been surprised by the fierce defense Guerra put up when they'd landed twenty feet below.

The Lord of Darkness was still alive and well, that he could sense. The sorcerer had shape-shifted back into his human form by now. At least Mace knew what animal Guerra had chosen. From now on, Mace would be extra watchful for a raven.

He cursed himself again for letting Guerra get away. Worse yet, the Dark Lord had veiled himself, so Mace could not pick up his energy trail. All he could do was wait for the sorcerer to reveal himself later. With Ana at large, Guerra would return.

Gripping the soap, Mace lathered his sweaty body. He couldn't stop thinking about Ana, how scared she must be. But he couldn't hang around to protect her, no matter how much he wanted to. He was injured himself and had to assess the damage to his shoulder.

Sending energy feelers to locate her, Mace had sensed she was still on the top of Huaynu Picchu, even though it was dawn. Why was she there?

That one kiss they'd shared had magically connected them to one another. Damn. He needed to keep his wits about him. Loss of focus would get them both in trouble.

After shutting off the shower, Mace wearily stepped out and reached for the yellow, fluffy towel. He looked into the steamy mirror and briskly rubbed his damp hair, feeling torn. It was 6:00 a.m. and he was due at the drilling site in an hour. But he wanted to get to Ana first and find out if she was all right.

Leaving the bathroom, he jerked open a dresser drawer, found a white shirt, clean jeans and socks and quickly donned them. Then, rubbing his jaw, he remembered he had to shave.

As he stood in front of the mirror again, electric razor buzzing, he could feel the Dark Lord's presence. Guerra was definitely nearby. But just because Mace could sense the master sorcerer, that didn't mean he could find him. Only when Guerra unveiled himself could he track him down.

Mace switched his psychic radar back to Ana. He could feel her—all of her. Every emotion. She felt better than she had last night, that was for sure. Far better than Mace himself felt at that moment. Every time he moved his shoulder, it pained him.

What with his jaguar shape-shifting energy, the area would be fully healed within twenty-four hours, he knew. Until then, Mace had to be careful. Being injured in either form was dangerous for a hunter-assassin, and he hoped the Dark Lord wouldn't come out of hiding while he was still healing, and therefore vulnerable.

He finished shaving and set the razor on the white countertop. Ana was on the move again. He could feel it. She was going somewhere.

Switching his attention back and forth between his two quarries, Mace got a really bad feeling.

Ana was in danger—again.

By noon, Ana had descended Huaynu Picchu via a small, slippery path down the sacred mountain. Grandmother Alaria's words from last night haunted her. "Go to the lunar temple at the *base* of the apu," she had said. "There are two temples—one above, on the peak, and the other below. They are mirror reflections of one another. As above, so below. You have been initiated on the top one. Now you must go to the one near the Urubamba River, and claim your birthright."

Moving carefully down the narrow trail, Ana saw the first tourist hikers of the day, just ahead of her. They were chattering and laughing, and she felt exhausted and frightened in comparison. The dampness of the morning made her shiver as she walked quickly down the uneven, rocky path. Ragged-looking clouds hung just above the jungle canopy, threatening rain.

Ana ate a protein bar to quiet her growling stomach. Was Victor alive or dead? Her own father had tried to kill her last night…

She decided the sorcerer was still around and continuing to stalk her. She didn't know how she sensed that, but trusted the instinct. Maybe her jaguar spirit guide had alerted her. She just knew Victor continued to be a very real danger to her.

Ana touched the jaguar claw hanging from the leather thong as a frisson of warning raced through her. For a second, she slowed her step. Victor was close. But where? She scanned the forest around her, the path ahead. She had no weapon with which to defend herself…either.

The possibility of dying was suddenly very real to Ana—and terrifying. She hadn't bargained on a life-and-death initiation. She wanted to live! And she wanted to find out who her mother was, why Magdelana had abandoned her.

This whole journey was turning into a perilous quest across quicksand, where shifting realities constantly obscured the truth. Ana had thought her parents might be Quero farmers, simple, benign people of the land. Her investigation was turning out to be anything but simple and benign. Rubbing her damp brow, she frowned. What orphan ever imagined she could come from such awful parents? The bitter reality left a sour taste in her mouth.

Continuing rapidly down the slippery trail, Ana passed the tourists, who said hello to her in German. She gave a wan smile in return, and wished Mace was with her. Just thinking about him brought her fear under control. And yet she couldn't stop replaying the events of last night. What about the jaguar she'd seen in that flash of lightning? The rifle shot and the bullet whizzing by her head had been as real as the cat itself.

The most brutal truth was that Victor wanted her dead. Ana wrestled mightily with that knowledge. Parents and children often had disagreements. But to kill her because she refused to be taught by him? Refused the power, fame and wealth he promised, in favor of life as a wildlife biologist? It seemed an extreme and sick reaction. *Loco.*

Reaching a fork in the path, Ana saw a small, hand-carved sign that said Lunar Temple. An arrow pointed down through the shadowy jungle below. Ana tried to remain alert as she made her way along the narrow, steep path, which was riddled with tree roots ready to trip her. The jungle walls closed in quickly, the path a narrow corridor between them. Howler monkeys screeched. Startled birds shrieked in alarm and flew off into the impenetrable interior.

Grandmother Alaria had told Ana she must find a cave with seven niches dug into the walls. She was to sit in each hollow in turn, where she would be given information by the Incan goddess or *nusta* assigned to it. At the end of the seventh session and her communication with the final *nusta,* Ana would know what to do, Alaria had told her. Ana would receive a gift for her next initiation.

Arriving at the river an hour later, she easily found the cave, even though vines and trees grew around the entrance. About two hundred feet away stood the partially destroyed lunar temple. Ana could see that the roof of the structure had rotted away over time, though the standing stone walls seemed strong. Each window ledge held a stone of a different size, shape and color. The roar of the Urubamba indicated the mighty river was very near, but the thick jungle wall hid it from view.

Ana ate a second protein bar, drank a pint of bottled water and then climbed the steep, rocky slope to the entrance of the cave. It was easy to spot the seven niches, for they were decorated with *despachos,* sacred gift offerings to the *nustas* left by Incan priests and priestesses of today. The Inca religion was thriving in South America, she was discovering, despite the heavy hand of the Spaniards who had brought Catholicism to the continent four centuries ago.

Ana had nothing to give to the *nustas* and she felt badly about that. Setting her knapsack on the floor of the cave, she stepped into the first small alcove and sat down, cross-legged. She grounded herself, took several deep, steadying breaths and closed her eyes.

Within seconds, she began to feel a spinning sensation, like a whirlpool, drawing her down into the earth. After last night's escapade with the triangular rock on Huaynu Picchu, Ana relaxed. She knew this signified her traveling in spirit to some other dimension.

But as she sank even deeper, she could still feel Victor nearby, closing in on her once again. She was torn between opening her eyes or surrendering to the energy that gently pulled her on into a white-gold light.

Victor Carancho Guerra smiled briefly. He stood just within the darkness of the jungle, less than ten feet from the lunar temple, which had been built by the Incas hundreds of years earlier. His rifle rested in the crook of his arm.

Cloaked and therefore undetectable, he saw his daughter coming out of the *nusta*'s cave. Victor's heart grew sad. He didn't want it to end this way. Why couldn't Ana see the positive side of working with him?

Having power, fame, riches and control wasn't bad. Everyone wanted those things. Why didn't she?

Victor shook his head. He knew he had to kill Ana if she didn't side with him and his goals for the world. Regardless of the guilt he felt, he had to do this. He had to fulfill the legend. Ana had made a foolish and deadly error in saying *no* to him.

The sudden appearance of that jaguar still bothered Victor, especially when he'd realized it was a hunter-assassin from the Warriors for the Light and not a true jungle animal. The shape-shifter—whoever he was—had torn through Victor's cloak, ripping five long gashes in the fabric. The unexpected attack had caught him off guard. He'd been too focused on stalking his daughter to be aware of anything else. As he'd become unveiled, Victor had been exposed, vulnerable. The hunter-assassin had located him precisely because of that fact. But Victor had had to release his energy in order to get to Ana. There was no other choice.

Staring down at the damp, leaf-strewn floor of the jungle, Victor knew that after killing her, he would then take her soul captive. Shooting her body came first. As she lay dying, he would entrap her spirit and transport her to the Land of the Dead. Once imprisoned there, Ana could never escape. She would never cause problems for him again.

Well, he wouldn't make any mistakes today. True, he had to unveil once more, but Victor was paying attention to everything around him this time, instead of just focusing on Ana.

He narrowed his eyes as he watched his tall, lean

daughter carefully pick her way through the temple entrance. She looked like her mother, Magdalena, without a doubt. Victor saw no trace of his own face in his daughter's features.

And then cold rage overwhelmed him. That bitch, his first wife, had completely deceived him. Him! Of all the sorcerers, Magdalena had tricked *him!* He had never dreamed anyone could outmaneuver him like that. He was, after all, the vaunted Lord of Darkness, come to life to fulfill a thousand-year-old legend.

Savagely, Victor squelched his rage. He had to pay attention. Had to keep his awareness open to all possibilities. He knew the jaguar shape-shifter was alive and would stalk him once more.

Time to act. Wiping his mouth impatiently, Victor saw Ana hesitantly step inside the ancient temple. She might be his daughter, but she wouldn't be much longer.

Looking around, the sorcerer sensed something else, but couldn't quite define the feeling. One second an energy was there; the next, it was gone. It had to be the hunter-assassin, searching for him. Victor quickly cloaked himself.

All he had to do now was wait until his daughter located the Emerald Key—a sphere-shaped emerald said to be buried here, at the temple. Victor had never managed to find it, but sensed it was present. The sphere had been hidden energetically, so that a *Tupay* could never locate its imprint or whereabouts.

The sphere was part of a powerful necklace created by the great Incan emperor Pachacuti. And Victor was going to get that ceremonial necklace, one way or another.

Shifting impatiently from foot to foot, he watched intently as Ana peered about in the murky depths of the temple. The Inca had sent seven jaguar warriors around the world, to bury the seven emeralds of the sacred necklace in seven countries. One of the spheres was here in Peru, where it had all begun. But even with his considerable powers and psychic ability, Victor hadn't been able to locate it. The spheres would only reveal themselves to a *Taqe* person.

Snorting softly, he watched as Ana carefully moved deeper into the roofless temple, continuing her search. She might be his daughter, carrying his blood within her, but she sure as hell wasn't choosing the right side.

But once she found the sphere, that wouldn't matter anymore.

Ana brushed aside cobwebs as she stepped into the northern corner of the stone structure. The dirt floor was dry here because a section of thick, rotting roof timbers remained intact. The *nustas* in the cave had given Ana a visual map of the temple floor. They had revealed the presence of a beautiful emerald sphere buried in a wooden box in a far corner.

Curiosity, excitement and dread warred within Ana as she sank to her knees. Digging with the knife she carried, she began to remove the packed top layer of red clay dirt. Grandmother Alaria had said that this initiation would bring her a gift, something she would need.... Ana wiped the sweat off her brow with the back of her hand, then continued digging.

Alaria had said Ana must use her heart during the

upcoming test, she recalled. If she was able to pass all the initiations, her life would change. She didn't know *how* it would change; she just wanted to know who her mother was.

Abruptly, the sounds of the jungle quieted, and Ana felt that terrifying stalking presence once more. Her father was so close that the hair stood up on the back of Ana's neck, screaming a warning.

Frightened and wary, Ana kept glancing toward the dim shaft of light coming through the doorway, half expecting Victor to be standing there, his rifle aimed at her once more. Mouth dry, heart pounding with fear, she saw nothing. She got back to work.

The point of her knife struck something with a *thunk*. It must be the wooden box! The last *nusta* had said Ana would find the emerald sphere inside it, in the north corner. Quickly, she continued to dig. A small, carved mahogany receptacle, about five inches long and wide, was gradually revealed. Gently prying it out of the ground, she felt her hands tingle wildly as she lifted the treasure from its resting place and set it on the floor. Her heart pounding, she wiped her dirty hands on her pant legs and then pried open the box with her fingernails.

As she opened the lid, bright, green-gold light shot out of the box, surrounding her and lighting up the entire interior of the shadowy temple. Wide-eyed, Ana stared down at the round sphere, about the size of a golf ball, nestled in a bed of tattered golden fabric. Green light blazed from its depths.

The energy bathed Ana. She felt infused with such love and peace that she closed her eyes and simply absorbed the incredible, healing vibrations exuding like a mighty beacon. Kneeling there, her hands resting on her thighs, she felt the energy encircle her thudding heart. Miraculously, all of her fear dissolved. In its place, Ana felt such sweet hope and harmony. Opening her eyes, she heard the spirit in the sphere whisper that she should pick it up in her left hand.

The moment her fingers curved around the object, Ana gasped again. That energy entered her palm, raced up her arm and flowed like a mighty river throughout her being, drenching every cell with a radiance that lifted and transformed her. The voices of women singing filled her mind as she clung to the sphere.

However long the beautiful, otherworldly experience lasted, Ana had no idea. As she continued kneeling there, the sphere seemed to throb with a cool and soothing energy. She couldn't explain what had happened to her or why. All she knew was that she felt reborn. The anxiety and acidic fear were gone. A sense of centering deep within made her feel connected to something incredibly healing and wonderful. Ana savored the moment, until a voice within finally told her it was time to move on.

After tucking the sphere carefully back into the box, Ana slipped the hook through its wire loop and closed the lid once more. She shakily got to her feet, reached for her pack and shrugged it on. Leaning down, she picked up the box and walked out of the temple.

Ana halted abruptly. Less than ten feet away was her father. Dressed all in black, he had his rifle in his hands—aimed at her.

"So, you found it," Victor rasped as he eyed the box.

Ana stared at him in alarm. This was the first time she'd come face-to-face with her father in broad daylight, in the flesh. Victor stared back at her, a sickening grin on his face. His canine teeth were like those of a feral animal. But it was his eyes that filled her with dread. Ana felt as if she were looking into a black hole.

Fear jagged through her like a bolt of lightning. Automatically, her grip tightened on the box she carried.

"Why are you here?" she demanded, her voice hoarse and unsteady. Her world was dissolving, she realized. The jungle sounds died away and the river went silent.

Victor lowered the rifle slightly. "I'm here to give you one more chance, Daughter. Come of your own free will and let me teach you what I know." He held his hand toward her, his voice hoarse and pleading. "Please, Ana. I don't want to hurt you. I want you to be my daughter once again. We can be such a good team, you and I." His voice dropped lower. "You are of my blood. My body. I'd rather work with you than harm you."

Breathing raggedly, Ana whispered, "I'll *never* work with you." She saw the hope disappear from his flat, dark eyes, felt him preparing to shoot her. There would be no escape this time. Absently, Ana wondered if her jaguar guide was near. She hadn't felt her around her since she'd entered the temple. Wasn't she supposed to protect her? As she cast a furtive glance at her surroundings, Ana knew they were alone. This was an out-of-the-way place where few tourists ever came, because it was such a long, dangerous, steep trek down to the ancient ceremonial site. *Alone.* And she was going to die.

Again, Ana realized how much she wanted to live. She felt the sphere inside the box she carried sending waves of tingles through her. There was a *reason* for her to live now. From what the *nustas* had told her, the sphere could only be given to someone of the light. Ana could never give it to the *Tupay*.

Suddenly, she saw a way to make up for the evil she carried inside herself. The sphere symbolized something good and clean and honorable—a positive gift to humanity.

She was not like her father, who stood before her like a thin, black scarecrow with a deadly smile. Compressing her lips, she snarled, "Get out of here! Leave me alone!"

"I can't. Not until you give me that box."

Ana's arms automatically tightened around it. She understood from the *nustas* that if this sphere fell into *Tupay* hands, it would be used for evil, not good. At all costs, she had to protect it. She would die trying.

"Give it to me and I'll let you live."

"You're going to kill me either way." Her voice was low, like the growl of a jaguar.

Victor said, "You could work at my side, as my consort. Together, you and I can rule this world." He gestured with the rifle. "I'm the most powerful sorcerer in the world. It is my destiny to rule the earth. And you could be at my side."

"I'll die first!" Ana answered. "I'm not evil. I want this world filled with peace, not war. The *nustas* told me that *Tupay* represent nothing but violence, war and death."

Stepping back, Victor scowled. His heart sank as he realized that the *nustas* were treating Ana as if she were

Taqe. Well, she wasn't! She had *his* genes, the *Tupay* heritage, within her! Rebuffed and hurt, he snarled, "You stupid girl. You could have everything—wealth, fame and power. You're just like your mother—a hopeless idealist. Well, idealists don't make it in this world." He waved a finger in Ana's direction. "And I'm not going to be lured again by your mother or her genetics. You look like her. You act like her." Victor snorted violently. "Do you know what happened to her? I'm going to tell you before I kill you."

Tears rushed to Ana's eyes. Her chest heaved with such violent emotions—grief, rage and despair—that it was all she could do to stand there. Her voice cracking, she cried, "What did you do to her?"

Victor smiled savagely. "I discovered that she wasn't *Tupay,* but *Taqe*. Magdalena was within a week of birthing you. Bitch that she was, she hid from me the fact she was a Warrior for the Light. I thought I had fulfilled the legend by marrying a *Tupay* woman who would bear my consort, a daughter as dark as I. Instead, a week before your birth, I saw the birthmark on the back of Magdalena's neck had changed from *Tupay* to *Taqe*." He pointed to his own neck. "I was holding her when I saw the symbol change. I had lifted her hair to kiss her there."

Victor muttered, "The sun symbol disappeared, replaced by the Vesica Piscis! The double ring indicated she was a Warrior for the Light. Before, she would shape-shift into a parrot, a *Tupay* spirit guide. I think her hormones during pregnancy had accidentally reverted her birthmark back to the real one." He took in a ragged breath and continued, "It showed me she was my enemy, not my wife."

"How c-could someone you love suddenly become your enemy?" Ana stammered in anger.

With a one-shouldered shrug, Victor narrowed his eyes speculatively. "Warriors for the Light are my natural enemies, girl. They are of the light energy. I am of heavy *Tupay* energy. I believe Maria Magdalena Sanchez knew exactly what she was doing when she sought me out, lured me into marriage and mated with me. I believe she knowingly gave her own life to supposedly 'save the world.' Or so she thought. You see, there's a legend that says when the Dark Lord mates with the Dark Mistress, a daughter will be born from that union. It will be she who becomes the consort of the Dark Lord, and they will go on to rule the world. Magdalena tricked me."

"How did you kill my mother?" The words were hushed and strained. Ana choked back tears and waited, her gaze riveted on Victor.

"Simple enough. I persuaded her to take a walk with me just before nightfall. Oh, she was having a few labor pains, but I sweet-talked her into it. Once I had her on the edge of a five-hundred-foot cliff, I confronted her about the *Taqe* symbol on her neck. I told her I'd found out her sneaky plan to bear a daughter who wasn't *Tupay*. Her last words to me were that I would never win the war against the light. I shoved her off the cliff for that."

Ana glared at him. "And the fall killed her?"

"I heard her body hit the rocks below," he answered calmly. "It was dark by then, so I couldn't see where she'd landed. I thought the fall would kill you both. But I was wrong. When you were four years old, I felt you unveil for the first time. I was shocked you'd survived. Your signature is one of a kind, and I recognized it for what it was. Children of the Light unveil naturally at around age four or five. *Tupay* children unveil at age seven or eight."

Victor smiled, as if congratulating himself. "I tracked you down by your energy signature. Somehow, your mother managed to give birth before she died. And from what I could make of it all, a mother jaguar came along and took you in as one of her cubs. For four years, you lived around here." Victor waved his hand toward the jungle. "You lived with the female jaguar and her cubs. She cared for and protected you. And I have no doubt you can shape-shift into a jaguar. Can't you?"

Shocked, Ana stared at him. "How could you know that?"

"Because Children of the Light begin to learn shape-shifting around age three or four. Your mother was of the jaguar clan, I discovered. You carry her genes." Victor shrugged lazily. "And you're just like her."

Ana now realized more than ever she truly was a daughter of the Light, not the Dark. And to her relief, she had leaned toward the genetics of her mother, not her evil father.

With a grimace, Victor said, "And here you are. Again. When I tracked you down in that farmer's field, I thought I had you. I saw the rainbow colors in your aura and knew you were of the *Taqe*. I was very disappointed. I knew then I had to kill you. When I fired my rifle at you, the female jaguar leaped in front of you and saved your life. Little did I know you'd survived a second time." He frowned. "It was as if some greater power was shielding your energy signature from me. Years later, I realized that you had lived after I thought I'd killed you in that field. I had a vision one night and saw you leaving Peru on an airplane, but I didn't know where you were being taken. I could not hunt you anymore because you were receiving protection that I couldn't penetrate. But I knew someday you would show up here in Peru again. And you did. You were unveiled, and it was easy to track you down.

"So here we are a third time, facing one another." Victor's look sharpened, his eyes growing even colder. "Now, give me the box. Because, one way or another, you're dying today, Ana. This is our final meeting. And I will be rid of you once and for all."

Chapter 11

Ana cried out in anguish. The truth about her mother's murder was a heavy burden. And her rage at this beast—her father—almost paralyzed her. She could barely stand the thought that she and Victor carried the same blood. Even as she realized just how much danger she was in, another part of her felt relief. So much made more sense now. Being adopted by John and Mary Rafael and raised in a loving household had made all the difference. That was why Ana had never tapped into the evil of her father's genetics. Not ever! Her head swimming with colliding realizations, Ana couldn't seem to control her breath. Tears brimmed in her eyes as she took a step back and hugged the box to her heart. "You don't deserve this gemstone. It's of the Light," she said unsteadily.

Victor chuckled. "The sphere has no say about its owner. It will work no matter who touches it." His voice grew harsher as he pointed at the box. "And I intend to find every one of the pieces and string that necklace together. Whoever wears it first will have the power and authority to rule this world." His mouth twisted. "And that will be me, girl. Now, hand it over."

All movement and sound ceased. Ana was again aware of the black emptiness in her father's slitted eyes. She saw him raise the rifle. Felt the pounding of her heart, as if it would leap out of her chest. He was going to murder her, just as he'd murdered the beloved mother she'd never known. And then Ana felt the dizziness. She was beginning to shape-shift. But what could shape-shifting do to save her from this man's bullet?

Victor's finger brushed the trigger. Bringing the rifle to his shoulder, he situated the stock firmly against it. A wrenching disappointment flooded him as he prepared to shoot Ana in the head, but his lust for power won out. He did not want to take a chance of shooting the emerald sphere pressed to her breast. No, the piece was far too valuable, and he had to be careful, observant.

Just then his ears caught an unusual sound. Hesitating fractionally, he jerked a glance to the right.

In that second, a huge male jaguar hurtled toward him, claws outstretched, mouth open, fangs long and curved. Ready to fight.

Ana gave a startled cry. She was in the middle of a shape-shift when it happened. The magnificent jaguar exploded out of the jungle and leaped directly at Victor. Frozen, Ana saw her father pause briefly.

Because she was in the most vulnerable state, between a jaguar and human, Ana was paralyzed and could not move. Instead, she became a target.

Victor's rifle roared, and Ana was lifted off her feet. She felt as if a fist had slammed into the center of her chest, just above where her hands clasped the box. The breath whooshed out of her mouth, and falling backward, she crashed to the jungle floor. Her hands flew outward, and the precious box tumbled into the mud near her head.

Something was wrong. Horribly wrong. Ana blinked, confused. Her vision began to go gray. She felt an odd, unexpected warmth rapidly spreading across her chest. Her fingers shook badly as she touched the numbed area there.

Senses heightened, she heard Victor scream. When she lifted her head, her breathing chaotic and forced, Ana saw the growling jaguar knock the sorcerer off his feet. The enraged cat's snarling reverberated through the clearing as he swung a paw and savagely sliced her father's exposed neck.

Ana saw blood spurt like a geyser out of the gaping wound in his throat. Her father fell back, unconscious. And then the cat turned, his green eyes connecting with hers. Instantly, the pinpoint black pupils enlarged, until Ana saw only a thin crescent of emerald surrounding them.

The jaguar had saved her life.

Her life.

Groaning, she felt the energy flowing out of her. Her father had succeeded. Surely the bullet in her chest would end her life. After all her monumental efforts to find herself, Ana felt a wave of sadness that her quest had come to this.

Numbly, she saw the cat walk up to her, its mouth open and panting. Was it going to kill her, as well as her father? She was already dying. Perhaps it would grab her by the throat and suffocate her. At this point, there was nothing she could do to defend herself. Her head fell back on the muddy ground.

Gasping for air, warm blood running through her fingers as she pressed her hand against her wound, Ana stared up into the cat's ferocious green eyes. Every breath required a huge effort, and Ana could feel herself fading. Her legs grew cold and numb, a sign of impending death.

And then something happened.

The jaguar began to waver and fade, resembling the heat waves she would see on a hot summer day across an asphalt highway. To her amazement, the cat morphed and changed—into Mace Ridfort. He stood over her, his face contorted in anguish, his blue eyes fraught with terror. Terror for her.

What was going on here? Ana closed her eyes, finding the effort to breathe a terrible struggle. She had to concentrate on pulling oxygen into her lungs. Panting harshly, she battled to suck precious, life-giving air into her body. And then she felt Mace's arms around her, drawing her against him. She was so weak now that her head lolled listlessly against the crook of his neck.

"Hold on, Ana. Hold on…." Mace whispered, his voice raw and unsteady. He placed one hand over her wound and pressed hard, trying to stop the bleeding. Ana's arms fell weakly to her sides. She closed her eyes, every breath a strained gurgle. Oddly enough, she felt safe now—finally. Mace was here.

She had to be hallucinating. He'd been a jaguar moments before. How could that be? Victor was dead. That, at least, was true. But Mace, a jaguar? That had to be her weakened mind playing tricks on her.

She couldn't worry about it now. She just closed her eyes and hoped she would wake up from this nightmare.

Mace jerked his head around. Panicked, he saw Ana's blood flowing over his fingers. She couldn't die! In the minute before he pounced upon the master sorcerer, he'd heard Victor say that she was the Light. That explained so much to him.

But he'd arrived too late. Too late! Ana was mortally wounded, dying. Tears burned in Mace's eyes as he allowed all the love he had for her to flow into her.

He had to save her. And yet Mace knew it was beyond him to do so. Spying the wooden box nearby, he noticed the green-and-gold glow throbbing around it. This had to be the emerald sphere he'd always heard about. Mace looked down at Ana's closed eyes. He understood she was the one who had found it. She was *Taqe*. Not *Tupay*, as he'd thought.

Oh, Great Mother Goddess! Help her! Save her! he called mentally to anyone from the Other Worlds who could hear his cry.

There was nothing he could do but hold Ana, rock her, whisper that he loved her. The blood purled through his fingers and her breath was shallow. Ana couldn't leave him. *No! No!* Mace looked up at the temple and surrounding jungle. They were alone here.

"Help us!" he cried out. "Help Ana! Let her live! She deserves to be saved!"

His sobbing words were quickly absorbed by the greenery around them. Ana took fewer and fewer breaths. She no longer moaned or moved. Mace felt her going limp in his arms, her head lolling back. The light that had burned so brightly in her beautiful green eyes was dimming rapidly. She was slipping away from him!

"No!" Mace screamed hoarsely. "Take me instead. Take my life. She's more important than I am."

He wept, unashamed, and held Ana tightly.

Out of the corner of his eye, Mace saw movement in the temple doorway. He blinked back his tears as an older woman in a blue-and-white robe appeared. Mace didn't know who she was—only that she was *Taqe,* with rainbow colors in her aura and a Vesica Piscis necklace. He felt sudden hope.

"Grandmother!" he cried. "Save Ana. Oh, Great Goddess, don't take her away from me!"

Mace choked back sobs, his attention torn between Ana, whose breath was now barely perceptible, and the old woman, who seemed to float effortlessly just above the ground. She glided toward him, the look on her aged face one of concern. Mace watched as she hovered over the box. A green sphere slowly rose from it, suspended in the air before Mace.

"Place this healing sphere upon her wound, my son. Do it now."

Without hesitation, he reached for the object. The

instant his bloodied fingers curved around it, a jolt of white-hot energy shot up his arm and into him. He placed it against the small bullet hole in Ana's chest and tried to stay calm.

Her face was white. Her eyes were open and distant. He felt her spirit leaving her, so he pressed the sphere more firmly against the oozing wound.

"Allow your love for her to travel into the sphere," the woman gently advised him. "Love will call her back, my son. Only pure love has the power to return her to you."

Mace choked again, nodded and closed his eyes. The sphere was red-hot in his palm as he held it against Ana's lethal wound. He could feel her spirit lingering nearby, waiting and watching. Opening his heart, he allowed all his desire, his yearning, the sweetness he held for Ana, to flow out of him, down his arm, into his hand. His love went through the glowing sphere into her lifeless body. If only she would live. She had to! Mace started sobbing once more.

He felt the tentative, warm touch of the old woman's hand on his shoulder.

"Call her back, my son. You know how to call her back."

Ana heard the musical trickle of a nearby stream. It sounded as if the water were singing to her. The pleasant, soothing burbling became clearer as her awareness continued to expand. The next thing she felt was weight. The weight of her body. Ana slowly became aware that she was lying on something soft but supportive.

The melodic call of birds registered next. And finally

the comforting warmth of a man's hand gripping her own cool fingers.

There was a sense of utter peace within and around her. Exhausted by her efforts to become conscious, Ana lay there, content just to feel Mother Earth infusing her body with a tingling, life-giving energy.

Someone pressed a cool cloth to her brow. Ana could hear hushed voices. She strained to make them out, but whoever was talking was speaking in low tones. Was she in the another world? Was this how it felt to die and be reborn into spirit?

Ana remembered being shot. Remembered her father killing her. Strangely, though, there was no emotion attached to the evil deed. It was as if her life was running before her like a movie film, and she was reviewing the last hours.

Most surprising, she saw Mace turning from jaguar to man. He scooped her up after she was shot, holding her, cried for her to come back to him, telling her he loved her. There was a lot of emotion in that moment, and Ana felt her heart swell with fierce love in return.

Her lips parted and she took a deep, ragged breath into her lungs. Mace loved her as much as she loved him! The discovery was meltingly beautiful and infused Ana with a renewed desire to live.

She felt the man's grip become more firm as oxygen flowed into her lungs once again. That cool cloth caressed her brow and her cheeks, removing the perspiration from her skin. The feeling of being love buoyed Ana, carried her and lifted her. With each breath she took, it was as if life itself was being pumped back into her chest. The delicious love she felt curled around her throbbing heart, and in her mind's eye she saw a lovely, sparkling rose-colored energy flowing into that organ.

Love. She was loved. Like a thirsty sponge, Ana absorbed the purity of the sensation into herself. And with each wave that flowed through her, she became stronger.

She loved Mace. She had loved him from the moment she'd first met him on that airplane, Ana realized. And it was a love so deep and unfathomable that it fed her like a wellspring flowing from deep within the skin and bones of Mother Earth.

"Ana?" Mace whispered. He cautiously watched as color flooded into her face. Her skin flushed with life, and he tightened his hand around hers. He felt more than saw Grandmother Alaria, the elder, kneel down next to him, near Ana's head. Earlier, Mace had been filled in on the Village of the Clouds, as well as those visiting this stronghold.

"Continue to allow your love to feed her, my son," she coaxed. "You're doing fine." She laid her trembling hand on Ana's smooth brow.

The moment Grandmother Alaria touched her, Mace felt a jolt of powerful energy flow through Ana and into himself. Though not uncomfortable, it was strong. This woman was much more than what she seemed. As he looked around the thatched hut, noting the gold woven rug upon the hard earthen floor, Mace knew that wherever they were, it wasn't on earth. His training told him that. Moving his gaze back to Ana, he continued to hold her hand and watched as Grandmother Alaria sent healing energy into her. He received some of it by proxy, because he was gripping Ana's damp, cool hand.

Silence enveloped them, but Mace was always aware of the small stream burbling happily just outside the door. The sound of birds calling to one another soothed his fractious state. His heart ached from the shock of almost losing Ana. Yet, now she was reviving. Mace had called back her spirit and somehow the emerald sphere had helped her return to him.

Ana was alive. And Mace knew, from the extent of her injury, she should have been dead.

"There," Alaria said at last, seeming pleased, as she lifted her hand from Ana's brow. "She's back. Fully in her body once more." She glanced tenderly at Mace and added, "You are exhausted, my son. Today you passed many tests, and moved higher in initiation as a result. Why not lie here at Ana's side? Sleep with her. Hold her. When you both awaken on the morrow, all will be well."

Mace nodded, his mouth working to hold back a fresh wave of tears. Alaria's face glowed with such goodness. He had no idea whether this woman was pure spirit and assuming a human form for his benefit. The bottom line was that she had saved his Ana's life, and he would always be grateful.

"Yes," he struggled to say. "I will. Thank you for *everything,* Grandmother. Especially for Ana's life. You have saved mine, too."

Straightening slowly, Alaria smiled and patted his shoulder. "Ah, my son, what brought Ana back to us was your love for her. You called to her spirit the only way it can be called back—with pure love. But you will realize this over time. Now rest. You are tired to your core, and so is Ana. Both of you have been through rugged initiations, and you've survived them. Now it's time to heal."

Ana stirred. This time, all the sounds outside the hut were clear and present. The stream's gurgle she remembered. The birds calling to one another gave her a sense of profound peace and of being swaddled in love. Ana pushed the light blanket away and opened her eyes.

The first thing she saw was Mace sitting on a three-legged wooden stool near her pallet, a cup of coffee in his hands. She was in a thatched hut of some kind, and a gold curtain had been pulled aside at the entrance.

Ana moved her attention back to Mace. His face was lined and tired looking, but a slight smile crooked the corners of his delicious mouth.

As she slowly sat up, the blanket she was wrapped in pooled around her hips. Someone had dressed her in a soft white blouse. She wore pale pink cotton slacks, but her feet were bare. Her palm grazed the area where she'd been shot. Frowning, she moved her fingers in explanation.

"You've been healed, Ana," Mace told her in a low, unsteady voice. "You're going to live." He saw her eyes widen and felt her relief.

Finally, she whispered, "It was so awful, Mace. I remember everything…." She wanted to dwell on the positive and not the terrifying last few hours.

"Where are we?" she asked in a hushed tone, her hand pressed over her heart. She couldn't see any evidence that she'd been shot. It was as if it never happened.

Mace held the hot coffee toward her. He wasn't sure if Ana was thirsty or hungry. "We're here in the Village of the Clouds. It's a special place, Ana, located in the Other Worlds. I heard of it during my training a long time ago, when I was very young. Grandmother Alaria and Grandfather Adaire filled me in after we arrived here. This is my first time here, and it's a *Taqe* fortress where we are completely safe."

Relishing the fragrant smell, Ana reached for the coffee. Being once more at the Village gave her a deep sense of security. She felt strong enough to hold the cup.

Their fingers met, and a warmth spread throughout her. Ana saw the love shining in Mace's blue eyes—toward her. He loved her. The feeling radiated from him to her like the sun's mighty rays. Ana felt incredibly protected and safe.

"Thank you for the coffee," she murmured.

Mace grinned and watched her cautiously take a sip. "You're welcome."

He had so much to say to Ana, and yet he knew she was still adjusting to being fully in her physical body. Coming back from death wasn't an easy transition. He understood it would take several days for Ana to feel whole, to feel "here" again. While he wanted to blurt out a ton of information, a million questions, Mace held himself in check and remained silent.

The coffee was sweet, creamy and warm. Ana felt the liquid slide down her throat and warm her stomach. The sensation was wonderful. Grounding. Wrapping both hands around the mug, she relished the heat radiating from the pottery. Her gaze never left Mace's face or those eyes that spoke so eloquently to her.

Ana felt an incredible connection with him, as if a telephone line were strung between them. It was so easy to know what he was feeling. He loved her with a depth that took her breath away. Could he feel her love for him in return? Judging from the scowl on his face, Ana wasn't sure.

She saw Mace's very male mouth curve a little more. His blue eyes glinted, as if he was reading her thoughts. Yet Ana felt no abrasive intrusion into her mind, as Victor had done. The feeling was completly different.

She took another sip from the cup. "I was dead, wasn't I?"

Nodding, Mace said, "Yes, you were. Your spirit left your body as I held you."

Brows drawing downward, Ana gazed at him. "Did I imagine you? I mean, I saw a jaguar kill my father. I saw it walk over to me afterward. I thought it was going to rip out my throat, as it had Victor's. And then it changed into you. Mace? I have such a terribly active imagination at times, so I have to ask."

Straightening, he ran his hands slowly up and down his thighs. "Sweetheart, I'm not who you think I am." This was the moment Mace had dreaded, second only to Ana dying in his arms. He'd felt helpless then, and just as helpless now. He had to be honest and tell her the whole truth. And he feared this truth would drive a wedge between them. He took a deep, steadying breath and told Ana of his birth, his mission and who he really was.

To complicate matters, Mace now realized that because of Ana's adoption, none of her spiritual training had ever been initiated. She had no understanding of the paranormal world he lived in.

When Mace completed his explanation, he saw Ana react. Frowning, she tucked her legs beneath her and set the cup next to her pallet. Inwardly, Mace could feel her wrestling with this shocking information.

Finally, she pushed her dark hair off her shoulders. The thick strands cascaded down her back. "Then, you were hunting me and Victor."

"Ana, I'm a hunter-assassin for the Warriors for the Light. There aren't a whole lot of us around, but we fulfill a need and we know our mission."

"And you knew I would lead you to my father."

"Yes," Mace admitted softly, meeting her shadowed, jade-colored eyes.

"I was bait."

"That's one way to put it."

Licking her chapped lips, Ana looked down at her hands. "And you thought I was *Tupay*...like Victor...."

"Yes. I didn't know that your mother was *Taqe,* of the Light, until your father said so at the lunar temple." Shifting his tense shoulders, Mace added, "It made sense to me, Ana. I never saw or felt heavy energy around you. Ever. And I couldn't figure out *why* I didn't. I should have. I know a *Tupay* person instantly by the energy signature of their aura. I wanted to hate you, as I did your father. But I never could." Mace gave her a helpless look. "Just the opposite." He fell silent. He wanted to say, *I was falling in love with you from the moment I met you, and I fought it with every breath I took.* But he kept those words buried in his anguished heart.

Nodding, Ana whispered, "I guess if I were in your place, I'd fight it, too. You couldn't afford to…well, to…"

"I couldn't like you." Mace held his breath as sadness came over her features. The truth was out. He had to risk telling the truth even if it meant losing Ana. She could walk out of his life—forever—at any time.

Ana could also refuse to follow her intended spiritual path, simply because she had never been trained for it. Legends and prophecies could be changed because human beings could exert free will. Ana could ignore who and what she was, but he hoped she wouldn't. Even more painful for him, Ana could say she wanted no part of him.

Mace was a jaguar shape-shifter, and Ana had seen him change before her dying eyes. How had she felt about that? She had to be confused, frightened and unsure. Anyone would be, given the terrible atrocity that she'd just experienced at the hands of her own father. And somehow, Mace had to prepare himself for any possibility.

But how? He loved Ana. Could he let her go without revealing the true extent of his love for her? His dream of having her as his mate—for life? Of wanting her to carry their children? Of sharing so many small but precious moments with her? He wanted to drown daily in those emerald eyes that danced with such life.

Hanging his head, Mace clasped his hands between his thighs and waited. Now he knew how someone felt with his neck on a guillotine block, waiting for the ax to fall.

Chapter 12

"Now, Ana, one more time," Alaria coaxed. The elder sat on a wooden bench in a small clearing not far from the village. Ana stood before her, dressed in a simple cotton dress of dark green to match her eyes, a bright yellow sash around her waist. Her hair was in braids.

Alaria saw the uncertainty in Ana's eyes. For days they had worked on her controlling her shape-shifting talent. "First thing in the morning what do you do?"

"I ground myself."

"And how do you do that?"

"I close my eyes and envision silver tree roots wrapping around my ankles, going down through my feet and deep into Mother Earth."

"Why do you do that, child?"

"Without being grounded completely in my body I can't control what I do in spirit."

"Exactly. What do you do next if you want to move from human into jaguar form?"

"First, I call my jaguar spirit guide to me." Ana was awed at the fact that she could now see into the invisible realms. For whatever reason, since her "death" she had been given the gift of psychic sight. Alaria had said it was a reward from spirit.

Ana saw her powerful female jaguar, Sage, sitting to her left. "Although, in times of danger, she will come over me automatically without my asking."

"That's right. But for today's lesson, there are no threats, and you want to command her to fit over your human form."

Nodding, Ana closed her eyes and sent a telepathic signal to Sage, asking her to fit over her. This time, she felt her move and lift into the air. Because her spirit guide was in the fourth dimension, she was unhampered by third-dimensional laws of physics or gravity. It was very easy for her to float up above her head.

"Very good," Alaria declared. "Now what?"

"Keep my knees slightly bent to allow the energy of Mother Earth to come up through my feet, into my legs, to connect with my jaguar spirit coming down over me. This will happen simultaneously," Ana said, feeling Sage beginning to ease like a heavy, warm blanket over her head and across her shoulders. "This tethers her spirit over my human form and keeps Sage in place for my protection."

"Correct. Mother Earth knows that you are her

daughter, and she will protect you. And what color comes from the earth and flows up into your legs?"

"It's a beautiful apple-green color," Ana whispered. She felt the cool green energy coming up through her feet with a tingling sensation. In the center of her brow—her movie screen, as she called it—Ana saw and felt the green energy swiftly gliding upward. And then the dark shape of Sage moved over her. The warmth of the jaguar and the cool green from Mother Earth mixed in her solar plexus, or stomach region. The dizziness began, but now Ana was prepared for it. By bending her knees, she was able to maintain her balance during the momentary chaos of the two energies integrating.

"Very good," Alaria declared, watching the morphing process unfold.

Ana felt joyous as Sage fully enclosed her. A locking sensation occurred, as if she had slipped on a pair of shoes. The spirit guide was fully in place around her, and she was in jaguar form.

"Open your eyes," Alaria instructed.

Opening them, Ana saw that she *was* a jaguar. She was standing on four legs, and seeing through Sage's eyes. Everything looked different.

Now you can talk telepathically to me, Alaria instructed Ana.

Ana emitted a low growl, meant to be a laugh, as she tried to switch from speaking aloud to thinking. She felt the primal brain of Sage, as well as her human one, as if two entities lived in the same body. Separate yet intermixed. The experience was interesting and strange, but not uncomfortable.

Okay, I'm now trying to speak to you, Grandmother. Do you hear me? Ana was trying so hard she could feel pressure in her head from the effort. She looked at Alaria, who beamed with pleasure. The elder clapped her hands.

Indeed I can, my child. Very good! Learning to telepath will take time, but practice often, and soon it will become as easy as breathing. All right, that's enough training for today. Shape-shift back into your human form. And then we'll go have breakfast with Mace. You've done well.

"It is time to speak with you at length," Alaria said to Ana after breakfast. They sat at the small wooden table that served as a dining area in Ana and Mace's hut. Cool morning air drifted through the opened windows. The sun hadn't yet risen above the trees to herald the new day.

"I'm glad, Grandmother. I've got so many questions." Ana had just finished her breakfast of papaya, guava juice, toast and eggs, which Mace had made for them. Ana sneaked a glance at him as he sat opposite her. In her eyes, he'd changed remarkably in the last three days. Everyone at the Village of the Clouds performed some kind of volunteer work, be it physical labor, or reading to and teaching the children. Mace had gone out daily to work in the corn and squash fields, an activity that seemed to lift the sadness Ana always felt around him. In the hut, they each had a bedroom, and slept on a pallet unrolled across a handwoven rug on the earthen floor. Ana had been sleeping dreamlessly, regaining her strength. But she didn't know what he was going through.

Mace poured Alaria a second glass of guava juice.

"Thank you, my son."

"You're welcome, Grandmother."

He started to push away from the table and leave them to talk in privacy, but Alaria held out her hand. "Stay, Mace. What I have to say is for both of you."

Surprised by the request, he hesitated, halfway out of his chair. He glanced at Ana, whose hair was plaited in two thick braids today, emphasizing her ephemeral beauty and those lovely eyes of hers. "Is that okay with you?" he asked.

Nodding, Ana wiped her mouth with her napkin. "Of course." She smiled at Alaria, who drank the pink guava juice with relish. Today, the head elder was dressed in farming clothes, just as Mace was. Ana did not know how old the leader of the village was, but she had surprising spryness and the energy of a twenty-year-old. That was amazing. Every day, Alaria spent time out in the fields alongside her husband, Adaire, working just like everyone else.

"Ana, it is time you know the rest of your life story," Alaria told her, setting the glass down on the wooden table. "Your mother, Mary Magdalena Sanchez, was a Warrior for the Light. She was one of us." Alaria lifted her hand and gestured toward the village. "And like every warrior, she had an innate gift, a skill that had been genetically passed down through her family to her.

"For example, a person might lay their hands on another individual or animal and heal them. Others become invisible at will, and no one can see them. There are others who can hold an object and tell you its entire history, such as who made it, who owned it, who touched it. That is called psychometry. Mind reading is another skill. As impossible as this may seem, there are warriors who can teleport themselves from one place to another, even from one country to another, without the aid of an airplane." Alaria smiled.

"Those are incredible gifts, Grandmother. What did my mother do?"

"Your mother had another skill. She was a shape-shifter."

Ana glanced over at Mace. His brows were drawn downward, his focus on Alaria.

"A shape-shifter," Ana murmured. That explained why she had the same talent. It made her feel good to know she was so much like her mother.

"Yes. When you were shot by your father," Alaria said, "you saw Mace in two different forms. He is of the Light, just as your mother was. His skill involves shape-shifting, too."

"I did see Mace change from a jaguar into a man...." Ana searched the woman's watery blue eyes for confirmation.

"You were not seeing things, child." Alaria reached out and patted Mace's arm. "He has the same genetic skill as your beloved mother did. In fact, Magdalena was born here and began to train with us when she was a very young girl. I taught her the elements of how to shape-shift from human to animal form, and then back again, just as I am teaching you now."

"You—you trained my mother?" The words seemed to jam in Ana's throat. She felt a sudden rush of unexpected emotion as she searched Alaria's wrinkled face.

The old woman nodded. "Yes, I did. Magdalena was an apt student. Her mother, Maria, allowed her to stay full-time with us. By the time Magdalena was in her teens, she could easily shape-shift back and forth."

"And she knew who she was? A Warrior for the Light?" Ana asked, grasping Alaria's thin, strong hand for support.

"Yes. Both her parents were Warriors. Magdalena had a very unique mission, my child. You need to understand that mission, because it involves you. We knew from our spiritual council, here at the Village of the Clouds, that Victor Carancho Guerra was destined to find a *Tupay* woman and deliberately breed with her in order to create a daughter who would then go on and help him rule the world. That was decreed by one of the legends that had been handed down to us before the Inca Empire was ever created."

Alaria took a sip of her juice. "We knew the time was upon us for this part of the legend to catalyze. Your mother volunteered to go undercover as a *Tupay* woman, marry the master sorcerer and become pregnant by him. The legend says there was only one chance of mating with the Dark Sorcerer, and no other opportunity would be given to fulfill this particular prophecy. We wanted Guerra's seed to go to the Light, not the Dark. That way, we could neutralize the legend."

Ana's eyes widened. "My mother was—"

"A spy. A mole, if you will. As do all of us who are of the Light, Magdalena knew the risks. She had such great love, hope and idealism that she could undertake this one-of-a-kind mission. She *wanted* to be that woman."

With her hand pressed against her throat, Ana stared agape at Alaria. "And then I was conceived? Is that right?"

"Yes, you were. Half Dark. Half Light. Magdalena was planning on raising you right under Guerra's nose, and, at the right time, turning you against him and his dark ways. She wanted to steal you away from him and bring you here to live and train in the Village of the Clouds. Magdalena knew Guerra would soon recognize you were not *Tupay,* and would kill both of you. Here, we could have protected both of you from him."

Taking a final drink of juice, Alaria set the glass aside and held Ana's gaze. "Something went awry in our planning, however. Laws of nature intruded. We can each make choices at any time."

The elder's mouth compressed for a moment and she said softly, "And sometimes, choice has terrible consequences." Alaria reached out and touched the back of Ana's neck, where her birthmark lay. "To fool Guerra, we had magically changed Magdalena's Vesica Piscis symbol of the double rings, into the *Tupay* symbol of the sun." The old woman shook her head. "What we did not know was that Magdalena's hormones toward the end of her pregnancy would change the sun symbol back to the real one. She wasn't aware of the alteration and neither were we. But Guerra saw it. And when he realized she was a spy who had infiltrated his life, he lured Magdalena out to a cliff. He deliberately pushed her off it to kill her—and you."

Ana closed her eyes for a moment, realizing how

much her mother must have suffered. When she caught her breath, she opened her eyes and settled her gaze on Mace. Tears were glimmering on his cheeks. He was no less moved by Alaria's story than she, Ana realized. Feeling the old woman's fingers tighten around her hand, she looked toward the elder.

"I remember none of this, Grandmother."

"I know, and that's why you need to hear what happened next. As Magdalena fell, she landed in a huge bush that broke her fall. Some of her ribs cracked, but the ground was only three feet below, and she suffered no more injury. Because it was nearly dark, Guerra could not see her. He only heard Magdalena strike something far below. He assumed she was dead, and left."

Eyes widening, Ana said, "I thought she did die! Victor told me she had."

Alaria said grimly, "Warriors for the Light are a lot tougher than Guerra gives us credit for. Your mother lay there giving birth to you beneath the protection of that huge bush. And once you were born, she shape-shifted into a jaguar. This would ensure that her injuries, which were not life-threatening, would heal within twenty-four hours. And she knew Guerra would come back to try and find her body the next morning. Even a master sorcerer, when overwhelmed by human emotion, cannot utilize his magical skills. Guerra, under other less daunting circumstances, could have shape-shifted and confirmed Magdalena's demise or not. But he was too emotionally involved and could not. And Magdalena knew that. So, it bought her time she needed to not only escape Guerra, but keep you safe."

The old woman leaned forward. "Magdalena became a jaguar and carried you off in her mouth to go live in the jungle. There was nothing we could do to help because of what we call 'house rules,' spiritually speaking. I went immediately to our council to ask for intervention on you and your mother's behalf, but they refused to grant it. I tried to help, but to no avail. We are all bound by the laws of spirit. Magdalena was on her own."

Ana gave the elder a grateful look. "At least you tried.... Couldn't Victor find my mother by her rainbow aura?"

Alaria shook her head. "Guerra couldn't pick up on Magdalena's energy signature at all when she was in jaguar form. The cat's aura is very different in color. He could only see her rainbow aura if she morphed back into human form. Because she didn't, Guerra thought you were both dead. And your rainbow colors would not be revealed until age four. He thought a jaguar had probably carried Magdalena's body off during the night. This would account for why he couldn't find her when he climbed down the cliff the next morning to make sure she was dead."

Alaria surveyed Mace and Ana. "Guerra was right—a jaguar did carry off Magdalena. So it was a perfect way for her to hide and protect you. Afterward, she decided to live in the jungle near her parents' home, a few miles from Aguas Calientes. Her mother, Maria, had died and he remarried."

Ana's mind reeled as a new realization dawned. "Don't tell me that was Juan Sanchez? The old farmer I talked to, he said—"

"That is your grandfather. He was Magdalena's father."

Stunned, Ana gasped. "But Juan said that the day the hunter came… I know the hunter was my father. Why didn't Juan recognize Guerra?"

"Because Guerra stole the body of a poor shoemaker in Cuzco and came back to Aguas Calientes in it. As a master sorcerer, one of the most powerful in the world, Guerra knew how to possess another person's body. That is how someone like him lives for thousands of years—he just steals and inhabits a younger, newer body when the last one starts to get older. When Guerra dispossesses of a body, however, that person dies when he leaves it. Juan would not recognize Guerra in the new form he'd stolen."

"I see." Ana shivered. "What an awful thing to do."

"It's a *Tupay* thing to do," Mace stated. "One of their favorite tricks. This is why there are many ancient, powerful sorcerers on earth right now. They continue to live through the ages, multiplying until there are enough of them to take over the world. They far outnumber Warriors for the Light, who would *never* possess another person. To do so is to rob them of their free will and kill their spirit. Both are wrong."

"I understand," Ana said. She now grasped why the *Taqe* were under such threat by the *Tupay.*

"Magdalena knew about the laws of spirit," Alaria continued. "She accepted what she had to do to survive. She was desperate to get you integrated with humans and civilization. Your fourth birthday was quickly approaching, and she wanted to acquaint you with your grandfather, Ana. It was a mother's wish for her daughter, pure and simple. She would bring you to the stream, near where her father worked in the fields during the dry season, and he got you to trust him."

"And yet my grandfather knew nothing of what happened to his daughter?"

Shaking her head, Alaria said, "No. Guerra told them shortly afterward that Magdalena had gone off for a walk at dusk and was never seen again. Guerra told them she'd probably been killed and dragged off by a jaguar. There was no body, so Juan and his wife accepted the sorcerer's explanation. They were, of course, heartbroken, because they'd not only lost a daughter, but they'd known about her pregnancy. They never realized Guerra was a master sorcerer. He kept his disguise firmly in place, and they never had a clue about who he really was. Maria died of a heart attack three months later. Juan remarried a year later to Juanita."

Mace stirred and looked at Ana. "Warriors for the Light can be fooled if a sorcerer is veiled. That is our Achilles' heel. They can take on a new body, a different aura, and we won't know who they really are. Even though Magdalena's parents were *Taqe,* they couldn't tell Guerra was a master sorcerer."

"Oh…" Ana whispered. "What an awful feeling, never being able to go see your parents again…." Tears burned in her eyes.

"Magdalena's sacrifice was greater than that," Alaria said. "At four years old, you were ready to move back with humans. You had become comfortable with your grandfather. He loved you. The one mistake, a free will choice, was that Magdalena shape-shifted back into human form just one time. She was going to leave you on the steps of her father's hut with a note asking him to care for you. She wasn't going to tell her father that you were his grandchild. Magdalena knew she had to keep your past a secret, to protect everyone in her family from Guerra."

Alaria pressed her hand over her heart. "Magdalena wanted you to be with your grandfather for a while before she took you to the Village of the Clouds."

"And once Magdalena shifted back to human form, Guerra picked up on her energy trail? That blew her cover?" Mace asked.

Alaria nodded grimly. "Yes, it did. Guerra instantly felt Magdalena unveil. He followed her energy signature to where she lived in the jungle near the Sanchez farm. He then realized that not only was Magdalena alive, but so was his daughter." Alaria gazed sadly at Ana. "And he came to kill both of you."

"Oh." Ana ran a hand over her damp forehead.

"All Magdalena had wanted to do, Ana, was let you spend a few precious days with your grandfather. It turned out to be a terrible mistake, but understandable. In her human form, in the jungle, she held you, kissed you, rocked and sang to you. And then she shape-shifted back into her jaguar form and led you to the edge of the field. You were toddling out toward your grandfather when Magdalena spotted Guerra in his black hunter's costume and a different body. Because she'd had sex with him, she could tell who Guerra really was. An intangible connection occurs between people who share sex. Guerra couldn't identify *her,* but Magdalena could recognize him, because of this connection. He was a stranger to Juan Sanchez, but Magdalena knew him, no matter what he looked like. In order to save your life, Ana, your mother ran out in front of you and took the bullet meant for you."

Ana buried her face in her hands. She was barely aware of a chair scraping across the floor. The next thing she knew, Mace was standing behind her, caressing her shoulders. Just his touch took away some of the searing pain, shock and grief rolling through her.

Finally, Ana mastered her emotions. Mace handed her his handkerchief and she blotted her eyes. Grandmother Alaria patted her hand. Ana felt healing energy move through her aching, broken heart, and more grief lifted. Mace never left her side, his hands resting gently on her shoulders. Gratefully, Ana looked up at him and murmured her thanks. She then thanked the elder for the healing.

Alaria sighed. "Guerra was confident he'd killed both of you with that one shot. But he didn't want to risk being identified by Juan, so he ran off before he could be positive. Your grandfather rescued you, Ana. He took you to his hut, cleaned you up and gave you clothes to wear for the first time. Your foster-grandmother had no idea who you were, either. And Juan never told her about the plan or about Maria being an Incan princess."

Mace sat back down in his chair, his gaze pinned on Ana. Her lower lip trembled and it tore at him. How badly he wanted to hold her, to protect her from the terrible truth, but he could not.

"That night," Alaria told Ana softly, "after Juan took you to the Cuzco orphanage, I sent him a lovely dream to lift some of the terrible guilt he felt about leaving you there."

"Thank you for doing that," Ana whispered brokenly, wiping her eyes. "He's such a kind person. Now I know why I was so emotional around him, why I wanted to hug him. I didn't want to leave, either. Now it all makes sense."

"Yes, he was your grandfather, but we had to get you out of Peru and away from Guerra. The council agreed to an intervention, something done only in extreme cases. We were allowed to cloak you so that Guerra couldn't pick up your signature and track you down again. We arranged for your adoptive parents to visit Cuzco, where they met and fell in love with you, Ana. John and Mary are not Warriors, but they are good-hearted people of strong moral fiber. They gave you high standards and values to live by, and brought out the Light in you as a result."

"But then," Mace said to Alaria, "that means Ana never received the training to shape-shift as she should have had from childhood onward."

Alaria nodded. "That's right. And it was the reason the council ordered the intervention. I knew her lack of metaphysical education could be remedied in the future, whenever Ana felt driven to come back here to Peru to search for her real parents." She reached out and grasped Ana's hand. "We weren't sure that Magdalena's ultimate sacrifice would ever have a happy ending, but it does. You are one of us now, Ana. You are a Warrior for the Light, and your mission, my child, should you decide to embrace it, could make a huge difference in this world. It may mean we have a chance to create that thousand years of peace, even though the legend has been changed by human intervention and free will."

Mace kept his feelings hidden. Ana didn't need to know the depth of suffering he felt for her. Her shock at the old woman's story was written across Ana's very readable features. And when Alaria turned to study him, he realized she was going to reveal his origins to Ana.

His gut clenched and he tasted fear. Afraid of losing Ana because of the raw honesty that would come from the elder's lips, he tried to wrestle his feelings into submission.

"Ana, you need to know that Mace was deliberately conceived by two Warriors for the Light to undertake a very unique mission of his own. We knew that if Guerra mated with a *Tupay* woman, the legend would be fulfilled. We could then lose the world to the Dark Forces. The council approved a plan to stop Guerra. We asked Mace's parents, both *Taqe,* to volunteer to bring back a strong, spiritually elevated old soul. We needed Mace born into this dimension, and they agreed. From the time he was four years old, he was trained by his parents for this mission."

"The mission being to kill me and Victor?"

"That's right," Alaria said. "Mace is one of a handful of hunter-assassins we have among us. In the days of the Incas, they were referred to as jaguar warriors. Mace's skills are necessary. You don't combat evil with a smile and goodwill. Sometimes you have to approach the evil ones on the field of battle. That is the only power they understand, unfortunately—brute force. And that was Mace's mission—to find you and Guerra. And by finding one, he would be led to the other. When you flew to Peru, Mace's jaguar guardian alerted him to your arrival. When you made the decision to find your real parents, the council lifted your protection. At that point you were unveiled, Ana, and Mace thought you were *Tupay.*"

Alaria frowned. "We did not tell Mace differently, Ana. If we had, it would have spoiled our efforts to find Guerra, who was cloaked and hiding. We had to use Mace, just as he used you, in order to find the master sorcerer. I feel badly that it had to be done that way. We wished for more options, but there were none available."

Mace sighed. "It makes sense you wouldn't tell me, Grandmother." Glancing at Ana, he said in a low tone, "Ana, I never felt anything but good energy around you. I kept fighting my own instincts about you. I'd been raised to think you were evil. But when I met you on the airplane, I sensed you were anything but."

"It must have been very confusing for you," Ana whispered. "To think I was one thing, and yet feel I was another."

Alaria nodded. "Mace has paid a heavy price in all of this, too, my child. Everyone has suffered. We had to let him do the work he was trained for, and locate Guerra. And when the sorcerer did unveil himself, we had to act."

Alaria pulled the emerald sphere from her pocket and placed it on the table. "You see, Ana, you were one of three couples whom we hoped would find the Emerald Key. Another legend said that you would one day string all seven emerald spheres into a necklace and place it around your neck. And when you did so, the thousand years of peace would have a chance to unfold."

Ana loved the energy throbbing and glowing around the sphere. It quieted her angst and grief. She watched as Mace's heavily lined features softened and relaxed, as well. "The *nustas* guided me to the sphere in the lunar temple. I had no idea what it was," she told the elder.

"We knew that. We never expected Guerra to find you there, by the way. Mace had an impossible mission to carry out." Alaria gave him an understanding look. "He was focused on the sorcerer, and yet, when he realized you were not *Tupay,* he wanted to protect you. So his mission became either to kill Guerra and eat his heart, or save you instead."

"Eat his heart?" Ana felt nauseous.

"The legend said that the heart of the Dark Sorcerer must be torn out and eaten by the Light in order to transform it and neutralize the Dark Forces." Mace's mouth quirked. "I didn't quite do that. Instead, I leaped, took a swipe at him and sliced open his jugular vein."

Ana felt her anxiety mount. "But if you didn't eat his heart, what does that mean?"

"It means," Alaria said, "that when Mace shapeshifted into human form to try and save your life, Guerra disappeared. Even though he died physically, his heart was saved. He is now alive and well in the Other Worlds, Ana. That means that although your father is not in a physical body anymore, he's just as dangerous, and in fact more powerful than ever. Guerra will gather legions of *Tupay* from around the world to battle us shortly."

Ana stared at Mace in silence. His eyes were turbulent and shadowy. She felt his anger, helplessness, grief, and something else she couldn't define. "You decided to try and save me instead of finishing your mission."

Mace's eyes fixed on hers. "I made a choice, Ana. I tried to save you and I blew my mission in the process. Free will in action. I'll live to see the results of my decision. And so will everyone else." Flexing his fist, he muttered, "And the war will begin shortly."

Holding up her hand, Alaria said, "My son, no matter how thorough your training, you are a Warrior for the Light. You live by your heart. You were taught that love and compassion trumps hatred, anger and prejudice every time. When you saw Ana wounded, you made a choice that probably would have been made by anyone else from the Light. It is in your genes, your heritage, to save those who are helpless and at the mercy of the *Tupay*."

Mace shrugged, "I know all that, Grandmother. Believe me, I've run the scenario through my head a thousand times." As he held Ana's gaze, Mace said flatly, "And you know what? I'm not sorry I made the choice I did, Ana. I *wanted* you to live." He turned to Alaria. "I know I failed my mission, Grandmother. I let the master sorcerer escape. Right now, he's building his *Tupay* army. I can feel it. I know you can, too."

"Yes, Guerra grows stronger by the hour," Alaria agreed. Sitting a little straighter, she gave Mace a sympathetic look. "My son, in the eyes of the council, your free will choice is not considered a failure. Rather, at the last moment, you returned to your heart. We feel you did the best you could in an unexpected situation that none of us fathomed."

"At least you saved Ana," Mace whispered to the elder, unable to meet Ana's gleaming eyes. "Something good came out of this botched mission, after all."

"Mace," the Alaria chided, "*you* saved Ana. Oh, you think it was the emerald sphere or my presence? It was your *love* that called her spirit back."

Shaken by Alaria's words, Mace held the elder's narrowed gaze. Then he glanced in Ana's direction. The look on her face was one of sudden awareness. Did she realize now that he loved her? Wanted no woman but her in his life?

Mace was uncertain. Only the coming days would give him that answer. But honesty had to come first. The question was, could Ana forgive him and allow his love for her to be unveiled?

Chapter 13

Mace drove his beat-up Land Rover toward Cuzco, where he and Ana would catch a plane for Quito, Ecuador, later in the evening. They had left the Village of the Clouds portal early that morning. By traveling swiftly between the dimensions, they'd found themselves back on Machu Picchu, at the Temple of Balance. Mace had made a call to his Cuzco office to leave his Land Rover in Ollantaytambo. From there, it was easy to catch one of many red tourist buses going down to Aguas Calientes. They then caught a local train to Ollantaytambo, where Mace had his car parked. His assistant project manager had smoothly taken over his drilling projects and Mace didn't have to worry about that, as well.

The road from there to Cuzco was rugged and daunting in some spots. The morning was clear, the sky a light blue. Only a few ragged white clouds hung low over the drab brown slopes of the Andes. Ana sat buckled into the passenger seat, the map laid across her knees.

Mace tried to keep his aching heart quiet, but it was nearly impossible. Ever since Grandmother Alaria had informed Ana of his mission, his dishonesty toward her had been like a wall between them. Not that he blamed Ana for her feelings toward him. He had lied to her, stalked her and used her to get to her sorcerer father. He had admitted his love for Ana, but he wasn't at all sure she loved him.

During the past week of her training at the Village of the Clouds, he'd seen Ana studying him, her gaze questioning. Mace had deliberately walled off the psychic connection between them. It was too soon for them to be together in the way he wanted. He'd also received confirmation that their kiss had connected them to one another for this lifetime. Grandfather Adaire, Alaria's husband and the other leader of the sacred village, had explained to him why he and Ana could feel one another's emotions and thoughts so quickly.

Mace didn't want to intrude into Ana's space right now. She had a lot on her plate, and she didn't need to deal with a relationship, too. What with discovering her father's history, her mother's murder and the truth about Mace, Ana was overwhelmed.

Despite all those emotional shocks, she had obviously thrived at the village. She had readily absorbed Alaria's tutelage of paranormal skills and had begun to learn the rudiments and protocols of shape-shifting. Ana was like a thrilled child, discovering that within herself. Mace had laughed and celebrated in that joyous moment with her, and been touched when Ana had reached up and impulsively kissed him on the cheek.

When Adaire and Alaria sat down with them mid-week to tell them that Mace and Ana had to go to the Vesica Piscis Foundation in Quito to meet the rest of their team, it was one more brick upon Ana's load. Mace had been trained from birth in the paranormal realms and its heavy responsibilities. She had not. Now she was playing catch-up of the most stressful kind. Because he had not taken Guerra's heart when he should have, the master sorcerer was building his army on both sides of the veil, and time was of the essence. Mace knew if he'd completed his task, they wouldn't be hurrying off to Quito after only one week recuperating at the Village of the Clouds.

He kept his gaze on the road curving up and over a mountain. Eventually, the route would descend from thirteen thousand feet down into the Sacred Valley. There, it would turn into a well-paved asphalt highway leading to Cuzco and the airport.

If he hadn't screwed up, Ana could have remained at the village for a year or two, developing her skills. As it was, she had to make contact with the foundation leaders, then return to the village for training on a monthly basis after that. Mace had left her vulnerable to attack from her father. He had to protect and defend her until she could get her armor and energy ready to fight him effectively. Ana was the only one who could defeat her father, if and when she embraced all her power. She had to train constantly to reach that level and confidence.

Adaire had warned Ana that Guerra would fight dirty and do anything he could to vanquish her and the Warriors for the Light. Further, Guerra was actively seeking the other emerald spheres. The foundation had one, and the second one that Ana had found was safe at the Village of the Clouds. Ana had taken a photo of it before they departed. That left five emerald spheres hidden elsewhere in the world, and the master sorcerer was sending out students to hunt for them. Obviously, the Warriors didn't have time to waste.

Feeling guilty, Mace slid a glance toward Ana. His heart swelled with such yearning for her that he nearly said something, but choked it back. Her hair was loose, a little frizzy from the high humidity, and emphasized her clean profile. It was her mouth Mace ached to feel beneath his once more, that made his lower body begin to heat and throb with need.

The road curved sharply. During the last rainstorm, boulders had fallen from the slopes of the craggy mountain. Mace slowed the vehicle to avoid them. There was hardly any traffic on this portion of the road today, though he'd often in the past encountered buses filled with passengers shuttling back and forth between Ollantaytambo and Cuzco. The road was so narrow it didn't allow for two-way traffic at times, a fact that set Mace's nerves on edge. He braked and eased the dark green Land Rover around a gray-and-black granite rock sitting near the edge of a thousand-foot drop-off.

"Nasty stuff," Ana commented, frowning.

"Very," he grunted.

As Mace rounded another curve, he saw several pieces of wood lying across the road. What the hell? It had obviously been put there by someone. But who? Bandits ranged along this road, as well.

"Get your pistol out," he warned Ana tersely.

She did as he ordered, pulling the Glock out of the holster she wore on her right thigh. Ana raised the pistol, snapped off the safety and got it ready. She was familiar with weapons. Wildlife biologists tracking dangerous jaguars had to be handy with a rifle and pistol in case of an attack.

Mace braked. He put the car in Park and climbed out. "Stay in the vehicle," he told Ana. "I'll move those tree limbs."

"I've got you covered," she murmured.

As he walked the ten feet to the first limb, Mace suddenly sensed evil nearby. He was tired and not as alert as he should be. And he hadn't erected his energy armor, the ultimate protection for a Warrior.

A flash of movement came from the right. Turning, Mace recognized Guerra's black aura. Only the sorcerer stood before him in the form of a young Quero man in his twenties. Guerra had possessed the unsuspecting Indian and was inhabiting his body.

Too late! Before Mace could shape-shift or even try to visualize his armor in place, he saw the sorcerer's triumphant look on the Indian's square face. Shooting his hand toward Mace, Guerra sent ten energy hooks into his heart chakra.

The moment that happened, Mace felt as if he'd been slammed in the chest with a sledgehammer. Instantly, he was flung off his feet. He landed hard on his back, dust rising where he slid across the hard, unforgiving road. Gasping for air, he struggled to breathe. He knew what was happening. The sorcerer was now pulling energy out of him, as if he'd cut him open with a knife and was bleeding him to death. It would kill him. In less than ten minutes, he'd die of a massive heart attack. Mace's vision began to grow gray.

He struggled and tried to resist the sorcerer's power, but he'd been caught off guard. Ana was screaming, and this only made Guerra laugh.

Ana! Mace twisted to look in her direction. She stood near the front of the vehicle, the Glock held in both hands, pointed toward her father.

"Stop it!" she shrieked. "Stop hurting Mace!" She knew Victor had possessed the poor Indian. It showed her that the sorcerer would do anything to get what he wanted.

Guerra kept his focus on the struggling Warrior who lay in the dirt, unable to resist his power. Victor held his hand steady, index finger pointed at the man who had killed him.

"Shut up, Ana! Get back into the car!" Guerra yelled.

Wildly, Ana looked toward Mace, whose face was growing gray, his movements weaker. He flailed about, clawing helplessly at his chest. The blood was draining from his darkly tanned face. Her father was murdering him before her very eyes! *No! No!*

Ana's mind went blank with horror. This was such a terrible misuse of power! Victor was her father, but a man she detested and feared. What should she do?

Revulsion roared through Ana. In order to stop him, she'd have to shoot and kill the poor Quero he possessed.

"Stop or I'll shoot you!" she screamed.

"Stupid girl!" Victor barked, concentrating on killing Mace Ridfort. "You can't hurt me. I'm invincible!"

Terror pulsed through Ana. She gripped the pistol and fired one, two, three times at her father. The gun roared, the sound hurting her sensitive ears. The shots echoed, the mountains reflecting the noise.

The young Quero was thrown backward, blood pouring out of his chest. And then he collapsed to the ground, dead. Ana saw a black, misty shape exit out of the Indian's head. The dark cloud grew to be ten feet high and three feet wide, and it pulsed with rage and violence. The energy buffeted Ana like waves of a turbulent tide.

It was Victor, she knew. Completely unaffected by the loss of the human body he'd possessed, he continued his attack on Mace.

Panicking, Ana tried to think. Bullets wouldn't touch the sorcerer in spirit form. What could she do?

Guerra roared with laughter. "You are so stupid!" he screamed at her, though his narrowed eyes never left Mace. "I'm not *real,* remember? I no longer have a physical form. Your bullets can't hurt me."

Breathing hard, Ana's stared at him. Guerra resembled a hologram. She vaguely saw a face, one she didn't recognize, triangular in shape. Jet-black eyes glowed a reddish color, and his skeletal hand pointed at Mace. Alarm gripped her. How could she stop Victor from killing the man she'd fallen in love with?

And then she knew the answer. Grandmother Alaria had given her a lesson in opening her heart and sending out energy to another person. Alaria had told her that love was the greatest power in the world and that, sincerely felt, emotion could stop the worst evil. Closing her eyes, Ana quickly grounded herself. She could hear Mace moaning. Her father was laughing, his voice hollow and echoing around her. Blocking everything out, Ana visualized her heart opening. She *felt* the love she had for Mace. And she aimed it into her father's dark heart, which looked like a bottomless black pit.

The instant Ana's energy struck Guerra, he shrieked in horror. The power of her love instantly broke his energetic connection to Mace.

Turning, the sorcerer rushed toward Ana. "Stop that!" he screamed, flailing his arms. He tried to send energy hooks into her heart, but they bounced off her aura. She had armored up, dammit! Guerra kept trying to push away her loving energy. It got closer and closer to his heart! He didn't dare allow that to happen, it could destroy him. Stunned by the mastery his daughter was displaying, Victor glared at her.

"You little bitch!" he shrieked.

Ana's mouth compressed. She held the laserlike focus of loving energy, moving it closer and closer to her father. His heart looked like a black, gaping hole in the center of his chest. She heard Mace gasp and then cough, but Ana couldn't risk switching her attention from Victor to him. She watched as Guerra floated higher in the air, making wild, swiping motions at the golden wave of energy coming toward him. Her love fought his hatred. And Ana knew without a doubt that if she didn't hold her concentration, her father would finish off Mace.

Victor cursed and suddenly willed himself out of the third dimension. It was the only way to escape.

Blinking, Ana watched her father disappear before her eyes. The black apparition simply faded and dissolved.

She again heard Mace coughing. Was her father gone? Ana carefully scanned the area to make sure. There was no energy signature of him anywhere. He'd gone back to the Other Worlds, behind the veil. Turning, Ana raced to where Mace was struggling to sit up, his hand pressed over his heart.

"Mace!" She fell to her knees and gripped his slumped shoulders. "Mace? Are you all right?"

He dragged deep drafts of life-giving air into his oxygen-starved body. Ana's hands were warm and steadying. She leaned over, her lips near his ear, her own breathing rough and raspy.

"Fine…fine…" he managed to croak. Glancing toward the cliff where Guerra had appeared, Mace knew the sorcerer was gone for now and that Ana had saved his life. He gripped her hand. "I'm okay, thanks. You saved me, Ana. He would have killed me…."

"Oh, Mace," she quavered. "I was never so scared. I didn't know what to do. The bullets…"

"Yeah," he rasped, his heartbeat still racing. "I know." He heard Ana whisper his name. She knelt in front of him, her hand trembling as she touched his cheek, his hair and then his arm, as if to make sure he was really going to live. Deeply moved, Mace reassured her in a husky voice, "I'm going to be okay, Ana. The hooks are gone. How did you get him to leave me alone?"

Wiping at her tears, Ana sat back on her heels and told him everything. Mace responded with the biggest smile, pride shining in his blue eyes.

"Grandmother Alaria is going to be very pleased," he said, his voice starting to sound normal once more.

As his energy began to return, he instantly armored himself. This was a lesson he'd never forget. He'd gotten lazy because of the safety at the village; no Dark Forces could ever penetrate that bastion of the Warriors for the Light. It was the one and only safe place in any dimension for them.

And being in Ana's presence had been a great distraction. Inattention could kill a Warrior. It had damn near killed him just now.

"I was scared, Mace. I panicked when the bullets killed that poor Quero he possessed. Victor exited the body and continued his attack against you." Ana couldn't make herself say "father," the word was so distasteful to her.

Reaching out, Mace gripped her damp hand. "You're learning on the job, Ana. Guerra is impervious to any third dimensional weapon when he's in spirit form. You didn't know that. The only thing he's allergic to is the feeling of love. He can't handle it. That is the one emotion, the one thing that can destroy him. And that's what you did—you sent love to him and he had to run. He couldn't stand and fight you."

Giving her a look of respect, Mace added, "You're more powerful than he is, with all his energy, all his students, and his thousands of years of experience." Squeezing her hand, Mace murmured, "All it took was a young neophyte with a pure heart, and he had to leave me alone. Thanks. You're something else."

Shakily, Ana pushed strands of hair away from her damp face. "I followed my jaguar instincts, I guess."

"Yes, you did. Our jaguar guardians are there to protect us and help us in moments of danger. It's a good thing Alaria was able to train you last week. You used everything she taught you just now. You're a fast study." Mace couldn't imagine the emotional trauma Ana must have gone through when she shot at her father and that poor Indian. Mace saw the sadness in her jade-colored eyes, and his heart contracted. No one should ever have to shoot his or her own father. Not even someone as evil as Guerra. Mace knew Ana wasn't taking her actions lightly, and chances were, after she came down off the adrenaline high, the impact of what she had done would strike her full force. Mace was determined to be there for her when it happened.

His quiet praise washed over Ana. She helped him to his feet. He dusted off his pants and she brushed off the back of his shirt. "I was scared," she admitted.

"In our job, we're often scared," Mace murmured. He reached out and drew Ana into his arms. She came eagerly, wrapping her arms around his waist. Surprised but relieved, Mace buried his face in her thick, dark hair as she pressed herself fully against him. He could feel the rapid beating of her heart, the lush fullness of her breasts.

Mace didn't take her embrace as capitulation or an admittance of any special feelings. He knew she was badly shaken by the sorcerer's attack. So was he. And right now, he wanted to give her what little comfort he could.

"Come on," he urged, pressing a light kiss to her hair, "we need to get going. Let's clear the rest of the tree limbs. I'll get a shovel out of the Land Rover. We need to bury the poor Quero your father possessed. And then we've got to catch that plane for Quito."

"The Dark Forces will continue to attack us," Mace warned Calen Hernandez and her husband, Reno Manchahi. He told them of the incident with Guerra on the mountain. Ana sat at his side on the veranda of their condominium outside Quito. After taking a sip of his iced tea, Mace completed his report to the executives of the Vesica Piscis Foundation. Ana quietly added that her father's treachery earlier had been a terrible shock to her.

"But you stopped him, Ana," Calen said, giving her a quick nod of approval. "He's *the* master sorcerer, the man who, according to legend, will gather the Dark Forces. If you could do that, there's hope for us, for the Light."

Shrugging, Ana said, "I didn't feel like I did anything. I just sent out the love I held in my heart." She smiled at the couple and looked around their lovely condo. It was filled with tropical greenery in brightly colored pots. The home was spacious and cool despite the high humidity and heat in the capital city of Ecuador.

Reno gave his wife a tender look, then turned to Ana. "Innocence always trumps a dark-hearted person."

Calen nodded. "We're so glad to have you on our team. The legend says we would meet and work together for the common good of the world." She pointed to a photograph of the second emerald. "I sent a photo you took of this to Professor Castillo at Quito University. She was able to transcribe the writing on it." Calen picked up a scribbled note. "This sphere has the word *honesty* etched upon it. It is one of the Seven Virtues of Peace."

Ana gave Mace a searching look. "Honesty. Doesn't that fit? My father was *dis*honest with me."

Taking her hand, Mace squeezed it, then reluctantly released it. "And I was *dis*honest with you, too, Ana. You didn't know who I really was and I didn't tell you."

Ana instantly missed the strength and warmth of his fingers around hers. "I know. The symbolic journey we took with one another was all about honesty, Mace. It makes sense to me now."

Reno sat up, elbows resting on his thighs. "If it makes you feel any better, Ana, the sphere was meant to be discovered by a specific couple. And the sphere relates directly to a life lesson they're trying to learn. Mace had a mission. He had to remain undercover. He couldn't be honest with you. But your father was a different story. Your entire history with him has been a saga of dishonesty. He was setting you up to kill you, since his *Taqe* wife had been dishonest with him."

Sadness filtered through Ana. "There was dishonesty following me from before my birth to just a week ago, when I began my trip. The truth came to light the moment the *nustas* revealed the emerald sphere to me in the lunar temple." She gave Mace a searching look and added softly, "I can forgive you, Mace. I can't forgive Victor. Not yet, maybe never. I can forgive my mother, because she sacrificed her life for me, for the Light, for the possibility of peace in our world someday."

Sweet and cooling relief rushed through Mace. "Thanks, I needed to know that, Ana. I know I hurt you, but I didn't know who you really were."

"In our business," Calen interjected gently, "we often feel like we're walking through a hall of mirrors. We don't know what's real and what isn't, and have to rely on our training, guts and heart to sort out the truth." She pressed her palm to her chest.

"You're a seasoned Warrior, Calen," Ana said. "I admire and respect you so much. Grandmother Alaria said I would learn much from you and Reno. I have to cram about ten years of training into the next few months in order to be ready for the attacks that my…er, Victor will start hurling at us."

"You're right," Calen agreed. "Grandmother Alaria appeared to me in a dream just a few weeks ago. Neither Reno nor I knew about the Village of the Clouds until then."

"She said that only when the four of us came together would they be permitted to reveal the existence of the village," Reno stated. He exchanged another warm look with his wife. "Calen and I thought we'd be starting from scratch, building the foundation here, but we don't have to reinvent the wheel, after all. Grandmother Alaria said once we were up and functioning, they would allow people who have the Vesica Piscis birthmark to train with them, too."

"That will lift a lot of the load off you two," Mace said. "It will free you up to do more defensive work out in the world, directing Light teams to protect people or sacred places from the *Tupay.* Plus focus your best teams on locating those other emerald spheres, before Guerra and his bunch find them."

"Exactly our thoughts," Calen said. "As we understand it, Grandmother Alaria said they have been waiting for this moment to arrive for a long time. And now it's here. The four of us have finally met," Calen gestured to all of them. "We each have a strength, a particular knowledge, and are spiritually trained to fight the *Tupay.*"

"Well, I feel like I've got training wheels on compared to the three of you, when it comes to metaphysical topics." Ana chuckled.

Reno smiled grimly. "Says the one who faced down the Dark Lord himself and made him retreat. No, Ana, you just aren't aware of your own power yet."

"But you will be. Sooner than you think," Mace said, his eyes full of emotion.

"But couldn't any of you taken on Victor, too?" Ana asked.

Shrugging, Calen said, "It all depends. Mace let his guard down and Guerra got to him. If we don't keep our energy armor in place all the time, The Dark Lord and his legions could hit us just like Mace was nailed."

"You must understand that we're all human beings," Reno said. "We aren't perfect. And because of this the Dark Forces will have the openings they're searching for. Just because a Warrior has a paranormal gift doesn't make him or her bulletproof."

Mace nodded and held Ana's gaze. "That means you, too, Ana."

"I'm trying to understand all this," she admitted. "I'm so new to it and you have a lifetime of training behind you, years of experience."

"Well, speaking of learning..." Calen reached toward the coffee table and handed each of them a file. "Our third team's coming in. Remember the legend? It said that three couples would form the Vesica Piscis Foundation. Take a look inside these dossiers. In two days, Professor Nolan Galloway from Princeton University and Dr. Kendra Johnson from Harvard's archeology department are going to be visiting us."

Ana opened her file and sat it in her lap. Color photos of both people stared back at her. "And who are they?"

Reno opened his copy. "They are experts on symbols and legends." He grimaced. "During our investigation of them, we found out the two are archenemies. Big-name universities like theirs are always in competition for an archeological discovery. They like getting the glory on a new dig."

Mace rapidly scanned through Dr. Johnson's book credits. *"Ancient Feminine Symbols Translated for the 21st Century,"* he said, reading one title aloud.

"Wow," Ana said excitedly, pressing her index finger to that title in her own report. "She's taken all the male definition of symbols throughout history and turned them into feminine ones. Hey, this looks interesting! What a concept!" She eagerly looked at Calen, who nodded with equal enthusiasm.

"Professor Galloway wrote a book called *The Suppressed Feminine Mystique in Male-Dominated Religion,*" Reno noted. "He's considered one of the most profeminine male archeologists in the world. And he's on a global lecture circuit to every big-name university in the world."

Ana scratched her head. "But if they both support the feminine in their books, why are they such enemies?"

Calen laughed. "We think part of it has to do with the competition between their schools, Princeton and Harvard. But there's a vague indicator that they worked on an archeological dig together, many years ago."

"We think that maybe they had more than just a professional relationship, and when it turned sour, they became enemies instead of lovers," Reno said.

Mace nodded and thumbed through the report. "Love and hate. Inexorably bound together."

Grunting, Reno agreed. "I'd rather love than hate." He eyed his wife fondly, and his gaze fell to her belly, which was showing a hint of the baby she carried.

Ana laughed. "Me, too. But I know enough about educators to realize most are academic warriors in their own right. They think they are always correct, and can be the worst intellectual snobs."

"Well," Calen murmured, "I don't believe these two are snobs. Whether they know it or not, they carry the Vesica Piscis symbol on their necks. Their lives don't seem to show service orientation, however. They also don't seem to have any paranormal abilities, or if they do, they're being tight-lipped about them."

"And that's what we need to find out," Reno confided. "Are these two people prepared to work with us? To be of service to something greater than their own considerable egos? Can they accept that paranormal skills are as normal as breathing? Will they go after the third emerald sphere? We know that Guerra is tracking the remaining spheres as we sit here. Calen and I are hoping these two educators will bury the hatchet and choose a higher calling."

Calen crossed her fingers. "And they can't be completely ignorant of the paranormal. Guerra will follow them, will send his sorcerer students after them, so they'll definitely have to deal with the Dark Forces. Another challenge, if they hope to locate that third sphere, will be trying to figure out the map I was shown in a dream."

"You had a dream about it?" Ana asked.

"Yes, I'm strong in vision dreaming. Last night, before you arrived, I was shown some cryptic symbols, and I saw the third sphere. In my vision, it was inscribed with the word *trust*."

Reno shook his head. "And isn't this following perfectly the pattern we've already seen between us? Johnson and Galloway *dis*trust one another completely. If they agree to go on this journey to find the sphere, they must learn to *trust* each other."

"At this spiritual level, every symbol is more than just a clever design," Mace said. "It is an activated energy expression in motion. In this case, those two will be challenged to trust each other so that they can survive this mission—and succeed in it..."

Ana gazed warmly at him. "And look at us. Our lesson was about honesty."

A wave of sadness flowed through Mace. "I know... and I am so sorry I lied to you, Ana. I can't forgive myself—"

She placed her fingertips against his mouth. "Shh… let's talk about this later. There's a lot to say, to share here, Mace…."

Calen glanced at Reno, one eyebrow raised. "I think we need to call it a night, don't you, my love?"

He nodded. "You both have gone through so much and must be exhausted."

Mace felt his lower lip tingle where Ana had grazed his flesh like a butterfly. The expression in her eyes was like heat lightning going through him, and the pleasurable sensation settled in his core. It made him hungry for her again. "Yeah. Honestly, I'm whipped."

"An honesty pun! There's our word again!" Ana laughed.

Calen grinned and rose from the couch. "Reno will show you to your rooms. This is a large condo, and you'll be across the hall from one another. If you need anything, let us know. Otherwise, we'll meet you in the kitchen for *desayuno* tomorrow morning. Our third team should arrive shortly after that."

Ana stood up, holding on to her dossier. She saw the dark smudges beneath Mace's eyes and the shadows within them, and her heart opened. She understood him so much more deeply now and looked forward to the quiet time they would have. She wanted to be close to him.

Because she had nearly lost Mace, had seen him suffer at her father's hand, Ana needed to come clean about her feelings. Gripping the file a little tighter, she climbed the polished mahogany steps to the second floor.

Ana was determined to tell him everything in her heart. And when she did, what would he do? Fear snaked through her, but she refused to allow her fear to deter her. No, she had to be a warrior for love as much as for peace. Mace was worth risking her life for…and equally important, worth risking her feelings for….

Chapter 14

"I want to sleep with you, Mace." Ana stood at his bedroom door, her hand gripping the frame.

"Are you sure?" he asked uncertainly. Dark shadows beneath her green eyes revealed her evident shock over the confrontation with Guerra on the mountain.

"I just need to be held," she whispered. "I want to hold *you.* I'll sleep better if I'm in your arms. If you want me."

The soft tenor of her voice poured sweetly across his beaten spirits, lifting them as nothing else could. He glanced at the king-size bed and then back at Ana, who still hesitated in the doorway. "That sounds really good, Ana." He held out his hand. "Come on, let's go to sleep. All I want—all I'll ever need, is you…."

* * *

Ana could not recall ever sleeping as deeply as she did in Mace's arms. The song of a nearby bird gently lured her out of the healing slumber. Mace's arms were around her and she was snuggled up against his chest.

As she lay there feeling his soft, warm breath against her neck and shoulder, she savored the exquisite moment. She opened her eyes and slid her hand down Mace's arm, which was wrapped around her waist. Though she felt so secure in his embrace, a ragged sigh slipped from her lips. She was still grappling with the fact that she was the woman in the legend born to help bring the world to peace, not destruction. She didn't feel important. Yet Calen and Reno had treated her as if this was fact. They seemed to have full faith in her.

Despite the pressures and expectations from Alaria and Adaire, Ana felt hope. It was a huge relief that they stood with her, supported her and would continue to train her to bring all her skills and abilities online. Reno and Calen were there to support her, too. And Mace. She was the one who had to adjust. And wrestle with the fact that her father was now—and always would be—her archenemy. She had to struggle with standing in the breach between the Light and the Dark.

There was so much to absorb. Before, she'd been a wildlife biologist. Now she was on center stage and indispensable in the coming war. Her thoughts turned to her mother, Magdalena, who had sacrificed her life so that Ana could be born. She could not fathom such heroism.

Heart swelling with pride and love for a woman she could not remember, Ana wished mightily that someday she might see Magdalena's face. To know more about her. Alaria had promised that she would—but not just yet. And soon, she would visit her grandfather, Juan.

Ana felt Mace stir, and a soft smile pulled at her mouth. She heard his breathing change, and his arm tightened around her waist, pulling her more surely against him. Ana felt his hardness pressing against her. Her mind left the complexity of her new life and shifted to him. The yearning to love Mace fully, to become a part of him, caused Ana to glide even more firmly against him.

Mace opened his eyes as Ana snuggled into his arms. He felt the insistent pressure of her breasts against the naked wall of his chest, felt her fingers slide tantalizingly across his collarbone, down his torso and ribs.

Her eyes smoldered with emerald heat. Like the jaguar she was, her warm body moved sensuously against him. "I like waking up like this," he mumbled, lifting his hand and sliding his fingers through her loose, tangled hair.

"I've been wanting this, dreaming of this, Mace." Ana leaned up and kissed his cheek, the line of his jaw, and finally his strong, masculine mouth.

"Mmm…" He groaned, feeling the urgent contact of Ana's lithe body against his. There was no question he wanted her. Opening his eyes wider, he absorbed her shining gaze, which held such love for him. "Are you sure? Is this what you want, Ana? This is no one-night stand…."

"I know that. I feel the same," Ana whispered, grazing his chest with her breasts. Her nipples hardened beneath the silk. Mace's eyes squeezed shut for a moment. His swift intake of breath satisfied her as a woman. "The only question left is, do you want to love me right now? Or should we wait?" She grinned wickedly as his mouth pulled into a boyish pout. Ana had her answer. She saw the feral gleam in Mace's eyes, the cerulean light focused fully on her. His sizzling look drove a delicious heat through her and created a wonderful dampness between her thighs.

Mace rolled her onto her back, his arm beneath her neck, her hair spread like a gleaming dark halo around her head. A fierce love swept through him for this woman who was so feminine and yet had a strength of spirit he could hardly fathom. "Want to? It's the most perfect thing in the world, Ana. Us. You and me." He leaned down and eased the pale pink silk camisole over her head, dropping it on the floor beside the bed. He gazed at her full, ripe breasts, the dark pink nubs begging for him to suckle them. Without a word, he lowered his head, pulled the first one into his mouth and captured the second between his thumb and forefinger. Ana moaned, her body arching up to meet his. Savoring the taste of her, the fragrance of her skin, Mace felt her fingers dig convulsively into his bunched shoulder muscles.

He wasn't surprised that her hands busied themselves first with his pajama bottoms and then with getting rid of her silky boxer shorts. When Ana pressed her hot, firm body against his fully naked one, Mace felt such unexpected pleasure that he released the captured nipple. Her hands framed his face and pulled him down to meet her questing lips.

Mace had had torrid dreams of loving Ana, but nothing could compare to the real deal. Having her in his arms, feeling the writhing, tempting movements of her flared hips, her soft belly and eager mouth, was better than his dreams.

And when she slipped her curved thigh across him, pushing him down on the bed and straddling his hips, Mace deepened the kiss. There was nothing passive about Ana. Somewhere in the spinning fog of his mind, he realized she was a jaguar mating with her male counterpart. Mace settled his hands on her hips with the errant thought that her body was perfect for carrying their children. It intensified the love he'd been keeping secret for so long.

As he watched Ana sheath his hardness, felt her wet warmth enclose him, he growled. It was a growl of ultimate pleasure. Of triumph in their coming together. He'd doubted this would ever occur, but it finally was. Here and now. With Ana. With a fierce feline glow in her emerald eyes, she moved downward, claiming him, claiming her right to him forever.

Each gliding, fluid movement brought Ana higher, closer to the light blazing above her. Even with her eyes closed, her lips parted and sighs of pleasure rippling from her mouth, she felt Mace's love drenching her, taking her places she'd never gone before. As his strong, callused hands gripped her hips and he thrust deeply into her, she rode a wave of shimmering desire that built and tightened. The moment that her heart opened and bathed Mace with its energy, Ana felt her body implode.

The pleasure was so intense, she cried out. Ana was weightless and experiencing a oneness no words could ever describe. She savored the feel of Mace releasing himself within her, a celebration of their joining. She could hear voices singing, and a cloud of white-gold light encased them. She felt Mace within her, around her, an inseparable part of her down to the cellular level…and beyond.

Ana saw them together in colorful pictures, like a movie running before her tightly shut eyes. It was of their past lives with one another. In some, they were warrior brothers, man and wife, and still others, siblings. She felt the thread of love that had always connected them over hundreds of years. Their coming together in this life was a culmination of past work. Only this time, they were teaming up for the greatest battle of all: saving the earth and helping peace to flourish.

A rainbow of light seemed to filter through the scenes that moved swiftly past. During all those lifetimes, her love for Mace had seeped through her on every level. She felt the deep, abiding passion he had felt for her over time. And now it settled down upon them once more. Ana absorbed the knowledge, as the heaviness of coming back into her physical body returned. Back to the here and now, back into Mace's arms, enclosing him, gripping him with her strong thighs as he prolonged their physical pleasure…

With a moan of utter surrender, she collapsed upon his chest, her head nestled in the crook of his shoulder.

Her hair, damp and curling, spread out across his broad chest. She closed her eyes, feeling the perspiration trickle down between her breasts, the rugged tenderness of Mace's hands now grazing her body. She tasted the salt of him. Kissed his shoulder and weakly moved her fingers up the thick column of his neck into his short, black hair.

"I love you with everything thing I have, Mace Ridfort," Ana whispered unsteadily. "I saw us, I saw our lives together just now…."

"I saw them, too, Ana." Weakness stole through Mace. But it was the best possible reaction a man could ever hope to have, that of sharing his body, heart and soul with the woman he loved. There was no greater feeling of partnering than this one. He closed his eyes, smiled and held Ana tightly against him. He relished the wild beating of her heart against the drumlike thud of his own. It only enhanced the power of his longtime love for this honorable woman warrior.

The moments flowed like light dancing off shimmering water. Rainbow colors continued to encircle them, and Ana was glad she had her sixth sense up and running. She'd have missed half the act of sharing their love, of coming together with Mace, if she had been shut down.

"I love you, Ana," he rasped against her brow. "Whatever happens from here on out, we have each other. We know we're strong together."

Ana smiled lazily. "I'm stunned by our love. I felt it through the ages…and I can feel it now. I don't ever want to stop feeling it, Mace."

"What we have now will only blossom with time, Ana," he whispered against her velvety cheek. "You can never destroy love. And love will destroy the darkness. What we have is special, something so rare. We're lucky to be together right now."

She pressed another kiss to his damp shoulder. "I do feel lucky—so lucky—that we have one another. It's all that counts and all we'll ever need."

Mace agreed. He felt her hot, fluid body still holding him tightly, a willing captive within her. The drive to be one melted Mace even more. It was as if he couldn't get enough of Ana, enough of her generous, honorable heart. As he held her, he silently promised to help her overcome the terrible realizations about her father. He ran his palm along her firm shoulder and down her strong, supple spine. He wanted to support Ana, hold her in moments of grief and weakness, and to celebrate the joy of their love. They could push back the darkness. A day at a time. An hour at a time.

Because of his metaphysical training, Mace understood how coming together with Ana—on a level of pure, unselfish love—made them a team to be reckoned with. Guerra might have slavelike minions and a gathering army, but Mace and Ana had love to combat him with. The Dark Forces hated an open heart, for there was no higher, greater power than love.

Leaning over, Mace smiled into her eyes. "Our love will see us through, Ana...and I will love you forever...."

His words cascaded over her and sank into her heart, which beat in rhythm with his. "I like what we have, Mace. I want you at my side. You're my other half." Ana caressed his bristly cheek and gazed fervently into his blue eyes. "I like the idea of being together for the rest of our lives. I look forward to it."

He gave her a teasing smile. "Right now, I'm centered on this moment." He glanced over at the clock on the bedstand. "Think we have time for dessert before *desayuno?*"

Giggling, Ana stretched like a lithe cat against him. "Oh, Mace, you *are* my *desayuno!* And I'm hungry… for you!"

Laughing with her, Mace felt himself thicken once more within her responsive body. "And I'm starving for you." As he helped Ana sit up, she locked her thighs against his hips and began to move with him. Mace didn't care if they shared breakfast with Reno and Calen or not. And if they didn't, he was sure their hosts would forgive them.

Right now, his whole attention was focused on the woman in his arms. The love burning in her emerald eyes for him touched his soul, and that sultry smile of hers told Mace she was his and his alone.

Chapter 15

Ana studied the blueprints Reno was showing her for the Vesica Piscis Foundation building that would soon be constructed. She stood in his office on the first floor of the condo, with Mace by her side. Absorbing Mace's closeness, she felt herself responding to his blatant masculinity. Though he was dressed casually in jeans and a red T-shirt, Ana couldn't stop looking at him. They'd shared so much of each other just this morning.

When Calen strolled in with a tray of coffee and freshly baked cookies, Ana looked up and smiled. The other woman's face was rosy and her willow-green eyes sparkled with happiness. She was about three months pregnant, and Ana witnessed the tender look Reno gave his wife as she entered the spacious room.

"Espresso and midmorning goodies, anyone?" Calen called, setting the mahogany tray on a nearby table.

Ana curved her hand beneath her hair, twisted it up, pinned it in place with a bright red plastic comb. She grinned at Calen and went over to help her with the tray while the two men continued to talk in low voices about the complex plans. "Nothing like South American espresso," she whispered with a wicked smile.

"I can't live without it," the other woman confided, pouring the fragrant liquid into small red cups. Her smile suddenly turned into a frown. "Ana? Did you see this?" She pointed to the birthmark on the back of Ana's neck.

"What? Oh, my birthmark?" Ana self-consciously touched her nape. She wasn't comfortable letting others see the symbol that marked her as *Tupay.* Even though she knew Reno and Calen accepted her as being of the Light, the mark was there. Out of habit, and without thinking, she'd put up her hair.

Calen came around the table and placed her hands on Ana's shoulder. "Did you *see* this?" she repeated.

Hearing her stunned tone, Ana couldn't keep the worry out of her own voice. "See what?"

Mace and Reno lifted their heads in unison and glanced over at them. Ana felt heat flood her cheeks when Calen touched the back of her neck.

"This is unbelievable. Mace? Reno? Come see this right now," she called urgently.

Confused, Ana twisted her head to look at Calen. "What?"

The other woman pulled her to a bathroom near the

office. She picked up a small, round mirror and placed it in Ana's hands. "Turn around and look at your birthmark!"

Unsettled by the sudden attention, Ana saw Mace walk toward her. Reno wasn't far behind. When she lifted the mirror and reflected it off the medicine cabinet mirror, she gasped.

"I don't believe this! Calen, is it true? Is my sun symbol...gone? Changed...?"

Mace eased into the bathroom and bent to look at Ana's neck. "Incredible," he murmured, and grinned down at her. "You've got the Vesica Piscis birthmark now. The *Tupay* symbol is *gone*." He rubbed the area with his finger. "Yeah, you've got the symbol for the Light on your neck now, Ana."

She stared at it in disbelief. "But how, Mace? I thought birthmarks lasted forever."

Calen gave a giddy laugh and patted her on the shoulder. "Hey, we live in a magical world, Ana. We just forget that. I bet if you ask Grandmother Alaria about this, she'd be able to tell you what happened. Don't forget, your mother's symbol changed, too. Why not yours?"

Mace leaned down and pressed a tender kiss on Ana's slender neck. "Now you're really one of us, sweetheart. You always were. Your birthmark has changed to make it official." He searched Ana's stunned green eyes as she lowered the mirror.

"I—I just can't believe this."

Reno checked it out, too, and grinned. "Your mother was a Warrior for the Light. You have her genes, and always lived in Light. Why isn't it possible that your own dark side would go away, become less pronounced in every way as you consciously chose the path? You agreed to help us find the Emerald Key. You fought your father and stopped him from killing Mace," Reno said. "Maybe it changed then? When you made a decision never to be like him?"

Calen smiled happily as she led Ana back to the office and handed her a cup of espresso. "We know our physical body conforms to our emotions and thoughts. That's why some people get sick and others stay well." She handed Mace and Reno their cups. "Those who get deluged by their emotions fall ill. Those who process and release them stay healthy. Why couldn't the symbol on your neck change? I think it's wonderful. Welcome to the club." She grinned broadly.

Ana was shaken by the discovery. She kept touching her neck and giving Mace questioning looks. When had the transfer taken place? Something deep inside her heart told her the change had occurred as she and Mace made long, passionate love that morning. Not that she'd been aware of it; no, she'd been floating in light and joy that suffused her inside and out.

Mace's heated look spoke volumes. He nodded briefly, as he was in touch with her thoughts on a telepathic level.

"Well," Ana said softly, settling on one of the wooden stools at the drafting table, "I just hope it never changes back to that *Tupay* symbol."

Mace came up behind her and kissed her neck. "Don't worry, you've turned a corner in your life, sweetheart. Many people come from less than healthy backgrounds, or from dark beginnings, but that doesn't mean they have to stay there. You're living proof change can happen. A real role model in every sense of the word."

Calen smiled across the table as she eased herself down on another stool, next to her husband. "If you ever had any doubts about who and what you are, this sign should convince you. It's a wonderful gift. A miracle."

Ana nodded and sipped her coffee. Calen had thoughtfully brought some warm lemon cookies that her housekeeper, Eliana Santos, had just baked for them. Nibbling on one, she felt Mace glide his hand comfortingly across her shoulder.

"Now you won't have to be ashamed of your birthmark," he told her. "You don't have to leave your hair down all the time to hide who and what you are."

"I was just thinking that." A giddy feeling of relief flowed through Ana. She saw the pride in the eyes of the group surrounding her. A sense of belonging swept through her, and for the first time in her life, Ana realized she had a *real* family. That didn't mean she didn't love John and Mary Rafael, who'd adopted her. They would always be the mother and father of her heart, and an integral part of her life. And, she had a grandfather who she was going to integrate back into her life shortly. But she relished the sense of being part of a larger, spiritual family who loved her, respected her and looked upon her as an equal. Ana was no longer the Daughter of Darkness, a pariah, an outcast shunned and feared by others. She was now, officially, a Warrior for the Light, fighting for the cause of peace.

Reno held up his espresso in a toast. "Welcome to our world, Ana. You're one of us now."

Feeling the heat of a blush stain her cheeks, Ana realized Reno, too, had read her thoughts. She saw the sparkle in his cinnamon-colored, intelligent eyes, felt the warrior energy exuding from him. Holding up her cup, she grinned in response. "Thanks, Reno…and everyone. It feels good to have such a beautiful spiritual home."

"Home," Mace murmured. He slid onto the stool beside Ana, embracing her. Looking at the other team members, he said in a suddenly emotional tone, "You know, we are *all* coming *home.* To here. Now. And our spiritual grandparents, Alaria and Adaire, are guiding us. It's nice to know we have a team not only here on this physical dimension, but in the Other Worlds, as well."

Ana leaned her head on Mace's shoulder. "After not knowing who I was, well, home feels wonderful to me," she confided in a choked voice.

"I was homeless until I met Calen," Reno admitted, with warmth in his gaze as he regarded his wife.

"And I was orphaned at age seven," Calen confided. "So you see, Ana, we were all lost in one way or another until we met." Her eyes glistened. "And now we're creating a new family of a sort. Only the mission we're undertaking isn't just for ourselves, it's for all our relations."

"It's for Mother Earth," Mace agreed in a serious tone. He gazed down at Ana's upturned face and absorbed the love she had for him. His heart opened even more, if that was possible. "The four of us bring unique talents and knowledge for our coming missions. And I know we're making a difference in the world."

"I agree," Calen said, slipping her arm around Reno's

narrow waist and squeezing. "The other two members of our cosmic family will be arriving this afternoon. I'm anxious to meet them. I know they don't yet realize any of what is going on in a greater spiritual sense, the war between *Taqe* and *Tupay* forces."

"But they will," Mace said grimly, sipping his espresso. "They might be from the educational branch, but each has special talents in areas we don't."

"I wonder what paranormal abilities they have?" Ana murmured.

"We'll find out shortly," Reno replied.

"In my dreams, they were clearly the two meant to help us," Calen said. "I trust the guidance I get that way."

"Grandmother Alaria said dreams are a wonderful pipeline of information," Ana said. "She said she'd help me develop in that area, too."

"Listen, you're a jaguar shape-shifter. You and dreams are synonymous." Calen laughed, giving Reno a knowing glance. "I'm sure Mace is a great dreamer, too."

Mace smiled at Ana. "As a child growing up, I received half my education in my dreams at night. And I dreamed of Ana after I met her. It shows dreams can and do come true."

Warmth suffused Ana's heart as she met Mace's gaze. His eyes were filled with love—for her.

Calen set aside her cup and pulled a piece of paper from her pants pocket. Opening it, she said to them, "Speaking of dreams, this is the one I had about where Kendra and Nolan need to start their search for the next emerald sphere." She flattened the paper on the desk before the group.

Ana frowned and studied the scribbled ink drawing. "That looks like a crop circle. Is it?" The beautiful geometric drawing showed two circles next to one another, one slightly smaller than the first. "It looks like the Vesica Piscis symbol, only with the rings pulled apart. They're not overlapping."

Calen nodded and stared down at the drawing. "I thought the same thing. I was also shown a windmill turning on top of a hill." She glanced around at her cohorts. "Anyone have an idea of what that's all about? I'm a dreamer, but not necessarily the best interpreter. What in the world would a windmill have to do with this crop circle symbol?"

Mace traded glances with Reno and Calen. "I know a little about crop circles. I have a great fascination for them. They most often appear in Britain, but have shown up all over the world. The most intense area of concentration, though, is around the Marlborough region in the southwest of England. At one time I wanted to go over there, walk into one and see what I could pick up, energy wise." He smiled at Calen. "That windmill you dreamed about? Well, one of the hottest areas for crop circles appearances is below Windmill Hill. There's an old Neolithic fort on top of this hill, and it's a real power center. There are farms on all sides, and crop circles continually appear in those field. I think your dream is trying to tell you that this symbol—" he pointed to her sketch "—will appear in the Windmill Hill area shortly. That's my gut feeling."

Reno nodded. "I've always had an interest in crop circles, too. But it looks like our third team is going to get to explore them up close and personal. And your dream does appear to indicate that specific area, Calen. I wonder if this crop circle has formed yet?"

She shook her head. "It hasn't. Before I brought the coffee, I jumped on the Internet and went to a crop circle Web site that shows pictures of all crop circles as soon as they're found and photographed. So far, there's no photo of this formation. Kendra and Nolan need to start their search for the next emerald sphere at the next formation. It's as if we're being given bread crumbs to follow."

"This is so fascinating!" Ana whispered, eyeing the drawing. "Crop circles are symbols, pure and simple. Energy in a symbolic form. All we have to do is figure out what they're trying to tell us."

"Not so simple," Reno warned. "Calen and I've been looking at several books of photos published by a group over in England that routinely flies a paraglider over every new formation. No one knows where they come from. Or what each symbol may mean."

Calen rubbed her hands together. "Fear not, intrepid family members, we have arriving shortly two of the world's most knowledgeable people on this topic. I'm *sure* they'll have an opinion or two about my dream." She grinned and added, "And I'm sure they'll probably fight like cats and dogs over the meaning. We might have to put them on separate planes bound for England!" She laughed heartily.

Ana didn't share Calen's obvious delight. "Victor is skulking around. I can feel him. He doesn't have the dream info you have, Calen, but that doesn't mean he can't send someone to covertly follow Kendra and Nolan. There's no guarantee he won't try and snatch the sphere from them once they find it."

Reno nodded grimly. "They have to understand how dangerous this game is," he stated. "They can't go into the mission blind or unprepared. We'll do the best we can to educate them about Guerra and his kind."

With a worried frown, Ana whispered, "Kendra and Nolan must be protected. What if Victor possesses one of them? They'll die…"

Mace squeezed her tense shoulder. "One step at a time, sweetheart. Let's get them here and explain things. We don't even know if they'll take on the assignment."

Calen sighed. "That's right, Mace. Kendra and Nolan are used to working with facts and pure science. Not mysticism, paranormal events or magic."

"Let's hope they've embraced quantum physics then," Mace murmured with a sly smile. "Because quantum mechanics does explain the invisible dimensions and mystical realms we all live in, whether we're aware of it or not. If they have, I think they'll leap at a chance to find the next emerald sphere. After all, they're archeologists. They live to discover the next important artifact. And it doesn't get any bigger than finding a piece of the Emerald Key."

Ana murmured her assent. With Mace tucking her against his strong, masculine body, she felt safe. And at home.

There was no question in her heart that in the next week, he was going to ask her to marry him. She'd picked up telepathically on his thoughts. He wanted her as his wife. He wanted her as the mother of their children.

Reaching over, Ana squeezed his hand. Mace was now her home and her family. And their children would have a loving mother and father, not to mention wonderful grandparents. Yes, life was suddenly good for Ana. Better than she'd ever thought it could be.

As she drowned in Mace's warm blue eyes, her heart blossomed fiercely with love—such great love that for a moment, only the two of them existed. She gazed at him adoringly, knowing she would love Mace—and he would love her—forever.

* * * * *

Don't miss Lindsay McKenna's next pulse-pounding romance, HEART OF THE STORM, available December 2007 from HQN.

Every Life Has More
Than One Chapter

Award-winning author Stevi Mittman delivers another hysterical mystery, featuring Teddi Bayer, an irrepressible heroine, and her to-die-for hero, Detective Drew Scoones. After all, life on Long Island can be murder!

Turn the page for a sneak peek
at the warm and funny fourth book,
WHOSE NUMBER IS UP, ANYWAY?,
in the Teddi Bayer series,
by STEVI MITTMAN.
On sale August 7.

CHAPTER 1

"Before redecorating a room, I always advise my clients to empty it of everything but one chair. Then I suggest they move that chair from place to place, sitting in it, until the placement feels right. Trust your instincts when deciding on furniture placement. Your room should 'feel right.'"

—TipsFromTeddi.com

Gut feelings. You know, that gnawing in the pit of your stomach that warns you that you are about to do the absolute stupidest thing you could do? Something that will ruin life as you know it?

I've got one now, standing at the butcher counter in King Kullen, the grocery store in the same strip mall as L.I. Lanes, the bowling alley cum billiard parlor I'm in the process of redecorating for its "Grand Opening."

I realize being in the wrong supermarket probably doesn't sound exactly dire to you, but you aren't the one buying your father a brisket at a store your mother will somehow know isn't Waldbaum's.

And then, June Bayer isn't your mother.

The woman behind the counter has agreed to go into

the freezer to find a brisket for me, since there aren't any in the case. There are packages of pork tenderloin, piles of spare ribs and rolls of sausage, but no briskets.

Warning Number Two, right? I should be so out of here.

But no, I'm still in the same spot when she comes back out, brisketless, her face ashen. She opens her mouth as if she is going to scream, but only a gurgle comes out.

And then she pinballs out from behind the counter, knocking bottles of Peter Luger Steak Sauce to the floor on her way, now hitting the tower of cans at the end of the prepared foods aisle and sending them sprawling, now making her way down the aisle, careening from side to side as she goes.

Finally, from a distance, I hear her shout, "He's deeeeeeaaaad! Joey's deeeeeaaaad."

My first thought is *You should always trust your gut.*

My second thought is that now, somehow, my mother will know I was in King Kullen. For weeks I will have to hear "What did you expect?" as though whenever you go to King Kullen someone turns up dead. And if the detective investigating the case turns out to be Detective Drew Scoones...well, I'll never hear the end of that from her, either.

She still suspects I murdered the guy who was found dead on my doorstep last Halloween just to get Drew back into my life.

Several people head for the butcher's freezer and I position myself to block them. If there's one thing I've learned from finding people dead—and the guy on my doorstep wasn't the first one—it's that the police get very testy when you mess with their murder scenes.

"You can't go in there until the police get here," I say, stationing myself at the end of the butcher's counter and in front of the Employees Only door, acting as if I'm some sort of authority. "You'll contaminate the evidence if it turns out to be murder."

Shouts and chaos. You'd think I'd know better than to throw the word *murder* around. Cell phones are flipping open and tongues are wagging.

I amend my statement quickly. "Which, of course, it probably isn't. Murder, I mean. People die all the time, and it's not always in hospitals or their own beds, or…" I babble when I'm nervous, and the idea of someone dead on the other side of the freezer door makes me very nervous.

So does the idea of seeing Drew Scoones again. Drew and I have this on-again, off-again sort of thing… that I kind of turned off.

Who knew he'd take it so personally when he tried to get serious and I responded by saying we could talk about *us* tomorrow—and then caught a plane to my parents' condo in Boca the next day? In July. In the middle of a job.

For some crazy reason, he took that to mean that I was avoiding him and the subject of *us*.

That was three months ago. I haven't seen him since.

The manager, who identifies himself and points to his nameplate in case I don't believe him, says he has to go into *his cooler*. "Maybe Joey's not dead," he says. "Maybe he can be saved, and you're letting him die in there. Did you ever think of that?"

In fact, I hadn't. But I had thought that the murderer might try to go back in to make sure his tracks were covered, so I say that I will go in and check.

Which means that the manager and I couple up and go in together while everyone pushes against the doorway to peer in, erasing any chance of finding clean prints on that Employee Only door.

I expect to find carcasses of dead animals hanging from hooks, and maybe Joey hanging from one, too. I think it's going to be very creepy and I steel myself, only to find a rather benign series of shelves with large slabs of meat laid out carefully on them, along with boxes and boxes marked simply Chicken.

Nothing scary here, unless you count the body of a middle-aged man with graying hair sprawled faceup on the floor. His eyes are wide open and unblinking. His shirt is stiff. His pants are stiff. His body is stiff. And his expression, you should forgive the pun—is frozen. Bill-the-manager crosses himself and stands mute while I pronounce the guy dead in a sort of *happy now?* tone.

"We should not be in here," I say, and he nods his head emphatically and helps me push people out of the doorway just in time to hear the police sirens and see the cop cars pull up outside the big store windows.

Bobbie Lyons, my partner in Teddi Bayer Interior Designs (and also my neighbor, my best friend and my private fashion police), and Mark, our carpenter (and my dogsitter, confidant, and ego booster), rush in from next door. They beat the cops by a half step and shout out my name. People point in my direction.

After all the publicity that followed the unfortunate

incident during which I shot my ex-husband, Rio Gallo, and then the subsequent murder of my first client—which I solved, I might add—it seems like the whole world, or at least all of Long Island, knows who I am.

Mark asks if I'm all right. (Did I remember to mention that the man is drop-dead-gorgeous-but-a-decade-too-young-for-me-yet-too-old-for-my-daughter-thank-god?) I don't get a chance to answer him because the police are quickly closing in on the store manager and me.

"The woman—" I begin telling the police. Then I have to pause for the manager to fill in her name, which he does: *Fran*.

I continue. "Right. Fran. Fran went into the freezer to get a brisket. A moment later she came out and screamed that Joey was dead. So I'd say she was the one who discovered the body."

"And you are…?" the cop asks me. It comes out a bit like who do I *think* I am, rather than who am I really?

"An innocent bystander," Bobbie, hair perfect, makeup just right, says, carefully placing her body between the cop and me.

"And she was just leaving," Mark adds. They each take one of my arms.

Fran comes into the inner circle surrounding the cops. In case it isn't obvious from the hairnet and blood-stained white apron with Fran embroidered on it, I explain that she was the butcher who was going for the brisket. Mark and Bobbie take that as a signal that I've done my job and they can now get me out of there. They twist around, with me in the middle, as if we're a

Rockettes line, until we are facing away from the butcher counter. They've managed to propel me a few steps toward the exit when disaster—in the form of a Mazda RX7 pulling up at the loading curb—strikes.

Mark's grip on my arm tightens like a vise. "Too late," he says.

Bobbie's expletive is unprintable. "Maybe there's a back door," she suggests, but Mark is right. It's too late.

I've laid my eyes on Detective Scoones. And while my gut is trying to warn me that my heart shouldn't go there, regions farther south are melting at just the sight of him.

"Walk," Bobbie orders me.

And I try to. Really.

Walk, I tell my feet. *Just put one foot in front of the other.*

I can do this because I know, in my heart of hearts, that if Drew Scoones was still interested in me, he'd have gotten in touch with me after I returned from Boca. And he didn't.

Since he's a detective, Drew doesn't have to wear one of those dark blue Nassau County Police uniforms. Instead, he's got on jeans, a tight-fitting T-shirt and a tweedy sports jacket. If you think that sounds good, you should see him. Chiseled features, cleft chin, brown hair that's naturally a little sandy in the front, a smile that…well, that doesn't matter. He isn't smiling now.

He walks up to me, tucks his sunglasses into his breast pocket and looks me over from head to toe.

"Well, if it isn't Miss Cut and Run," he says. "Aren't you supposed to be somewhere in Florida or something?" He looks at Mark accusingly, as if he was covering for me when he told Drew I was gone.

"Detective Scoones?" one of the uniforms says. "The stiff's in the cooler and the woman who found him is over there." He jerks his head in Fran's direction.

Drew continues to stare at me.

You know how when you were young, your mother always told you to wear clean underwear in case you were in an accident? And how, a little farther on, she told you not to go out in hair rollers because you never knew who you might see—or who might see you? And how now your best friend says she wouldn't be caught dead without makeup and suggests you shouldn't either?

Okay, today, *finally,* in my overalls and Converse sneakers, I get it.

I brush my hair out of my eyes. "Well, I'm back," I say. As if he hasn't known my exact whereabouts. The man is a detective, for heaven's sake. "Been back awhile."

Bobbie has watched the exchange and apparently decided she's given Drew all the time he deserves. "And we've got work to do, so…" she says, grabbing my arm and giving Drew a little two-fingered wave goodbye.

As I back up a foot or two, the store manager sees his chance and places himself in front of Drew, trying to get his attention. Maybe what makes Drew such a good detective is his ability to focus.

Only what he's focusing on is me.

"Phone broken? Carrier pigeon died?" he asks me, taking in Fran, the manager, the meat counter and that Employees Only door, all without taking his eyes off me.

Mark tries to break the spell. "We've got work to do

there, you've got work to do here, Scoones," Mark says to him, gesturing toward next door. "So it's back to the alley for us."

Drew's lip twitches. "You working the alley now?" he says.

"If you'd like to follow me," Bill-the-manager, clearly exasperated, says to Drew—who doesn't respond. It's as if waiting for my answer is all he has to do.

So, fine. "You knew I was back," I say.

The man has known my whereabouts every hour of the day for as long as I've known him. And my mother's not the only one who won't buy that he "just happened" to answer this particular call. In fact, I'm willing to bet my children's lunch money that he's taken every call within ten miles of my home since the day I got back.

And now he's gotten lucky.

"*You* could have called *me*," I say.

"You're the one who said *tomorrow* for our talk and then flew the coop, chickie," he says. "I figured the ball was in your court."

"Detective?" the uniform says. "There's something you ought to see in here."

Drew gives me a look that amounts to *in or out?*

He could be talking about the investigation, or about our relationship.

Bobbie tries to steer me away. Mark's fists are balled. Drew waits me out, knowing I won't be able to resist what might be a murder investigation.

Finally he turns and heads for the cooler.

And, like a puppy dog, I follow.

Bobbie grabs the back of my shirt and pulls me to a halt.

"I'm just going to show him something," I say, yanking away.

"Yeah," Bobbie says, pointedly looking at the buttons on my blouse. The two at breast level have popped. "That's what I'm afraid of."

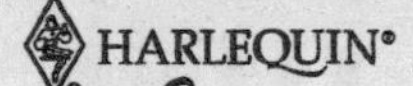
HARLEQUIN®

Silhouette®

nocturne™

COMING NEXT MONTH

#21 FAMILIAR STRANGER • Michele Hauf

Dark Enchantments (Book 1 of 4)

P-Cell agent Jack Harris was recruited to fight the Cadre—instead, he fell in love with their most free-spirited member, the girl with the green cat eyes, Mersey Bane. Their joining leads to a whirlwind of passion and adventure that will deliver them deep into a world of danger.

#22 DAMNED • Lisa Childs

Witch Hunt (Book 3 of 3)

Ty McIntyre saw Irina Cooper's murder before it ever happened. But with a witch killer on the hunt, Ty has to put his disbelief in his newfound abilities on hold so he can save Irina—and end the Cooper family curse—before it's too late.

SNCNM0707